The Co... Unexpected Love

Wade and Sierra

The MacFarlands
Book One

By SJ McCoy

A Sweet n Steamy Romance

Published by Xenion, Inc

Published by Xenion, Inc.
First paperback edition February 2022
www.sjmccoy.com

Cover Design by Dana Lamothe of Designs by Dana
Editor: Kellie Montgomery
Proofreaders: Aileen Blomberg, Traci Atkinson, Becky Claxon.

ISBN: 978-1-946220-83-7

Dedication

For Sam. Sometimes, life really is too short, few oxo

xxx

Chapter One

"Thanks for switching with me. For offering to drive home," said Wade.

His brother, Ford, glanced at him then returned his focus to the road. "That's okay. The second I saw Josie corner you, I thought you'd need a drink."

Wade blew out a sigh and turned to look out at the mountains. They glowed in the last rays of evening sun under a sky streaked with crimson and gold. "My days of hitting the bottle over her are a long way behind me."

"I noticed. I should have had one myself when I realized you weren't drinking. Want to talk about it?"

He let out a short laugh. "There's nothing to say. At least, nothing new."

Ford turned the truck off the highway and pointed it south, down East River Road. "She's determined. I'll give her that."

"Yeah. She was determined that we'd get married, and we did. She was determined to have kids, and she did."

"Do you ever regret it?"

Wade took his hat off and leaned back against the headrest. "Which part?"

"Not wanting to have kids."

"No. I don't. We got married too young." He shot his brother a rueful smile. "You were right about that. If I regret anything, it's marrying her in the first place. Having kids would have made things worse, for everyone. I regret that we didn't make a clean break when it was obvious that we wanted different things in life. I regret a lot of things, but not having kids with her isn't one of them."

"Good. So, you're not thinking about giving in to her, are you? Getting back together?"

"Hell, no! I don't know how many times I'll have to tell her before it sinks in, but there's no way on Earth I'd ever get back with her. Even if she didn't have Harland's kids. There's nothing there. I have no feelings for her anymore."

"None at all?"

"Maybe a touch of resentment for what she did. She still claims she never cheated, but she sure moved on quickly with Harland when we separated."

The way Ford's jaw tightened reminded Wade that his brother had his own opinion on whether Josie had cheated on him. Thankfully, he didn't bring it up. Instead, he punched Wade's arm. "How about when we get back to the ranch, we hit the bourbon? We can drink to our future as the old bachelor brothers of MacFarland Ranch."

"I'll happily put a hurting on a bottle of bourbon with you. But …" He smiled through pursed lips. "I'm not ready to throw in the towel and commit to dying a lonely old man just yet."

Ford laughed. "What are you, a glutton for punishment? Are you saying that you'd get married again?"

Wade shrugged. "I don't know why we're on this deep and meaningful track this evening, but while we are, then yeah. You know me. I'm soft, I guess."

Ford snorted. "You're a damned romantic is what you are."

Wade shrugged again. "I guess I am. See, if the right woman came along, and I'm not saying she ever will, just that if she did, I'd want to marry her. Make her my wife." He grabbed onto the door handle when the truck swerved.

"What the hell?" Ford was pointing through the windshield.

Wade peered out, wondering if he was imagining things. An SUV was off the side of the road. Its wheels on the passenger side were down in the drainage ditch. Standing next to the vehicle was a woman – a woman in a wedding dress.

Ford laughed beside him when the woman slapped the side of the SUV and then gave the tire a few good kicks. "Be careful what you wish for, huh?"

Wade cocked an eyebrow at him.

"You just said you wanted to find a woman you could marry and boom, the next minute there's a bride on the side of the road."

Wade laughed. "Yeah. I don't think that was my doing."

Ford brought the truck to a stop behind the SUV and looked over at him before he got out. "Maybe not, but you can deal with her. You know how well I do with emotional women."

~ ~ ~

Sierra looked up at the big sky – Montana! She could hardly believe she was here. She shouldn't be. She was supposed to be at her wedding reception right now. Instead, here she was underneath the famed *Big Sky,* which was streaked with quickly fading red and gold. The artist in her wanted to appreciate the beautiful sunset, but she had a few more pressing things on her mind.

She pulled her phone out of the little clutch bag that sat on the passenger seat. Thank goodness she'd had the presence of mind to at least make sure she had that with her when she'd fled. Then again, she wouldn't have gotten far without it.

She hit the speed dial for Cassidy's number and held her breath as she waited. *Please pick up. Please pick up. Please – Shoot!*

"Hi, you've reached Cassidy Remington ..."

Sierra cursed as she ended the call. She'd already left a message and she had no doubt that the second Cass heard it she'd call back. She probably sounded hysterical – heck, she felt hysterical.

She'd thought this day couldn't get any worse, but it just kept on giving. It was supposed to be the happiest day of her life ... She looked down at the phone in her hand, and the tears started to fall again. She should have been cried out by now. She'd spent the last, who knew how many hours, on the road crying.

She shouldn't have been driving, she knew that much. But she had no choice. She'd had to get out of there. Had to leave the plush hotel where her friends were no doubt wondering what had happened to her. Perhaps it was all just a nightmare, and she'd wake up soon. It'd be the morning of her wedding day and the last several hours would never have happened. She sniffed and wiped her face on the now grubby, and far from white, satin handkerchief. No such luck. She was definitely living a nightmare, but it was a very real one. There'd be no waking up from it.

She put the SUV in neutral and opened the door. She might as well have one more try at pushing it out of the ditch. It was futile, and she knew it, but she had to do something. Cassidy wasn't answering. The fading sunset warned that it would get dark soon, and she had no clue what she was going to do. She was in the middle of nowhere, Montana and ... she shuddered at the sound of a screech that tore through the air. A bird? What if it was a wolf? They had those in Montana. She let out a sound that was half laugh, half sob. Maybe a wolf would come and eat her; that would be a fitting end to this nightmare of a day.

She gave up trying to push the stupid SUV. There was no way she was going to get it out of the ditch. Maybe if she hadn't swerved to avoid the deer that had jumped out in front of her, it would be lying here in the road waiting for a wolf to come and eat it instead of her. No. Even with the mess she was in, she was glad she hadn't hit the deer, glad that it had bounced on its merry way not even looking back at her as she ran off the road. She was happy that the deer got to go on with its life; it probably had a brighter future ahead of it than she did. It would go on to have babies, raise its children – shoot! She couldn't die out here, eaten by a wolf or otherwise. She was going to have children to raise soon, too – even if she didn't get to have babies.

She slammed the door shut and slapped the stupid vehicle in frustration. "You were supposed to be the safest vehicle on the road." That's what the man at the rental desk in the hotel had told her. She gave the tire a kick and then another for good measure. She knew it was unreasonable to take it out on the poor SUV, but at least expressing her anger felt better than sitting there sobbing and feeling helpless.

Movement on the road behind her made her stop kicking and look. A huge pickup truck was pulling up behind the SUV. Uh-oh. Maybe she was going to die out here after all. Did serial killers drive pickup trucks?

Oh my! If serial killers looked like this guy … Had there ever been a cowboy serial killer? He got out of the driver's side and tipped his hat before starting toward her. He was big, muscly, handsome as the devil himself. Dark and broody good looks had never been her thing, nor had cowboys, but she could be persuaded to reconsider for this guy.

She jumped nervously and tore her gaze away from him at the sound of the passenger door closing. And what the heck? Maybe she was dreaming after all, but rather than a nightmare, this was a girl's cowboy fantasy come true. Cowboy number two was just as tall and built as the first, but he was much fairer. Where the first one looked dark and broody, this one looked open and friendly. And then he smiled – and she'd swear that the sun came back out, even though it had just set behind the rugged mountains that towered above them.

"Ma'am." He touched the front of his hat with two fingers and came striding toward her. All she could do was stare. From the top of his hat, her gaze slid down over him. He was breathtaking. Broad shoulders, narrow hips, muscular thighs encased in workworn jeans. Wow! She looked back up at his face. The lines around his eyes crinkled as he smiled. He had a dimple in one cheek that made him look friendly, approachable. She glanced back at the other man, the darker one. He smiled, too, he was possibly, technically, just as handsome, but the warmth wasn't there.

He had the same straight nose, high cheek bones and strong, square jawline. She looked back at the fairer one for comparison. They must be brothers. The looked too much alike to …

"Are you all right?"

Shoot. She really needed to pull herself together. After the shock of what she'd seen and heard this afternoon and then spending the last several hours alone in her head on the road, she seemed to have lost the ability to interact with reality. The friendly cowboy was still smiling at her, but he was starting to look worried now. He shot a glance at the other one.

She let out a laugh at the ridiculousness of the situation. She was supposed to be at her wedding reception – sipping champagne at the St. Regis in Park City, Utah with trust fund kids and hedge fund managers. Instead, here she was, by the side of the road in who knew where, Montana with a couple of cowboys.

Those cowboys were starting to look a little wary. Who could blame them? It wasn't every day you ran across a bride by the side of road – kicking her vehicle, no less. That thought made her laugh again; they must have seen that, and they really must think she was a crazy. Oops. And laughing the way she kept doing probably wasn't helping any.

She took a deep breath to steady herself and pulled herself together. She had an entire lifetime's worth of training in how to appear calm and gracious in the face of adversity, no matter how far from calm she might feel.

She smiled at them both, but then focused her attention on the fairer of the two. "I'm sorry. I promise I'm not as crazy as I look."

There went that smile again. It warmed her insides and made her relax a little. How could that be?

"You don't look crazy." His eyes were so kind. "You do look as though you might be having a tough day, though." He jerked his head at the SUV which was, of course, still stuck in the ditch.

At least he didn't comment on her wedding dress. She knew she'd have to explain, but she'd stick with her more pressing predicament to start with. "I had the choice between going off the road or hitting a deer." She lifted one shoulder. "I chose the ditch."

The darker one chuckled. "You're lucky that you got to choose. More often than not you hit 'em before you know what happened."

She laughed again. She couldn't help it. "Well, if you call this lucky, then I'll take it. I thought luck wasn't on my side today, but maybe I just wasn't seeing the blessing through the disguise."

They both gave her sympathetic looks. Yeah. They were decent men, good guys. They had to be. No serial killer could ever muster the kind of compassion that she saw in their eyes.

"We should be able to haul you out of there." The friendly one walked around to inspect the way the SUV was sitting in the ditch. "Do you have a spare?"

She stared at him until she figured it out. "Oh, a spare tire? I don't know. I should. They all come with one, don't they?"

She didn't miss the look they exchanged. They thought she was stupid, she could tell.

"It's not mine," she explained. "I only rented it this afternoon. I had to get out of there!" She closed her eyes, trying to keep the stupid tears from falling. Shoot. Crazy, stupid, whatever they thought of her, they were right. She was.

Her eyes flew open when a hand came down on her shoulder. It felt warm, reassuring, and it spread a glow all through her. She looked up into a pair of kind, green eyes and her breath caught in her chest. "Hey. It's okay. It's all going to be okay. We'll get your car out of the ditch, and we'll get you on your way. Where are you headed?"

She drew in a big, shaky breath. "I … I don't even know. As you can probably tell by the dress, I didn't exactly plan to be here. I just started driving and when I realized where I was, I remembered that I have a friend here in Montana. I thought I'd maybe land on her tonight and then figure out what I'm going to do tomorrow."

His hand was still on her shoulder; it felt like reassurance, like he was lending her strength to lean on. "Where does your friend live? Have you spoken to her?"

"According to the GPS, her house is only about five miles farther down this road. But I can't get hold of her."

The darker cowboy stepped forward. "What's your friend's name?"

"Cassidy. Cassidy Lane. Oh wait, no. Cassidy Remington now. She got married." Sierra's eyes welled with tears again. Of course, Cassidy had gotten married. To a wonderful man by all accounts. She now had a cowboy all of her own. Unlike Sierra, who hadn't even made it to the altar. At least, she'd found out before she walked down the aisle that the man she was about to marry wasn't her own. She shuddered at the images that flashed through her mind – the graphic details of …

"You're a friend of Cassidy's?" The cowboy's question dragged her back to the present.

"Yes. Do you know her?"

"We do. And you can't get ahold of her?"

Sierra sniffed. "No. Her phone just goes to voicemail."

The two men exchanged another look. "I can call her husband, Shane."

"You know them?"

"We do. Hang on." She watched, feeling a little bereft when he took his hand off her shoulder and pulled his phone out of his back pocket.

"Shane? … Yeah. It's Wade."

Wade? Hmm. It was a nice name. It suited him.

"Where are you guys? … Oh. I see …"

That didn't sound too hopeful.

"Ford and I just ran into a friend of Cassidy's …" He put his hand over the phone and looked at her expectantly. She stared back at him, wondering what he wanted.

"What's your name, sweetie?"

"Oh! Right. Sierra. Sierra Hartford." She watched him repeat her name into his phone, then his expression changed, and he held it away from his ear before turning and holding it out to her. "Cassidy wants to talk to you."

Her heart pounded as she took it from him. "Cass?"

"Sierra! What are you doing in Montana? I would have sworn this weekend was your wedding. Tell me when it is? I only turned down the invitation because I couldn't get out of this conference. But I must have had the dates confused. If you can still fit us in, I'd love to come! I won't pretend that I like Jared, but I'd love to be there for you."

"Oh. No. You didn't have the dates confused."

"Damn, girl. So, you're calling me on your wedding day? I'm honored. Wait … why are you in Montana? Shit. What's going on, Sierra?"

"You were right about Jared."

"What happened?"

No way was she going to tell the whole sordid story. Not over the phone and not standing here by the side of the road with two big, handsome cowboys watching over her. "I'll tell you about it when I see you. For now, let's just say that I came to my senses just in time."

"What, and you called it off and decided to take a vacation instead?"

Sierra couldn't hold in a bitter laugh. "Not quite. When I said just in time, I mean literally just in time. I ran out of there, rented a car and started driving."

She should have known what to expect from Cassidy. She laughed. "Good for you! I'm proud of you. What happens now?"

"Well, that's the part I don't have figured out. See, I got on I-15 and just drove for hours. Then I realized that I'd have to stop before I hit Canada. I don't have my passport. Then I remembered that you live up here now. I was on my way to your house. I forgot about your conference. And then I managed to land my rental in a ditch." She looked at the two cowboys. "Then I ran into some friends of yours and they said they'd call Shane, since I hadn't been able to get hold of you."

"Damn, girl. I'm so sorry I'm not there. But you're okay with Wade and Ford."

Sierra looked at the two men again. "Apparently."

Cassidy chuckled. "They'll take good care of you."

"They offered to get my car out of the ditch."

"Yeah. And then they can take you back to their place."

"Cass!"

Cassidy laughed. "Our place is all locked up. Those MacFarland boys have plenty of room. They have a guest ranch. They'll be able to put you up. We'll be back on Monday. I'd come right now if I could, but I have a meeting tomorrow that I can't miss. Say you'll stay till Monday?"

"I …" Sierra looked at the two men – the MacFarland boys, apparently. Cassidy was out of her mind. She couldn't just ask complete strangers if she could stay with them for the weekend.

"Sierra?"

"What?"

"Give the phone back to Wade, and trust your Auntie Cassie to sort this out for you, would ya? You'll have a place to stay and some time and space to get your head on straight. I'd come straight back for you if I could. But I'll be there on Monday. They're good guys. They own a guest ranch. It's not like I'm suggesting that you should stay in their house or anything. Trust me?"

Sierra looked at Wade and then at Ford. They were friends of a friend. Not strangers. And it wasn't as though she had any other options.

"Trust me, okay?" Cassidy said again. "I'll talk to them, get you set up with a place to stay, and I'll be there on Monday."

"Okay. Thanks. I'll see you then, then."

"You will. Relax. You'll be fine. You did the right thing, you know."

"That's about the only thing I'm certain of right now."

"I'd say it's the only thing you need to know. You'll be fine. I promise. Let me talk to Wade and get you set up. I'll turn my phone back on and you can call me any time you need, okay?"

"Thanks, Cassidy."

"Hey, that's what friends are for. Talk soon. You're going to be okay. I promise."

Sierra handed the phone back to Wade. She was glad Cassidy sounded so confident. The way she felt, she wasn't sure that she'd ever be okay again.

Chapter Two

Wade held the passenger door of the SUV open and smiled at Sierra. It hadn't taken him and Ford long to get the vehicle out of the ditch and change the flat. But in that short time, it had gone dark, and the woman in the wedding dress – Sierra – seemed to be going downhill fast. She was shaking now.

It wasn't that cold. But then what did he know about how it felt to her? She looked kind of delicate. She probably wasn't used to cold or heat. She looked like the kind of woman who lived a climate-controlled kind of life.

Since she wasn't getting into the SUV, he strode back to the truck and grabbed his jacket from the backseat. Ford followed him and raised an eyebrow. "Do you think she's cold or in shock?

"Probably a little bit of both."

Ford nodded. "If you're okay with her, I'm going to head back to the ranch."

Wade laughed. "Coward!"

Ford grinned back at him. "Hell yeah. And I don't mind admitting it. Emotional women scare me – and that right there is one emotional woman."

"Ah, come on. You can hardly blame her."

"Nope. Not saying I blame her. Just saying that I'm not getting involved. You're the one who wanted a bride. Now, you've got one." He grinned. "Maybe dealing with this one will be enough to bring you to your senses."

Wade glanced back to where Sierra was still standing beside the vehicle, shivering. "It's not like we could leave her out here."

"I know. I'm not saying I would. Just that I'm glad you're here to play the good Samaritan so that I don't have to."

"Yeah. I'm going to give her the jacket. I'll see you back at the ranch once I get her settled at the lodge."

"Okay. You still up for a drink when we're both done?"

"Yup." For some reason, Wade felt as though he was going to need one.

Ford pulled away, and Wade went back to Sierra. He held out the jacket, but she just looked at it.

"Are you cold? You're shivering."

"Oh. Sorry."

He smiled. "There's no need to apologize." He moved closer, wrapping the jacket around her shoulders. Whoa. Not a wise move. She was an attractive woman, a fact he'd been trying to ignore since she was wearing a wedding dress and obviously traumatized. But standing this close to her, wrapping his jacket around her, it was impossible to ignore the way his body reacted to her. And didn't that make him an asshole? What was supposed to be the best day of her life had gone horribly wrong somehow. She was stuck by the side of the road in the middle of nowhere. The last thing she needed was a horny cowboy getting ideas about her.

Just as he tried to talk himself down, she looked up into his eyes and stole his breath. "Thank you."

He struggled for air before he could make himself speak. "You looked cold." He pulled the lapels of the jacket together under her chin, partly because he didn't want to move away from her, and partly to cover up the tantalizing yet tasteful display of cleavage that he was struggling to ignore.

Her eyes were a beautiful gray color. At first, they seemed flat and dull but when they met his, they seemed to light from within, like there was lightning in the clouds. Damn.

"I don't mean for the jacket. Well, not just the jacket. I mean thank you for ..." She looked around, taking in the fields and the river and the mountains under the now dark sky. "For everything. For finding me. For offering me a place. For ... being so kind. I don't know what I would have done if you hadn't shown up."

She looked small and lost and he wanted nothing more than to wrap her up in a hug. She looked like she could use one. Instead, he patted her shoulder awkwardly. "You'd have been fine. This might look like the back end of nowhere, but someone would have come along. Folks are neighborly out here. Anyone would have helped you out."

She was still shivering as she met his gaze again. "Really? I was starting to think I might be eaten by wolves or found by a serial killer."

He chuckled and tightened his hold on her shoulder. "Nah. Like I said, pretty much anyone out here would help you out."

Her tongue darted out and moistened her bottom lip. Yeesh. He should not be letting his mind go there. "I'm glad it was you." Her voice was little more than a whisper, but it hit him full force.

His breath got stuck somewhere in his chest again. He needed to stop it. She was just being polite, thanking him. He didn't need to get carried away, didn't need to think about kissing those pink lips as he watched her roll them together. He needed to get her into her car and get her to a room in the lodge. He didn't see any harm in telling the truth, though.

"I'm glad it was me, too. Come on, let's get going." He helped her up into the passenger seat and pulled out the seatbelt, though he did manage to resist reaching across and fastening it for her. Instead, his fingers brushed against hers when he handed her the buckle. He froze. How could such a fleeting touch have such a profound effect on him?

"Thank you." She held his gaze for a long moment. Her cheeks were flushed and her eyes wide. Was he some kind of idiot? There was no way she was reacting the same way he was. The poor little darlin' was more likely freaking out, wondering what he was up to.

He made himself give her a friendly smile, before closing the door and jogging around to the driver's side.

~ ~ ~

Sierra looked up at the wooden arch across the entry to the driveway. The name *MacFarland Ranch* was carved into it. White post and rail fence lined the long driveway. Even in the dark, the place was impressive. She could make out the shape of horses in the field to the right, and cows to the left.

"Is it a working ranch?"

"It is. It's been a cattle ranch for fifty years. We only opened the lodge last year." Wade glanced across at her. "Don't worry. It's nice." He looked hesitant for a moment before he added. "The lodge, I mean. It's high end."

She smiled at him. She couldn't help it. He'd been so good to her already and here he was reassuring her that his home – his guest ranch – was somewhere that she'd feel comfortable.

He brought the SUV to a stop when the driveway split. He pointed to the left. "The house is over there." Then he turned to the right. "The lodge is this way and beyond it are the stables."

"Do you have a lot of horses?" It felt strange to be making small talk, but what else could she do? She could hardly pour her heart out to him. No matter how kind he was, he was still a stranger. He didn't need to hear her sorry tale or to see her break down, and she knew that as soon as she was alone, she was going to do just that.

He glanced over at her again. "We do. There's the stud … we run a breeding operation," he explained. "And we have a bunch of trail horses that the guests ride. And then there are the cow horses." He smiled and explained again, "The horses that the hands ride to work the cattle."

Either he was really good at knowing what would need to be explained to someone who knew next to nothing about horses and cows and ranches, or her face gave away her cluelessness. Either way, she was grateful.

He stopped in front of a beautiful, big log-built lodge. It was much larger than she'd expected. A porch ran along the front of the building. It was lined with rockers, and planters filled with flowers hung on the railing. It looked like the perfect place to sit and relax. Though, she wondered if she'd ever relax again. She shuddered at the memory of what she'd heard Jared say this afternoon. She'd be safe here, for the weekend, until Cassidy came. But she was going to have to pull herself together and figure out what to do. Could she call the police?

Should she? Was what Jared had planned for her a crime if he'd only planned it and didn't get the chance to see it through?

Wade turned in his seat, looking concerned. "Are you still cold? Do you want to wait here while I go in? Anita's on the desk tonight. I'll ask her what we have available. I think one of the cabins is vacant. If it is, I can get the key and take you over there without you having to go inside the lodge."

She frowned, wondering why he wouldn't want her to go inside. Then she remembered. She was still wearing her freaking wedding dress. The skirt was streaked with dust and dirt, and the rest of her didn't look much better.

He smiled. "If you want to come in, you're welcome. I was only thinking about how you might feel."

She nodded and had to swallow around the lump in her throat. How could a man she'd known for an hour at most be more considerate of her feelings than the man she'd been about to marry? Only last Sunday morning, Jared had invited his golf buddies into the kitchen to wait for him while he finished getting ready, even though she'd been sitting there bleary-eyed in her pajamas. "Thanks. I'd rather wait here."

She watched Wade run up the steps. Phew. He was one heck of a cowboy. And didn't that just show how traumatized she must be? How could she be ogling another man's butt right now? Even if it was encased in tight blue jeans.

He stopped and looked back at her before he pushed the door open. His smile settled her insides. What was it about him that made her believe what he'd said – that everything was going to be okay? Her whole world was about as far away from okay as it had ever been, but Wade's smile made it not seem so bad after all.

His smile was noticeably absent when he came back down the steps. He didn't look happy at all. He opened the door and got in, then turned to face her before he spoke.

"What's wrong?"

He smiled, but it wasn't as comforting as before. "I'm afraid the lodge is full. Anita took a last-minute booking from a couple traveling down the valley to the park and gave them the last cabin, too."

"Oh." She hated that her voice wavered, but she had no idea what she was going to do now. But it was hardly his problem. Maybe there'd be a room available in one of the motels in the little town she'd seen when she left the highway. She could drive up there, she'd have to. She reached for the door handle. He'd been so good to drive her here, but he was home now, and she needed …

"Hey," he reached across and rested his hand on her arm, "slow down. Where are you going?"

She looked back at him. "To get back in the driver's seat." She made a face as she said it. She needed to do that both literally and metaphorically. It'd been nice to let the sexy cowboy take the wheel for a while, but she had a life to figure out, starting with finding a place to spend the night – and that was hardly his responsibility. He'd already done more than could be expected of him.

Her mind stopped its chattering and slowed down when he squeezed her arm. "It's okay. I still have a place for you."

"You do?"

He looked at little uncomfortable, but he nodded. "I hoped that you'd be able to go straight into a room that was ready for you. But since that's not an option, there is a cabin you can have."

"But didn't you say they're all booked?"

He gave her a sheepish smile. "Not all of them. I've been staying in one, but I can clear my things out and you can have it."

She stared at him. "You can't do that. Where will you sleep?"

"It's okay. I can go back up to the house."

"But ..." Her eyes filled with tears. She didn't want to be a weak and weepy woman, but it had been one heck of a day. She was tired, and all of a sudden hungry, and this kind, sexy wonderful man was now offering her his bed. She hiccupped out a half laugh half sob, at that thought. Not like that. He wasn't offering to *share* his bed with her. She looked up into his kind green eyes; the lines around them were etched with concern. She had to admit that if he were offering, she'd be tempted to take him up on it.

"Come on. I'll drive you over there. You must be exhausted."

She simply nodded. That must be it. Exhaustion must be the reason she was having thoughts no woman in her situation should be having – no matter how hot the cowboy who'd rescued her might be.

~ ~ ~

Wade held the cabin door open and gestured for Sierra to go inside. He'd been using this cabin while he fixed it up. It was one of the original buildings on the ranch and he hadn't planned to use it to accommodate guests. But between the fact that he needed all the beds he could get and the way so many guests had commented on how *quaint* it was, he'd decided to renovate it. Fortunately, the work was almost finished. There was no way he would have brought Sierra here even a few weeks ago.

He went inside after her and found her turning in a circle, taking it all in. "This place is lovely. I can see why you'd want to stay here. Are you sure you don't mind, though?"

"Of course not." He looked around, glad that he'd taken the time to straighten the place up before he went out this morning. His laptop sat on the coffee table in front of the sofa. His mug was still on the counter in the kitchen, but at least none of his clothes were strewn around.

"Can I get you anything? Are you hungry? Do you want a drink?"

Her pained expression made him wonder what she was about to say. "The first thing I need is to use the bathroom."

"Ah. Of course." He pointed to the hallway that led off the living area. "Second door on the left."

"Thank you." Her dress rustled as she walked. Her cheeks were pink when she stopped and looked back over her shoulder at him. "It may take me a while. Don't think I've fallen in or anything."

He cocked an eyebrow, not sure what to say to that.

She gave an embarrassed little laugh. "I'm going to have to do battle with the dress."

"Ah!" Shit. He should have thought. "Do you have a bag in your car – something to change into?"

"No. I …" She drew in a big shaky breath, making him want to go to her and wrap her in a hug – he needed to stop thinking about that. "I left in too much of a hurry."

He nodded, and she turned and rustled down the hall until he heard the bathroom door close behind her. He'd seen enough movies where the bride had a bridesmaid go to the bathroom with her to help do battle with the dress as she put it, but he could hardly offer to do that.

He took off his hat and hung it on the hook by the door. He could find her something to change into. She had to be a good six inches shorter than him, maybe more, but he could offer her a shirt, maybe some sweatpants.

He went into the bedroom and started digging through the drawers. After leaving a few choices on the bed for her, he went to the kitchen. There was beer – if a woman like her drank the stuff – and there was a frozen pizza, if she needed food. He could maybe call Tyler and ask him to rustle something up for her at the lodge, but no, he decided against it. Sierra didn't need to have to deal with people tonight. That was the only reason. It wasn't that he wanted to keep her here to himself or anything – that would be crazy.

Chapter Three

When she came out of the bathroom, Sierra startled at the sight of Wade standing right there. He was looking in the linen closet in the hallway.

He looked stressed but gave her a half smile. "I thought I had extra bedding in here, but don't worry. I'll run back up to the lodge and get fresh sheets for you."

She looked at the door across the hallway. "What's in there?"

"It's a second bedroom, but it isn't finished yet. You can't stay in there. You can have the master, but I've been sleeping in there, so I need to change the sheets."

She was starting to wonder if the universe had put Wade on that road this evening – brought him into her life however briefly – just to show her how a good man was supposed to behave. To prove to her beyond a shadow of a doubt that the way Jared treated her was so much less than she deserved – even before what he had planned for her and what he had going on with Lori. She shuddered at the memory of what she'd seen.

"Hey. Are you okay?"

She looked up into Wade's kind eyes. "Strange as it may sound, I think I'm better than I've been in a long time. Or I will be once I have the chance to process it all."

He nodded; the poor man obviously didn't know what to say. How could he?

"Thank you so much. For everything. You've done so much – gone way above and beyond. You really don't need to change the bedding."

"It won't take me long to run up to the lodge. If you're okay here?" He smiled, and the warmth of it washed over her again. How could he have that effect on her? How could the smile of a man she'd known for a couple of hours make her feel better – make her feel that perhaps he was right and that everything was going to be okay?

She realized he was watching her face, waiting for an answer.

When she didn't speak, he asked again, "Are you okay? What else do you need? Are you hungry, thirsty?" He ran his hand through his hair, making her notice that he'd taken off his hat. His hair was a sandy blond, and watching him run his fingers through it made her want to do the same – what the heck was wrong with her?

"Oh, and I put some clothes out on the bed for you. I'm guessing you might want to get out of that dress."

She rolled her eyes and leaned her head back against the wall. "You're an angel, aren't you? Sent to me in my hour of need."

He laughed, and the sound of it reverberated in her chest. It was the best sound she'd heard all day, probably all week, maybe ever. "I'm no angel, believe me."

Tension coiled in her stomach at those words, but he didn't mean them the way she wanted to interpret them. She had to get a grip, otherwise she'd be throwing herself at him and dragging him into the bedroom with her – and asking for his help to get out of the dress.

That thought sobered her and brought her back to her senses. She was indeed going to have to ask him to help her out of the dress, though not in the way that her frazzled brain wanted to imagine.

He took a step back. She was probably freaking him out. "Do you want to change while I pour you a drink? There's frozen pizza if you're hungry. I can heat the oven."

"Thanks. That all sounds wonderful, but first, could you …" Her cheeks heated, but she had to ask; there was no way she'd be able to get out of the dress if he didn't undo all those fiddly little pearl fasteners for her.

His smile was back. "Whatever you want. Name it, and I'll do it."

If only! She turned around and held her hand as far up her back as she could get it. "See all these pesky little things, could you undo them for me? I'll never escape this darned dress otherwise." She was glad she wasn't facing him when she heard his sharp intake of breath. "I'm sorry. I …"

"No. Don't apologize. It'd be my honor to help liberate you from the demon dress."

She couldn't see his smile, but she could hear it in his voice. His words made her smile, too. "Thank you." She liked the idea of him being the one to free her from the dress and all that it represented. She could hardly tell him that, though.

"Do you want to come back into the living room? The light's better in there."

She followed him back and stood in front of the sofa, underneath the main light fixture, which was a chandelier made of some kind of antlers.

She sucked in her breath when his warm fingers brushed over the bare skin on her back.

"Sorry. Cold hands?"

"No! I …" She couldn't exactly tell him that far from feeling cold, his fingers sent a rush of heat through her. "It's fine."

She'd swear his fingers trembled as they worked their way down her back. She'd thought the two dozen tiny pearls and the loops that held them were overkill when she'd chosen the dress. She knew Jared wouldn't have had the patience for them; she'd planned to have Amelia help with them when she changed into her evening dress. What did it say about her that she was grateful for every one of those little pearls as Wade's hands slowly worked their way down her back?

"There you go. That's the last one."

"Thank you." She held the bodice tightly to her front. The dress didn't need a bra and there was no way she was going to flash him by letting it fall. She scurried back to the bedroom before she made a fool of herself.

Wade turned on the oven to preheat and then grabbed himself a beer. He didn't know if she'd drink one but he sure as hell needed one – some of Ford's bourbon sounded even better right now. He needed a stiff one. He stifled a laugh at the thought that he'd had to hide the fact that unfastening her dress like that had given him a stiff one.

He took a long slug of his beer and tried to recall baseball stats, hoping that would settle him before she came back out. He had no right to be thinking about her that way, but whoever she was supposed to marry today must be the biggest fool on Earth. How he could have let her get away was beyond Wade. Her skin was so pale and delicate. She smelled so damned good, and she was so responsive. If she quivered and trembled the way she had while he was unfastening all those little pearls, he could only imagine what she'd be like in bed.

He shook his head. He shouldn't be imagining anything of the sort. Back to baseball stats – and beer. His phone rang, and he pulled it out of his back pocket, grateful for the distraction until he saw Ford's name on the display. His brother was about to give him some shit, no doubt about it.

"What's up?"

"I was calling to ask you the same thing. Where are you? Did you get your jilted bride settled at the lodge?"

"She wasn't jilted. She's a runaway bride."

Ford laughed. "Uh-oh. You're jumping to her defense already?"

"No, I ..." He ran his hand through his hair. "I just feel bad for her."

"Why, what's the story?

"I don't even know yet."

"Yet? Does that mean you still plan to find out? Haven't you dropped her off yet?"

"No. I ... err ... the lodge was full so ..."

"So? Where are you? Where are you taking her?"

Wade glanced at the hallway, but Sierra hadn't emerged from the bedroom. "We're fully booked, so I offered her the cabin."

"*Your* cabin?"

"It's not mine. You know that. And it's almost ready for guests anyway. And ..."

Ford's laugh cut him off. "Whatever you say, bro. I take it I shouldn't expect you to come over for that drink?"

"I'll be there, but later. I'm going to make sure she gets something to eat, and ..." He totally forgot what he was saying when Sierra came padding down the hallway barefoot, wearing just his T-shirt. She gave him an apologetic look when she saw that he was on the phone. He put his hand over the speaker. "What do you need?"

She cringed as if she was about to ask for something outrageous. "Would it be okay if I took a shower?"

Wade swallowed, hard. Neither baseball stats, nor his brother on the phone could stop his mind from conjuring up images of droplets of water running down over her naked body. He swallowed again and nodded. "Of course. There are clean towels in the linen cupboard."

"Thanks." She smiled and turned to go back the way she'd come. He watched her ass and her long, shapely, bare legs every step of the way.

"Bro!" Ford's voice coming out of his phone brought him back to his senses.

"Yeah?" His voice sounded hoarse even to his own ears.

Ford laughed. "I'll leave you to it. But I'm going to want a full report when you get back here – or tomorrow after she leaves."

Wade's heart thudded to a stop.

"You still there?"

"Yeah."

Ford laughed again. "You need to get your shit together."

"I'm not denying that. But she can't leave tomorrow – where would she go? Cassidy said she'll be home on Monday. We have to keep her till then."

"Jesus, Wade. She's not a stray puppy you brought home from the shelter. You don't get to keep her or not keep her. It'll be up to her what she wants to do. And I think you need to remember that whatever's going on with her, she was supposed to get married today. Don't let your inner romantic get carried away. She's got to be a mess. If she's going to stick around, all she needs is a friend. Nothing more."

"I know." He couldn't even make himself sound angry. Ford was only looking out for him, and he could use all the help he could get. It'd be all too easy to get carried away around the beautiful but fragile woman who was currently in his shower, and Ford was right – if it weren't for whatever had sent her fleeing from her wedding, she'd be with *Jared* tonight and …

no. He stopped his mind before it got to thinking about what newlyweds would be doing on their wedding night.

"You're not planning on spending the night there, are you?"

"No! I'm just going to make sure she's settled, then I'll be up to the house."

"Okay."

"Okay." Wade glanced at the bathroom door. If he had any sense he'd leave now before she came out. But he couldn't do that to her. He'd wait and make sure she was settled, just like he'd said.

Ford blew out a sigh. "We should probably call Jane tomorrow."

"Why?"

"Because she's a girl, dipshit. And I may not know much about them, but I do know that when they're upset, they like to talk – to other girls."

"Yeah. You're right. That's a good idea."

"Ugh. But you think it'd be a better idea for her to talk to you, don't you? I'm going to hang up. Don't do anything stupid."

Wade chuckled. "I won't. See you later." He ended the call and went to put the pizza in the oven.

Sierra checked herself over in the mirror before she opened the bathroom door. Her damp hair hung around her shoulders, her cheeks were pink, and her eyes were rimmed with red from all the crying, but she looked better than she did before.

She felt like a little lost orphan dressed in Wade's clothes. She'd had to turn up the bottoms of the sweatpants three times over, the same with the sleeves of his Henley. But the way they looked mattered less to her than the way they felt. They were soft, and warm, and clean, and they smelled like Wade. She smelled like him too, which was both comforting and disconcerting at the same time. Since she'd fled from her wedding without even going up to her room to collect her bags, she had nothing with her. Her purse had only contained her wallet, her phone, lipstick, and eyeliner. The ridiculously expensive perfumed toiletries that had been part of Amelia's wedding gift to her still sat in the bathroom of the hotel room where she'd gotten ready this morning. Wow. That was this morning? It seemed like another lifetime already.

She hadn't thought about it until she'd stepped into the shower, but once she was there, she'd had no choice but to use Wade's toiletries. His shower gel smelled like sandalwood with a hint of citrus. It didn't look particularly expensive, but it smelled divine. Perhaps it was simply because it smelled like him. She pushed away from the counter. Obviously, her brain was addled after a long and stressful day. She'd had no food, not even anything to drink since the water she'd sipped while she and Amelia got ready.

Shoot! She needed to call Amelia. It was time to face reality. Even though being here with a cowboy, in a cabin, in Montana felt nothing like any reality she'd ever known.

Wade was in the kitchen, drinking beer from a bottle. The bottle stopped halfway to his lips when he saw her coming.

All of a sudden, she felt stupidly shy, though why she had no idea. "Hi," was all she could manage to squeak out.

"Hey." His voice was low and gravelly, and he cleared his throat before he spoke again. "What can I get you to drink? I put a pizza in. I figured you must be hungry."

"I am. I'm starved. And I'd love a beer, please."

He cocked an eyebrow. "I wouldn't have had you down as a beer drinker, but it's all I have here. You should probably have water, too." He handed her a bottle of water and popped the top off a beer before handing her that. "When was the last time you had anything to eat?"

"This morning. Before … before everything happened. I didn't feel much like stopping anywhere on the road – I didn't want to endure the odd looks people would give me in the dress – or heaven forbid, have to answer any questions."

He nodded. "I figured as much." He gestured toward the sofa. "Want to sit? The pizza still has ten minutes."

"Thanks." She sat at one end of the sofa and curled her legs underneath her. Wade took the armchair opposite her. She felt her skin heat as he let his gaze travel over her. Was it possible that he felt the same kind of attraction she did?

He let out a short laugh, and that combined with his words convinced her that she was being ridiculous. "Sorry about the clothes."

"Oh." Shoot. She really shouldn't sound disappointed – shouldn't *feel* disappointed. She could hardly expect him to find anything attractive about a makeup-free woman, with damp hair who was dressed in his sweatpants. "They're very comfortable," she offered. As if that might help somehow.

He chuckled. "Good. That was my intention. I figured you'd need something comfortable after your dress." His smile faded. "After the day you've had."

She nodded. It was a good thing he'd brought that up. She'd been more concerned about what he might think of her in his clothes than anything else. His mention of the day she'd had reminded her that she needed to call Amelia. Her best friend had covered for her while she made her exit. She'd blindly accepted that Sierra knew what she was doing and that she had to do it, but she had to be going out of her mind with worry by now.

She reached for her purse, which she'd left on the coffee table. "I don't mean to be rude. But I need to call my friend."

"Of course." He jumped to his feet. "I can go. You're all set now. The pizza just – "

"No!" She said it so forcefully she surprised them both. "Sorry. But please don't go. I was hoping that you'd stay and help with the pizza and …" She didn't know what else she wanted him to stay for, but she knew that she didn't want him to leave. Not yet. She smiled, hoping that would be enough. "I wasn't trying to get rid of you. I could use the company if you wouldn't mind, but I really need to call my best friend, let her know that I'm still alive."

"Of course. I can wait outside if you like. Give you some privacy."

He was something else. She lived amongst and rubbed shoulders with the so-called elite of society every day of her life, yet she'd never met a man as considerate as the cowboy standing before her. "It's okay. Please don't go outside. I'm only going to let her know that I'm okay, that I'm safe."

He nodded, but still looked uncomfortable. He jerked his head toward the kitchen. "I'll set us up for the pizza."

She took a big breath to steady herself and then dialed Amelia's number. Her best friend picked up on the second ring.

"Sierra! Where are you? Are you okay?"

"I'm fine. Honestly. I'm okay."

"Thank God for that! Where are you? Please tell me that you're still here? Did you go over to the Waldorf Astoria?"

Sierra couldn't help but laugh. Of course, Amelia would expect her to have gone all of five miles across the resort town to the next best hotel. "No, actually I went a little farther."

"Oh, Sierra! Did you go all the way down into Salt Lake? Where are you staying? I'll come to you."

She laughed again. "That'd take you a while. I'm in Montana." She had to hold the phone away from her ear when Amelia squealed.

"Oh, my gosh, Sierra! Did you get on a plane? Did you stop and buy clothes? What did you do?"

Sierra sneaked a glance at Wade. He had his back to her, but she'd bet he was listening. It'd be hard for him not to. For some reason, she wanted him to hear about the way her day had gone. But she doubted that he'd ask, so this worked out well.

"Remember the old guy on the concierge desk? The one who was so nice to us yesterday when we asked about the spa."

"Yes."

"Well, after I left you, I went straight to him and told him that I had an emergency and needed to rent a vehicle."

"Oh, my gosh, Sierra. Don't tell me that you drove all the way to Montana? And don't tell me that you paid for the rental with your credit card? Jared will for sure track you down."

Sierra glanced at Wade again. "I didn't use my credit card. I was worried about Jared tracking me, too. I told Francis, the concierge, that I didn't want anyone to know that I'd rented a vehicle." She was fairly certain Wade's shoulders tensed at that. "He was so sweet. He told me I could pay with cash and then he'd bill it through the hotel."

"Do you think that's safe?"

"I do. He knew what I was doing – that I was running away from the wedding. Although, that didn't take much figuring out given that I was wearing a wedding dress. He was so sweet. He squeezed my hand and wished me luck. Said he knew it was none of his business but that he hadn't thought much of the groom when he met him."

Amelia giggled. "He's a smart man."

Sierra's smile faded. "Yeah. Way smarter than I am. Francis met Jared for just a few minutes and took a dislike to him. I've known him all this time and almost married him."

"Almost, that's the important word there. You didn't marry him. And that's all that matters. You escaped from a fate worse than death."

"More than that, Amelia. I literally escaped death. I told you what he said. If I'd married him ..." she shuddered.

"Yes, but you didn't. You had a narrow escape, but you still escaped."

"What if he comes after me?"

Wade swung around to look at her, and she gave him a wan smile.

"You think he would?" asked Amelia.

"I hope not. It seems logical to me that since his plan was to kill me in order to inherit everything, there won't be any point in killing me now – because we're not married, so he wouldn't get my money."

"I hope you're right. But Sierra, I think you should stay hidden away for a while. You didn't see him when he realized that you'd gone. That there wasn't going to be a wedding. He looked ready to kill all right."

Sierra shuddered. "How did everyone else handle it? I feel so bad, letting them all down."

"Ugh! Don't! What else could you have done? Your life is way more important than their travel plans."

"I know, but so many people went out of their way to be there for me today and ... How was Barney?"

"He was less shocked than most of them. I think he was secretly glad that you called it off."

Sierra let out a short laugh. "I hardly called it off. I just ran. After seeing Jared and Lori together like that and hearing what he had planned for me and those poor little children ... I had no choice."

"I think you need to tell Barney exactly what you heard – and saw."

"I know. I will. I had enough to deal with just trying to keep the car on the road today." She gave Wade a rueful smile. Amelia might not know that she hadn't actually succeeded in keeping the car on the road, but he did. He smiled back.

"And where exactly are you?"

"Oh. Remember Cassidy Lane?"

"Cassidy! I should have realized when you said Montana. It turned out to be a blessing in disguise that she couldn't make it for the wedding then."

"It did." Sierra didn't like to lie, but technically she hadn't. She only mentioned Cassidy, and Amelia had assumed the rest for herself.

"What did you say to Jared before you left?"

"I didn't say anything. I heard him talking to Lori – and saw what they were doing, and then I came to you. And thanks, by the way. You're the best bestie in the world. I can't think of anyone else on Earth who would be as supportive as you were. After what I'd seen and heard, I had to run. And you didn't even question me. You just wished me luck, told me to call and let you know I was safe, and said you'd cover for me." She didn't for one moment think that Amelia needed a recap of those frantic few moments, but it couldn't hurt for Wade to hear it.

"Aww. You know I'd do anything for you. I was as stunned as you were at what he said – and at Lori, if not him, for what they were doing. I should have gone with you, though."

"No. It was better that you stayed. And I really am okay." Wade was slicing the pizza now. "I'll call you again tomorrow, okay?"

"Okay. I hope you get some sleep. And say hi to Cassidy for me."

"Will do." She ended the call and looked over at Wade, hoping that he'd ask what had happened. She wanted to talk to him, to tell him, but he just smiled and held up the pizza. "Stay there. I'll bring it over."

When he served her a slice on a plate and then sat back in the armchair, she waited. But he didn't ask. So, she didn't tell. Between the beer and the food and the stress of the day finally taking its toll, she was yawning by the time he took her empty plate away.

"That should set you up to be able to sleep."

"I hope so."

"I'll leave you my number. Call me in the morning when you're ready for some company."

"Thanks." She watched him write his number on the pad. She didn't want him to go. How crazy was that?

When he straightened up, he met her gaze. "Are you going to be okay?"

She shook her head. "I know I shouldn't ask, but please would you stay?"

He froze and his eyes widened.

Oh, Lord! She'd gone and done it now. "I don't mean like that, I just mean here, in the cabin. I don't want … I'm scared."

He nodded slowly. "Sure. If you want. I can take the second bedroom." The lines around his eyes were etched with concern. "But only if you're comfortable with me being here?"

She nodded. "I feel so much safer with you than I did with the man I was supposed to marry today."

His lips pressed together. "I gathered as much. I didn't want to intrude. But if you want to talk about it, I want to listen."

"Thank you. I'd like that." She couldn't hold in a huge yawn and then flushed with embarrassment when he laughed.

"Tomorrow will be soon enough. Tonight, you need to sleep."

Chapter Four

Wade pulled the cabin door closed as quietly as he could. He was hoping that Sierra would sleep for a while yet. He'd left her a note just in case. He didn't want her to wake up and wonder where he was – didn't want her to feel like she was all alone in a strange place. But he had to take the risk of leaving her. He wanted to talk to Ford, to tell him what she'd said last night. His brother was probably going to give him grief for having stayed the night with her, but he'd get over it when Wade told him what she'd said to her friend.

She'd literally escaped death. His jaw clenched as he remembered the look on her face while she talked to her friend. This Jared had planned to kill her? And from what Wade had pieced together, he'd been with another woman, someone named Lori.

He shook his head and pulled the keys to her SUV out of his pocket. He really had to hope that she didn't wake up before he returned. He didn't want her to panic and think that her vehicle had been stolen on top of everything else.

Ford was standing in the kitchen, a mug of coffee gripped in his hand when Wade entered. He pursed his lips but didn't say anything.

Wade poured himself a mug. "Before you say anything. I only stayed because she asked me to."

Ford sputtered coffee as he snorted.

"Not like that!" Wade felt bad that for a moment, when she'd asked him to stay, he'd thought she meant *stay* with her, too.

"So, you stayed to comfort her?"

"No. I stayed because she was scared."

Ford's smirk disappeared. "Of what? What's her deal?"

"I don't know the full story, but she called her friend last night. She said that she used cash to rent the car because she didn't want him to be able to find her. She also said that she hoped he wouldn't see any point in killing her now – "

"What the fuck?"

"I know, right? Apparently, she overheard him talking to another woman, and I'm guessing that they were doing more than talking. Either way, she heard that he planned to kill her once they were married – so that he'd inherit all her money."

Ford frowned. "And that's why she thinks there wouldn't be any point in him killing her now? Because he wouldn't inherit?"

Wade nodded. "That's what it sounded like."

"But she didn't tell you any of this?"

"No, like I said, she talked to her friend on the phone." He took a sip of his coffee. "I offered to go outside and let her talk in private, but I kind of got the impression that she wanted me to overhear. That she wanted me to know but didn't want to tell me."

"I can see that. So, what are we going to do?"

Wade smiled. His brother might not have wanted to have to deal with the emotional woman they'd brought home. But now he knew that her troubles were very real, he showed no hesitation. "I haven't figured that out yet. She's still sleeping, and I wanted to let you know what the deal was. I doubt we'll have an angry groom show up on the ranch, but just in case we do, I wanted to let you know."

"Right. I'll let the hands know to keep an eye out for any strangers around."

"Thanks. Mind if I use your laptop?"

"Go ahead. You going to look her up?"

Wade nodded. "I figure if she has enough money to be worth killing for it, then there's probably something online somewhere about the wedding. I want to see what I can find out about this Jared asshole." He went and sat at the big kitchen table and flipped open Ford's laptop.

"And what you can learn about her, too?"

"Yeah." There was no point in denying it. Especially not to Ford. He hadn't slept well. He'd been too busy alternating between thinking about and trying not to think about the woman lying just a few feet away from him. He'd wanted to get on his own laptop to see what he could learn about her, but that had felt wrong somehow. Up here at the house with Ford, it seemed more reasonable. He wasn't stalking the woman he was attracted to; he was researching her background to figure out how they could help her.

"Want me to call Jane and ask her to come over now?"

"No!" He answered too quickly, and he knew it.

Ford just laughed. "You've got it bad. All right. You can keep her to yourself this morning, but I think you should bring her up here for lunch with everyone. Then afterwards she can decide for herself if she'd rather stay here and hang out with Jane for girl talk or let you whisk her back to your cabin."

Wade just made a face at him while he waited for the search results to load. "Holy shit!"

"What?" Ford came to stand behind him. "Damn! That's not just any old runaway bride you've got stashed away in your cabin, little brother. She's a real-life billionaire heiress."

Wade nodded slowly as he read over the article. Her father, Sebastian Hartford was one of those rich old men who showed up on the TV whenever there was big news in the financial markets. At least, he had been. The article reported that he'd died almost three years ago. Wade frowned as he read on. His son, Sebastian Hartford II, had taken over Hartford Enterprises. Wade clicked the link to read more about him. Damn. It led to an obituary. He'd died just over a year ago, in a boating accident.

"That poor girl's been through hell," Ford muttered, still reading over Wade's shoulder.

"Yeah. She lost her dad, then her brother in such a short time. Makes me think that this Jared saw her as an easy mark."

"No, look." Ford pointed at the screen. "I bet that's him. Barney Hollinsworth appointed Jared Hanson second-in-command at Hartford Enterprises."

"Great. So, he's into her business as well."

"As her pants?" Ford smirked.

But Wade wasn't laughing. "I meant as well as her life. If he works for the family company then it's not going to be so easy for her to just get him out of her life, is it? I'm sure she mentioned someone called Barney last night. Hopefully, he's a good guy." He ran his hand through his hair. "I should get back to the cabin before she wakes up."

"Sure. You should probably ask her if she knows Hope."

"Hope?"

Ford rolled his eyes. "Hope Davenport, well, Malone now. Chance's wife. Think about it, her dad, Seymour, was into all that high finance stuff, too. There can't be that many billionaires around. They probably know each other."

"Yeah. Right. I will."

"You need to find out exactly what she heard. We need to know how likely it is that this Jared is going to come after her and what we need to do to keep her safe."

Wade smiled at him. "Thanks."

"Hmph! I'm saying it for the sake of keeping her safe, not for your sake or the sake of … whatever it is you're thinking about you and her."

"No! I'm not! I mean. I do … she is …"

Ford laughed. "You like her. I get it. But I think this is a bit bigger than you getting laid."

Wade scowled at him. "Yes. I find her attractive. But no, I'm not that much of an asshole that I'd …" He blew out a sigh. "This time yesterday she still thought she was getting married. Now she's scared her jilted groom might want to kill her. And even apart from all of that, we now know that she's way out of my league. So, no matter how attractive I find her, I can assure you, this isn't about me hoping to get laid."

"Yeah. Sorry. For what it's worth, she seemed kind of taken with you, too, yesterday."

Wade's heart leaped in his chest. There had been a few moments when he'd wondered if she'd felt the same attraction between them that he did. "You think so?" he asked a little too eagerly.

Ford smiled through pursed lips. "For what it's worth, I do. But for all the reasons you just listed, I don't think it matters, does it?"

Wade's heart sank. "No. You're right. It doesn't. The only thing that matters is making sure that she stays safe."

"Yup. And she's probably not going to feel too safe if she wakes up alone in that cabin and wonders where her knight in shining armor has taken off to in her SUV. You should get back. Bring her up here when you're ready. Tyler said he'll do lunch for one-thirty. Jane should be back from visiting the old man by then."

"Okay." He held his brother's gaze. Just the mention of the old man was a downer. "We're going to have to go and see him sometime, you know."

"Hmph." Ford shook his head. "It's not like he gives a shit. How the hell Janey keeps going week after week is beyond me."

Wade shrugged. "I guess it's a girl thing."

"I don't know about that. Laney's not been back to see him once since the last surgery, and she swears she won't come again until he's in the ground."

"Well, Laney's a different story. And maybe it's a Jane thing rather than a girl thing. But it's probably good that at least one of us has a big enough heart to go and sit with the old bastard every once in a while."

"Yeah. She's too kind for her own good, our Janey. I bet she'll take Sierra under her wing, too."

"Probably." Wade knew it'd make more sense to let his sister step up and become Sierra's point of contact and comfort. He should back out. But he didn't want to. As he drove back to the cabin, he tried telling himself that it was only because he was concerned for her safety. But it wasn't.

He opened the cabin door quietly and peeked around it.

"Morning!" She was standing in the kitchen, pouring herself a mug of coffee. "Thanks for leaving the pot all ready to go. I have a Keurig at home. I'm not sure I would have figured this thing out by myself."

He was aware that she was talking, saying something about the coffee pot, but his brain was incapable of deciphering her words. It had frozen at the sight of her. She was wearing his shirt – making him wish he'd given her a shorter one – and from what he could see, nothing else.

Her feet were bare. Her long, tan legs seemed to go on forever. At least, until they met the curve of her butt cheek, which he could see just enough of to render him speechless. She turned to face him, and he had to guess that between her bare ass cheek and the way her nipples greeted him through his shirt, she really wasn't wearing anything else.

"Are you okay? Do you need coffee?"

He nodded dumbly, hoping that she'd assume that his muteness was due to a lack of caffeine rather than a rush of desire. Lust – that was the word. His whole body was on high alert. His heart was pounding, his palms were sweating, and his dick was wide awake and pressing uncomfortably against his zipper. Shit!

"Yes, please, to a coffee. I'll be right back." He turned and fled back out through the door. He needed the cold morning air and possibly a slap upside the head to bring him back to his senses. He stuck his hands in his pockets and adjusted his jeans. Baseball stats – nope, not a chance in hell of conjuring any of those. The thought of that asshole plotting to kill Sierra for her money? Yeah, that sent a cold rush of anger through him, and brought out all his protective instincts. That might not be ideal since Sierra wasn't his to protect, but it was a step in the right direction. Since she most definitely wasn't his for what his little head had been thinking.

He took a few deep breaths before going back inside.

"Is everything okay?" Sierra looked worried.

He forced himself to smile, though it was no great hardship while he was looking at her. "Everything's fine. Did you sleep okay?"

"I did. I lay there for maybe five minutes with my brain swirling, convinced that I'd never be able to sleep and the next thing I knew I was waking up and it was morning. How about you, did you do okay in that smaller room?"

"I was fine." His breath caught in his chest again when she came closer. She looked like she hadn't been awake long, her eyes were still puffy, and her hair was a mess. It was brown with honey blonde streaks through it. It looked like she'd spent the summer on the beach. Her lips were ... curved up in a smile.

"Do you want this?" She was holding a mug of coffee out to him.

"Oh. Sorry. Thanks." He took it, and she went to sit on the sofa. He wanted to go and sit beside her, so he took the armchair instead. His brain was obviously fried, and his body was overheating again. He needed to keep his distance.

"Do you mind if I keep these things?"

He had no clue what she was talking about.

"The shirt and the sweatpants. I'll have them cleaned and mail them back to you when ..."

"Whoa!" He held his hand up. "What are you talking about?"

~ ~ ~

Sierra's heart was pounding. She needed to leave. The man sitting opposite her had shown her nothing but kindness. He'd be mortified if he knew what she'd been thinking about him as she lay in his bed last night – and again when she woke up this morning.

He hadn't ended up changing the sheets on the bed. That had turned out to be a terrible thing – and a wonderful thing at the same time. His bed smelled like him. It smelled like sandalwood and citrus, but then so did she after using his shower gel. But his bed smelled of him, not just shower gel, but him – it smelled like the man. She'd wrapped herself up in his comforter, imagining that it was his arms around her. She'd buried her face in his pillow and imagined that she was burying her face in his neck and breathing him in.

Heat flushed her cheeks. Exactly. She needed to leave before she embarrassed herself, or worse, embarrassed him.

He was still staring at her, his hand up in the air. He was rightly wondering why she was talking about mailing his clothes back to him.

She gave him an apologetic smile. "I'm sure I'll be able to buy clothes up in town, but I'd really rather burn the dress than try to get into it again."

He shook his head. "I'll take you to town. I'll buy you clothes. You can keep those. But please don't leave."

Her heart leaped into her mouth. Did he feel it too?

As if to answer her unspoken question, he shook his head. "I mean … all I mean is that you're better off staying here. For now, at least. Cassidy will be back tomorrow. I'd like you to explain what happened. I heard what you told your friend last night. I'd like it if you stayed here … until we know you're safe."

She sucked in a deep breath and let it out slowly. Of course, he'd want to make sure she was safe. He was just that kind of man. You could tell. She nodded slowly. It made sense. She needed some time to figure out what she was going to do. Hiding out here was better than any other option she could think of. And as he'd said, Cassidy would be back tomorrow. It'd make more sense to stay here than to leave in search of somewhere else to wait until her friend returned.

She met his gaze. "I don't want to intrude. You've already …"

He held his hand up again, but this time he did it with a smile and waggled his finger at her. "I'm already involved." He frowned. "I mean, we are. I talked to Ford this morning. He thinks you should stay here, too. And since it's Sunday, you'll get to meet two more brothers and a sister. We all have lunch together on Sundays."

She raised her eyebrows. "There are five of you?" That's a big family.

He chuckled. "There are five of us who live in the valley these days. There are another three who don't."

"Oh, my goodness! Eight children! Your mother must be a saint."

His smile vanished. "Yeah. She deserved a sainthood. She died a long time ago."

"I'm sorry."

He shook his head. "No need. She was glad when her time came. She might have been a saint, but my dad – " He stopped abruptly. "So, yeah. You already met Ford. He runs the cattle. Tanner and Tyler both got out of the military recently. Tanner's our horse whisperer and Tyler's the chef – he'll be making lunch. Then there's Jane. She's a veterinarian, and an absolute sweetheart. Ford thinks she'll be just what you need – you know, another girl to talk to until Cassidy gets back."

Sierra blinked. Was he going to palm her off onto his sister? She hoped not. But then maybe it would be better all around. The way she felt about him was completely inappropriate given her circumstances. She knew that sometimes hostages fell for their captors – it was some kind of syndrome. But she didn't think there was any such explanation when it came to runaway brides and their rescuers.

"You like that idea?" He held her gaze so earnestly, looking as though he was trying to do whatever would make her comfortable.

What the heck. If he wanted her to be comfortable then he needed to know. "Honestly, I'm sure your sister is lovely, but I'd be more comfortable with you. If you don't mind? If you have the time. If … if I'm going to stay here." Good grief. She must sound like an idiot. She laughed, hoping to ease the awkwardness of the moment. "I think what happened yesterday hit me harder than I realized. When I saw them, when I heard what Jared was planning to do …" She shook her head. "I think I went into shock, and then I drove all that way."

"Over four hundred miles," Wade interjected.

"Really? That far?" She shook her head again. "See. I must have been in shock. I had no idea. I only really came out of it when you and Ford stopped for me. I feel like a baby duckling. I formed an attachment to the first person I saw when I came back to the land of the living." She gave him a rueful smile. "I'm sorry, but I've kind of come to …" What word could she use? She'd come to what? Want him? Need him? Depend on him? They were all true. But if she spoke any of them out loud … She didn't need to figure out which word to choose.

He saved her by laughing. "I love that explanation. So, you see me as your mama duck?"

She had to laugh. That wasn't it at all, but it was funny and much easier to go with than any of her explanations. "I suppose I do. I hope that doesn't offend you?"

He laughed again. "Not in the slightest. In fact, I kinda like it."

"You do?"

He grinned happily. "Yeah. As long as it means that when I waddle my ass over to the big house this afternoon, you'll follow. And if I get a bit clucky around you, you won't mind."

Her heart melted a little bit at the thought of him getting clucky over her. "I won't mind one bit. In fact, I'll be very grateful. I shall happily waddle my little ducky butt after you wherever you want to go."

He met her gaze and held it for a long moment. His green eyes bored into hers. She was only imagining it, but it felt like the connection between them was more about a man and a woman than a mama duck and her duckling.

Chapter Five

Wade narrowed his eyes at Tyler. He'd had Sierra talking in the kitchen for the last ten minutes. He was making her laugh, too. It was a beautiful sound that tugged at Wade's insides. The only trouble was, he wanted to be the one who caused it.

He spun around when someone slapped the back of his head. Tanner stood there grinning at him. "Quit shooting daggers at Ty and come out back with me."

"Why?" Wade didn't want to go outside. He wanted to stay close to Sierra – just to make sure she was okay.

Tanner laughed. "So that you can tell me all about her. And don't worry. She might look like she's chatting away with Ty, but it's you she's into."

That got his attention. "You think? Why?" Out of all the brothers, Tanner was the ladies' man. If he thought Sierra was interested …

"Come outside with me and I'll tell you."

Wade followed him out onto the back porch. "Well?"

Tanner chuckled. "You've got it bad, dude. And I wasn't messing with you, she is interested. She's smiling and nodding with Ty, but she keeps looking around for you. When she spots you, she smiles, and her shoulders relax."

"You think?"

"I don't just think, I know. But I wouldn't get too excited about it. She's probably got some kind of hero worship thing going on. You know, since you're the one who rescued her."

Wade couldn't hide his smile. "She admitted that much. Only it was cuter the way she said it."

Tanner raised his eyebrows.

"She said that she was in shock after she ran out on her wedding and that she wasn't really with it while she was on the road. I was the first person she saw when she came out of it, and she was like a baby duck locking in on its mama."

Tanner threw his head back and laughed out loud. "Jesus, Wade. You have got it bad. You're right, though. That is cute." He looked in through the kitchen window, where they could see her still talking to Ty. "*She's* cute."

"Hey!" Wade scowled. "It's bad enough watching her with Ty; if you set your sights on her, I may as well be a duck." It seemed all Tanner had to do was smile at women and they threw themselves at him.

"Nah. Like I said. You're the one she's interested in." Tanner smiled and waggled his fingers in a little wave.

Wade followed his gaze to find Sierra looking out the window at them. Her cheeks flushed when she met his gaze.

"See?" said Tanner. "She'll wave back at me, but you're the one who makes her blush."

Wade felt as though he grew two feet taller at his brother's words. Tanner was right; she had been looking for him. His smile faded. "Yeah, but what does it matter? She's not in a position to do anything about it. I like her, it seems she likes me. But Cassidy will be back tomorrow. She'll no doubt go and stay with her. And that's if she even sticks around. She'll probably want to go back to her life. And Ford told you who she is. She's way out of my league."

Tanner grasped his shoulder. "Stranger things have happened, bro."

"Really? Stanger things than a billionaire heiress and a cowboy getting together? When?"

Tanner laughed. "Err, a couple years back. Hope and Chance. Remember them?"

Wade stared at him. He had a point. "You're right. Except Hope hadn't just run away from the man she was supposed to marry."

Tanner shrugged. "True, and no one was trying to kill her either."

Wade blew out a sigh. "Yeah."

"What's going on with all of that? It seems weird to me that she could just run out on her wedding and then sit around here having Sunday lunch with us."

"I guess it is weird. But I'm glad she is. She was supposed to be away for two weeks on her honeymoon, so she's not going to be missed in her real life. She has no family left. I know Ford told you about her dad and her brother. The guy who runs the company seems to be the closest thing to family that she has – Barney. She called him this morning and he told her to stay put and lie low while he sees what he can dig up on Jared."

"Hey guys!"

They both turned and smiled at Jane when she stuck her head out the French doors that led onto the back deck where they were standing. She looked back over her shoulder before coming out to join them.

She greeted Tanner with a hug and then turned to Wade. He wrapped her up in his trademark bear hug and lifted her off her feet, spinning her around. "It's good to see you, Janey."

"You, too." She glanced through the kitchen window. "Ford called and gave me the short version. Are you going to introduce me to your friend?"

"Sure, come on in."

Tanner chuckled. "But no matter what Ford told you, don't think you're going to get yourself a new girlfriend out of the deal, Jane. Wade doesn't let her out of his sight for more than a few minutes at a time."

Wade made a face at him, but Jane smiled. "Aww. Don't tease. I can understand why he'd be taken with her. She's such a lovely person."

They both stared at her. "You know her?"

Jane laughed. "Not personally, of course. But I've read a couple of articles about her, and she gave a few interviews on TV when she had her big exhibition in San Francisco ... What?"

"Exhibition?" Wade was lost.

"Yes. You know. Her art. Her paintings. Some of them sold for over a million apiece."

Wade exchanged a look with Tanner who said, "No shit?"

Jane laughed. "I shit you not." She gave Wade a puzzled frown. "Didn't you know that either?"

"Nope." His heart felt as though it had sunk all the way down into his boots. He had to get a lid on his attraction to the woman standing in the kitchen. How many signs did he need? Not only was she supposed to be on her honeymoon right now, but she came from the kind of wealth that he couldn't even imagine and now, it turned out that she was a talented artist who'd made millions in her own right. He rubbed his hand over the stubble on his jaw. Damn. And he was just a cowboy on the family ranch who hadn't even shaved today. He blew out a sigh.

Tanner caught his eye. "She's still looking for you, dude. You should go in and introduce her to Janey."

Sierra felt her cheeks heat yet again when Wade pulled a chair out for her at the dining table. He was such a gentleman. To be fair, they all were. She looked around at the MacFarland brothers. Ford didn't seem quite as dark and broody today. He was the least friendly of the bunch, but he'd made her welcome. He just seemed less approachable than the others. Tyler, who had prepared lunch for them all, was a lot like his eldest brother. He was dark, too. She'd say he was more intense rather than brooding, but he definitely gave off the same kind of vibes as Ford. Tanner was absolutely stunning. There was no other way to describe the man. He was the kind of good-looking that could have made him a model if he chose. He was charming and confident, too. From what the others had said, he was the ladies' man of the family, and she could see it.

When her gaze settled on Wade, who'd taken the seat beside her, she felt herself relax. He was the one who made her breath catch in her chest. He smiled back at her, his eyes holding hers for a long moment before he asked in a low voice, "You okay?"

She nodded. "I am, thanks." She looked around the table. "Thanks for bringing me here. This is good."

Jane sat down opposite Wade and gave her a friendly smile. Jane had been a surprise. With all these good-looking men in the family, Sierra had expected their sister to be a beautiful cowgirl. Jane was nothing of the sort. She was very welcoming and friendly, but ... Sierra felt bad even thinking it, but she was plain. Homey looking was a nice way to put it. She was a little taller than Sierra, which would put her at around five-six. She was on the heavy side, to be polite about it. Her hair was a mousey brown color and didn't look like she'd done anything to it – like she'd washed it and left it to do its own frizzy thing. Her face was pleasant, but she could make so much more of herself with a touch of makeup. And the thick, black rims of her glasses did nothing to lift the overall impression.

Sierra felt terrible. She shouldn't be judging the woman's looks. Looks were purely superficial and she knew it. Jane's warm smile made her beautiful in all the ways that mattered. Sierra smiled back at her.

"Wade told me you're a veterinarian."

Jane nodded. "That's me." She chuckled. "I take care of all the sick animals around here – including my brothers."

Tanner nudged her with his elbow as he sat down beside her. "That joke wore thin years ago, honey. Ford said you went over to see the old man this morning. How was that?"

Jane shrugged. "The same as usual."

"I don't know why you keep going," Tyler said as he placed a bowl full of bread rolls in the center of the table. "Dig in, everyone."

He'd served up the meal family style and everyone reached for a bowl to start serving themselves mashed potatoes and carved beef and vegetables. Sierra sat and watched. So, this was what it was like to be part of a big family. She'd envied one of her friends at school who had a brother and two sisters – they were the biggest family she knew.

Wade turned to her. "Do you want me to serve you?"

She pressed her lips together to hide a smile at the way her corrupt little mind wanted to interpret his words. "Yes, please." She wouldn't know how to begin taking part in what seemed like highly choreographed chaos as everyone grabbed dishes and served themselves before exchanging with their neighbor.

Wade loaded her plate up with way more than she'd be able to eat, but she smiled gratefully and thanked him.

She watched and listened as the conversation bounced around the table. They were a lively bunch and from what they said, they needed to be. They had so much going on between the cattle, and the hands who took care of them, and the guest ranch, where Tyler apparently was working as the chef, and the stud – the horse breeding. She couldn't help smiling at the thought that it was appropriate that Tanner was in charge of that. He was a stud all right.

They all seemed to be involved in every aspect of the ranch, even though each of them was in charge of something separate. Even Jane talked about visiting the horses and the cows in the coming week.

It was a whole new world to Sierra, and she was happy to let the conversation wash over her while she ate and listened.

She jumped at the sound of her cell phone ringing in her purse, which she'd hung over the back of her chair. How rude! Normally she would have put it on silent during a meal, but she hadn't even thought about it. And she should probably at least check to see who it was.

Her cheeks heated yet again as she looked around at the now silent MacFarlands who all were looking at her. How embarrassing. "I'm so sorry. I ..."

Tanner gave her a reassuring smile and waved his hand at her. "No problem."

Wade already had her purse and was handing it to her. "You should probably get it."

She nodded and got to her feet, pulling her phone out as she hurried from the room. She didn't even look at the display, she was just in a hurry to get out of the room. It was deeply ingrained in her that cell phones at the dining table were a major faux pas.

"Hello?"

"Where are you?"

She stopped in her tracks. She hadn't expected him to call. "Jared?" She hated the way her voice wavered and sounded so ... fearful.

She'd only made it as far as the door, and Wade was beside her before she had time to remember to breathe.

"Are you okay?" Wade mouthed the words silently.

She nodded.

"Yes. Of course it's me." Jared's voice sounded weird. Like he was angry but trying to sound pleasant. "They all talked me into letting you have some space yesterday, my love. And I'll admit I was a little ... overwrought. But I thought you'd call when you came to your senses. Was it all too much? Did the stress get to you? It's okay, you can tell me. I forgive you."

Sierra was so stunned by his words that she held her phone out in front of her and stared at it.

"Sierra?" She brought it back to her ear when she heard his voice squawking out of it. "Are you still there?"

"Yes."

"Tell me where you are, baby, and I'll come get you. We can still get married, we can have a small private ceremony, just you and me and Amelia and Lori and a couple of the guys. That's all we need."

"I … err …" Her brain wasn't working properly. It couldn't process what he was saying. What he was trying to do. He still wanted to marry her? Because he still wanted to kill her so he could get her money.

She started to shake. Wade stepped toward her, his eyes full of concern. He held his hand out for the phone, but she shook her head. "I need some time to think."

"You can think back at home with me."

"No." She shook her head again as a thought struck her. "I have to go."

"Sierra, just tell me where you are." The edge to his voice sent shivers down her spine – he sounded like he wanted to kill her. "I'm on the road. I'll call you when I stop again." She hit the end call button and immediately turned her phone off. Then she turned it over and slid out both the sim card and the battery, which was quite an achievement considering the way her hands were shaking.

Wade put his hand on her shoulder. How could such a simple touch make her feel better – safer? "Are you okay? What did he say?"

She let out a laugh that sounded way too high, then glanced at the table, where the rest of the MacFarlands were all watching her.

"He forgives me!" She laughed again. "And he still wants to marry me." She looked up into Wade's eyes. "So, that means he still wants to kill me, doesn't it?"

He pursed his lips but didn't disagree.

She held out her phone. "Can you smash this?"

He cocked an eyebrow. "I can if you want, but do you want to tell me why?"

"He can track it. I know he can. I should have thought of it before. He asked me where I am, but I don't know if that means he hasn't tracked me or if he wants to see if I'm lying. That's why I told him I'm driving. I need to leave. I don't want to bring him here."

Wade gave her a puzzled look. "Even if he has tracked it, this is the safest place for you to be." He looked over at his brothers, who all nodded.

"If he's looking for you, you're better off here on the ranch with us than out driving by yourself," said Ford.

"And if he has tracked your phone, there's no point in smashing it," said Tanner.

Tyler smiled at her. "That's right. But if you don't mind giving it up, we can use it."

She stared at him, not understanding what he was thinking. "I'm happy to give it up. But how will you use it?"

"I'm headed up to town this afternoon to meet with a friend. He's a wine distributor. He's on his way to Minnesota. He can take your phone with him – and leave it on."

"Oh!"

"Thanks, Ty." She could hear the relief in Wade's voice.

"Yes. Thank you." Sierra nodded. "But what am I going to do? I thought – hoped, I suppose, that he'd give up. That he'd know that he'd missed his chance at the money." She looked up at Wade. "He said he still wants to marry me – that means he's not given up. And it means that he doesn't know that I saw him and Lori, or that I heard what he had planned for me and the children."

"The children?" Wade's eyes were wide, and the room went totally silent.

Sierra nodded. "Yes. Dax is going to bring them to me in two weeks. When Jared found out about them, he simply added them to his plan. He wants to kill them, too, so that he'll get everything. Or he would – if we were married."

"You have children?"

Oh. That was right. She hadn't actually told him about the children yet. She hadn't thought she'd need to. They wouldn't be arriving for another couple of weeks and … she looked up at him and nodded. "Yes."

Chapter Six

Wade's mouth opened and closed a couple of times. He had nothing. The list of reasons why he shouldn't be interested in Sierra had kept growing since the moment he met her. And the hits just kept on coming.

This one might prove to be the fatal blow. She had kids. He continued to stare at her, knowing that the silence was lengthening but apparently incapable of saying anything to break it. He was grateful when Ford finally spoke.

"Why don't you come and sit back down. You look like you need to."

Wade wasn't sure if Ford was addressing him or Sierra. Either way, his assessment was right. Sierra was pale and shaking, and his own knees felt as though they might give out.

He led her back to the table and held out her chair, before slumping down in the one beside her.

Ford raised an eyebrow at him, giving him the opportunity to speak, but he still had nothing.

Ford gave the slightest hint of a nod before turning to Sierra. "You're welcome to stay here. I'm glad that we found you and glad that you're here. But I think it's time you tell us the full story. What's going on with you?"

Wade wished he'd used a gentler tone, but that wasn't Ford's way. He liked to get straight to the point – and he also liked to get shit done.

Sierra sucked in a deep breath. "You're right. I do owe you all an explanation."

"You don't owe us anything." Wade couldn't help himself. He hated that she felt that way.

She smiled and his heart hammered in his chest when she reached out and took hold of his hand. "I do. You've all been so kind, especially you. You deserve to know what's going on." She sucked in another breath and then reached for her glass of water.

"Do you want something stronger than that?" asked Tyler. "I've got a decent bottle of cab stashed away if you do."

"I could murder a glass." Her laugh felt as though it might turn to tears. "I should probably rephrase that, shouldn't I?'

They waited for Ty to come back and pour her a glass. He poured another for Jane, but the others shook their heads. Tanner went out and came back with beers for the brothers.

"Okay," Sierra said when everyone was settled. "I feel as though I should start at the beginning, but I'm not really sure where this all began."

"How long has Jared worked for Hartford Enterprises?" asked Ford.

Wade wasn't surprised that Ford was going to guide her. He just hoped that it wouldn't feel like an inquisition.

"Err. I think he worked for the company even when Daddy was still alive." Sierra nodded. "I think so. But I didn't know him then. He came onto the management team just over a year ago. Just before …" Her fingers tightened around Wade's, and he squeezed her hand, guessing that he knew what she was about to say. He was right.

"Just before Seb died. That's my brother. At least, he was."

Wade wanted to move his chair closer so that he could put his arm around her. She looked small and lost as she sat there. He made do with lacing his fingers through hers.

She turned and gave him a weak smile before she continued. "I don't really get involved with the business. After Seb died, I had to go in for meetings and things. But Barney's the mastermind. I met Jared a couple of times in the office, and then he came to one of my openings. The first night of an art show," she explained when Tyler looked puzzled. "I thought it was odd. He didn't strike me as being very arty." She made a face. "I was right. He's not. He doesn't understand. Well, he doesn't understand the art; he understands the money side well enough."

"Tell me he doesn't manage your finances?" asked Ford.

"No! He did offer to. But Barney does it all for me."

"And we trust Barney?" Tanner asked.

"Absolutely. He was Daddy's best friend. He's been like an uncle my whole life."

"So, you've been dating Jared for less than a year and you were about to marry him?"

Wade wished Ford didn't look so disapproving. Fortunately, Sierra either didn't pick up on it or chose to ignore it.

"Yes. I …" She looked around at all of them, "I must seem so stupid to you guys. But I was lost. I had nothing." She dropped her gaze. "I know that probably sounds like the poor little rich girl whining. I know I have so much, financially, and materially-speaking. But believe me, when you never knew your mom and your father and brother both go and die within two years of each other, you realize just how little the material stuff is worth. I had no one. I *have* no one. My parents were both only children, so there's no family." She looked around at them. "I envy you guys."

Wade squeezed her hand again and had to stop himself from offering to make her part of their family. Ford glanced at him before smiling at Sierra. "You don't need to envy us. From today on you can count on every one of us as your family." He looked around at the others. "I say Sierra is now an honorary MacFarland; agreed?"

Wade loved his siblings more than ever as they all grinned and nodded at her. Tanner winked at her. "Don't look too pleased. These guys can be a pain in the ass."

It was good to hear her laugh, but he didn't dare look at her. He was having crazy thoughts about wanting to make her more than just an honorary member of the family. And that was too dumb for words.

"I just wish I'd met you guys before I met Jared." Wade wholeheartedly shared that sentiment.

"I suppose I was flattered. He made no secret that he was interested in me, and he went out of his way to let everyone see and know that he was in love with me and wanted us to have a future together."

"Do you mind if I ask you something?"

Wade looked at Jane. She was the smart one, and perceptive, too. He wondered if she'd picked up on the same thing he had. He hoped so, because if not, he was going to have to ask a question of his own, and he knew what his brothers would think. They'd be right, too, but the fact that he was interested in her himself wasn't the reason that he needed her to clarify what she'd just said.

He was relieved when Sierra nodded, and Jane spoke again. She was on the same track he was. "You said that Jared went out of his way to let *everyone* see and know that he was in love with you. That struck me as odd. If I were you, I'd want a man to let *me* know that he was in love with me. Did he do that for you or was it like it sounds – more for show?"

Sierra shrugged. "I didn't even realize that I'd said it that way, but you're right. My friend, Amelia ..." She looked at Wade. "The one I talked to on the phone last night. She's never liked him. She used to say that he put on more of a show when there were other people around. I used to get upset with him, but he made out that I was overly sensitive, you know, since I was still a mess over Seb."

Wade clenched his jaw. He already had Jared down as a predator who'd been out for what he could get. Sierra was sweet, probably too sweet. She didn't seem to have any edge to her at all. It'd be too easy for a man to prey on her and manipulate her. The looks his brothers exchanged told him they were thinking the same thing.

"I know. I was stupid, right? I can see it in your faces."

"No!" Jane beat the guys to it. "What you're seeing on their faces – and take it from one who knows – they're not mad at you or thinking any less of you. They're angry at – probably wanting to kill – the asshole who took advantage of you."

Ford chuckled as he looked at Jane. "Can I remind you of this conversation the next time some low-life tries to take advantage of your good nature?"

Jane made a face at him and turned back to Sierra. "See what I mean?"

To Wade's relief, Sierra smiled back at her. "I do."

"And you'd better get used to it," said Tanner. "Now that you're an honorary little sister, you'll have us four and a couple more brothers looking out for you. And I think Jane and Laney will both tell you that I wasn't joking when I said we can be a real pain in the ass."

Wade was feeling anything but brotherly toward the woman sitting beside him, but he could hardly say so.

"Anyway," Tyler got them back on track. "So, we know that he made a move on you, and you went along with it. And then you found out just before the wedding that he was only after you for your money, right? Where do the kids come in? Who's the father?"

Part of Wade wanted to punch him to shut him up – did he need to be so blunt? At the same time, he was more than interested to hear her answer.

Her fingers tightened around his. "I only found out about them a few weeks ago myself." She let out a little laugh. "That must sound weird. I mean, if I were a man then it's feasible that I might have children that I didn't know about but that's kind of impossible for a woman. Obviously, they're not my children." She squeezed his hand again at that. Had she known how much it had been freaking him out?

"My brother, Seb, didn't always work with Daddy. He joined the Navy and went on to become a SEAL."

Wade looked at his brothers and was glad that none of them interrupted.

"He was injured a few years ago. His knee blew out and he was medically retired. But his teammates were like brothers to him. And to me. They kept an eye on me after he died, but they're away most of the time. Out of the country. Seb's best friend, Dax, was kind of the team representative – it was his job to keep in touch. I've known him for years."

"Are these his kids?" Ford asked.

"No. Well, not exactly. The team was on a mission – I don't know the details, no one's allowed to – it's all classified, you know?"

They all nodded – they knew only too well.

"All he told me was that their parents had been killed. And the team had taken responsibility for them – because they had to, because there's all kinds of human trafficking down there. Dax was going to retire to be their dad. He's a good guy, you'd like him." She looked up at Wade, but he wasn't sure that he agreed. He was reserving judgment on that one for now.

"I told him I'd take them. I always wanted children. And I thought that since I was getting married, it'd work. I told Jared, and he went crazy. I was shocked. I mean, I know it's a big thing to land on someone. But it's important, you know? Two little people who I could give a good life to – not just the money; I'm going to love them with all my heart and do everything I can to be a good mom."

Wade could believe that.

"I thought that Jared would come around. I mean, he'd talked about us having a family – or at least, he'd agreed vaguely when I talked about it. But he was adamant that I couldn't take them on. That Dax would have to retire and take them himself. He acted like Dax was awful for letting me do it, but it was *my* idea. Dax didn't want me to at first. I had to talk him into it. He still has his career, and he isn't married.

"In the end I told Jared that we should call off the wedding. I should have stuck with that. I should have known that I didn't really love him when I was prepared to give him up –

the children were more important to me than he was. But when I told him that I didn't want to marry him, he came around and said that he'd gotten over it and that it would all work out. That he'd take on the children." She shook her head. "I suppose what he actually meant was that he'd take *out* the children at the same time he took me out."

"Are you going to tell us what he planned?" asked Ford.

"And how you found out," Tyler added.

She took a big swig of her wine before she nodded. "Okay. Well, we were going to get married in a hotel. The St Regis, in Park City."

Ford glanced at Wade, but it was hardly surprising. She had money; she was bound to be getting married somewhere like that.

"I spent the morning getting ready with my friend, Amelia. We have another friend, Lori, who was supposed to be with us. But she called on Friday and said that she wouldn't be able to get in until Saturday morning. Wow. That was only yesterday. Anyway. I thought it was strange that Lori said she couldn't get there, because I thought I'd seen her in the hallway.

"So, it was just Amelia and me getting ready in the morning and Amelia was talking about the kids and about Jared. She never really liked him. It seems that none of my real friends did, but they put up with him for my sake. She told me that I needed to be one hundred percent sure that he was okay about the children coming – that it wouldn't be fair to them to bring them into a home where the man who was supposed to be stepping up to be their father didn't want them.

"She was right of course. So, I decided that I should go and talk to him. I felt that maybe I'd railroaded him into something that he didn't want for his life. I needed to give him the chance to back out.

"We weren't supposed to see each other before the wedding. I know it's silly, but I like that superstition. I'm glad I ignored it now, though. I went to Jared's suite and knocked but he didn't answer. I thought maybe he was down at the bar with his friends. But I had a room key. The concierge gave it to me when I checked in. Even though it was a mix up, he told me that I may as well keep it, since it was to my husband's room."

She frowned at Wade. "That was Francis, the man who helped me get a rental without using my credit card. I wonder if he knew – if he had a feeling that I might walk in on something if he gave me the key?"

Wade shrugged. He didn't know, but if he ever met this Francis guy, he'd buy the man a drink.

"Anyway. I used the key to let myself in. I don't even know why. I'm not a snoop or anything; I'm usually very respectful. But I just wanted to see if he was there. When I went in, I heard him in the bathroom, talking. I was about to call out to him, until I heard someone answer him. A woman." She blew out a sigh. "It was Lori. At first, I couldn't figure out why she'd be there talking to him. I'm so stupid. I thought they might be planning some kind of surprise for me. Well, they were. But not a good one.

"She was asking how long it would take. Jared said that they'd have to wait a while. That he didn't want it to be as soon as the children came. That they should wait a couple of months, even though he was dreading having to spend all that time married to me and even more so having to put up with a couple of brats."

Sierra shook her head sadly. "I just stood there trying to wrap my head around it. I couldn't understand what he meant. Then Lori asked how he could be sure that I'd die in the accident and if he was absolutely sure that he'd get everything when I died. He said that Aiden, that's his friend who's a lawyer, had assured him that as long as the children died with me, there'd be nothing standing in the way. He told her that she was amazing for having talked me out of getting a prenup. I feel so stupid. She did talk me out of it. Jared and I had had a fight when I asked him to sign one. Then Lori kept telling me that I didn't need one and that if a man asked her to sign one, it'd feel like he didn't love her. She thought Jared was in the right, and I was in the wrong. I thought she was looking out for me, trying to save my relationship. It turned out she was looking out for him – and for herself, since she expected him to be with her after he killed me. I think I've been a very weak woman these last few years. I let them manipulate me, and I went against my own instincts because they made me feel bad about myself."

Wade squeezed her hand. He knew how easily that could happen – and not just to women.

"So, I stood there outside the bathroom, listening to them talk about how long he'd have to put up with me before he could kill me and the children. And then he was praising her for talking me out of a prenup. And then …" Sierra's lip curled in disgust. "He said he wanted to show her how pleased he was with her." She shuddered. "I really couldn't imagine that he was going to do what it sounded like. So, I peeked through the crack in the door. I so wish I hadn't. He had her bent over the vanity and …" She shuddered again. "Yeah." She looked at Tyler. "So, that's how I found out. I wanted to throw up, but I just turned around and ran. I went back down to the concierge desk and told Francis that I needed to get out of there. I called Amelia but I didn't even stop for her. I panicked. I know logically that there'd be no point in him killing me before we were married, but I had it in my head that if he caught me, he'd do it anyway. I rented the SUV and started driving. I was heading north on I-15 before I knew what I was doing, and that's when it occurred to me that Cassidy lives up here. I put her address in the navigation and I was heading for her house when I lost a game of chicken with a deer and ended up in a ditch."

She gave Ford a rueful smile and then looked up into Wade's eyes. "And you guys know everything that's happened since then."

She looked around at them. "So, there you have it. My sorry tale."

Wade squeezed her hand. "I'd call it your lucky escape."

She smiled. "Thanks. You're right. I need to look at it that way. I am lucky. I escaped with my life."

"And what do you plan to do next?" asked Ford.

Sierra shrugged. "I don't know. I talked to Barney this morning. He's angry. He said he's going to look into it. But he thought it was best if I stay out of the way. And I agree. I don't want to go home, and no one expects me back in my life for the next two weeks anyway – I'm supposed to be on my honeymoon. My friend Cassidy said she'll be home tomorrow. I'll go and see her and then, I don't know. Knowing Cass, she'll want to catch up. But after that … I guess I'll try to get in touch with Dax. I could go and stay at his place. He's away and Jared doesn't know where he lives."

Wade's heart sank. He didn't want her to leave. This time he didn't wait for one of the others to speak first. "You should stay here."

Her gray eyes glowed from within as they looked into his. "I …"

His heart was pounding as he waited to hear her answer.

"He's right," said Ford. "I doubt Jared would come looking for you. At least not to harm you. Since it sounds like he doesn't know what you heard and saw, he might think he still stands a chance of persuading you to go home and marry him. But I don't think you're likely to go for that, are you?"

"Oh, heck no!"

"Then I think this place is your best bet. Jared doesn't know we exist. You have all of us to look out for you. Plus, it's a big ranch. He wouldn't be able to get near you because he won't be able to get on the property."

Wade looked down into her eyes and nodded. Everything Ford had said made sense, but none of it was the main reason he wanted her to stay. "Say you'll stay?"

She ran her tongue over her bottom lip and nodded slowly. "Thank you."

He was lost in her eyes, mesmerized by her plump pink lips. It'd be all too easy to lean in and kiss her. Her eyelids drifted closed. She felt it too, he could see it.

"Welcome aboard, little sis!" Wade sat back in a hurry and Sierra's eyes flew open at Tanner's words. He'd raised his bottle in a toast and was smiling at them.

"Thank you, guys." She smiled around at them as they all clinked their bottles against her glass.

Ford caught Wade's gaze and cocked an eyebrow at him. Whatever his question was, Wade didn't know the answer. All he knew was that he was thrilled that she planned to stay at the ranch – even though he also knew that he shouldn't be.

Chapter Seven

"I'm glad we're the same shoe size, but you might want to keep Wade's clothes on when you see mine."

Sierra followed Jane up the steps to her cottage and waited while she let them in. "You're all so kind. I appreciate it more than you can imagine."

Jane stopped inside the living room and smiled her warm smile. "Honestly, I can't imagine what you've been through. I can't believe how well you're holding up. You're amazing."

"I'm an idiot, is what I am. While I sat there telling you and your brothers everything that's happened, I heard it the way it must sound. It's so easy to see it now. I was just a stupid, stupid woman too caught up in grief to be able to see that I was being set up all along."

Jane patted her arm. "It might be easy to see from the outside, but it's not so simple when you're the one going through it. Don't be hard on yourself. No one thinks badly of you."

Sierra rolled her eyes. "Your brothers could see it. And they're right. I was too trusting. I let Jared and Lori manipulate me. I mean, come on. Who in their right mind would let their friend talk them out of asking for a prenup?"

Jane chuckled. "I'm probably not the right person to ask about that. I don't have anything that anyone would want to take from me in a divorce – except maybe custody of my fur babies. But then I'm hardly likely to get married anyway so …" She shrugged.

"Why not?" asked Sierra. "You don't want to?"

Jane laughed. "Have you seen me? No guy's ever going to fall for me. I'm the frumpy dumpy one. I'm the kind of girl who guys turn to to talk about the girls they are interested in."

Sierra felt bad. She'd had some uncharitable thoughts about the way Jane looked when she first saw her. But she was an absolute sweetheart. "Any guy would be lucky to get you."

Jane just laughed again. "It's okay. I know what I am. I'm okay with me. Achilles! Come down!"

Sierra startled at the sudden change in Jane's tone. She followed her gaze to see a huge orange cat sitting on top of the curtain rail. "Oh, my goodness!"

Jane laughed and went to the curtain. She held her arm up and the cat stretched before walking nonchalantly down her arm and proceeding to drape itself around her neck, looking for all the world like a fox stole.

"Sierra, meet Achilles. Achilles, Sierra. He's the main man in my life at the moment."

Sierra jumped when a low woof came from the kitchen.

"You weren't supposed to hear that, Boo." Jane jerked her head toward the kitchen. "He thinks he's my main man. Come on. I'll introduce you."

Sierra watched in wonder as the cat stayed wound around Jane's neck as she walked into the kitchen. There, a big old hound dog greeted them. He rubbed against Jane's leg and then came and sat himself down in front of Sierra. He looked up at her with big soulful eyes and held out his paw.

Sierra looked at Jane, not sure if he was begging for a treat, or what he wanted. She wasn't used to animals.

Jane laughed. "He wants to shake hands with you. He's pleased to meet you."

"Oh! Well, forgive my manners." Sierra took hold of his paw and shook with him. When she let go, he shuffled his butt across the floor until he was right next to her and then leaned against her leg, still looking up into her eyes.

"You old devil, Boo!" said Jane.

"Is he okay?"

Jane laughed. "He's happier than a pig in … mud! You have just gotten yourself a new admirer. He's gone and fallen in love with you."

Sierra looked down at him. His tongue was hanging out the side of his mouth as he panted, and his big eyes looked back adoringly into hers. "Well, I'm flattered. I think." She looked at Jane. "Forgive my cynicism, but given my recent experiences, I hope you'll understand me asking: does he do this to everyone? Is this his way to get me to feed him?"

"No. I can see why you'd ask. But Boo's not that kind of guy. He ignores most people. Doesn't have the time for them. And he's not the type to be motivated by food. It seems that he's just taken a shine to you. He doesn't do ulterior motives, so you can relax and enjoy some straightforward adoration."

Sierra rubbed the dog's ears, warmth spreading through her chest as he seemed to smile back at her. "Well, thank you, Boo. Straightforward adoration is like a balm to this girl's heart right now."

Boo let out another low woof, which seemed to convey that he understood and was happy to help.

When she straightened up, Jane was trying to hide a smile.

"What?"

"I probably shouldn't say it, but Boo isn't the only one who adores you."

Sierra's heart leaped into her mouth. She'd tried to keep her mind off Wade all day. Tried to not notice the way he made her feel. Shoot. Jane might not even be talking about him – but what else could she mean?

"Sorry. I shouldn't go there. Should I?" Jane tilted her head to the side in question.

"I ... I'm not sure where you're going. So, I don't know how to answer."

Jane laughed. "I think you have an idea. I'm talking about Wade. He's besotted with you. And that's not like him."

"It's not?" She shouldn't feel so relieved. But he was a good-looking guy. Maybe he took a shine to a lot of girls.

"No. He doesn't date much. And I've never seen him act the way he is with you."

Sierra dropped her gaze and looked up at Jane from under her lashes. "I know it's crazy, given the circumstances, but I may have the teeniest bit of a crush on your brother."

Jane laughed and clapped her hands together. "I wasn't sure. I can see how he feels. But I wasn't sure if you were just grateful to him for helping you out."

"Oh. I'm definitely grateful. In fact, at first, I tried to convince myself that that's all it was. But it's not. There's something there." She looked over her shoulder as if there might be someone waiting to hear her confession. "There's this connection. It's crazy. I feel more drawn to Wade than I ever did to Jared. I don't know. Maybe it's just a reaction to everything that's happened. Maybe it's some kind of hero worship because he found me on the side of the road and came to the rescue."

"Maybe. But Ford was with him. You don't feel that way about Ford, do you?"

Sierra shook her head a little too rapidly. "No!" And then she remembered that Ford was Jane's brother, too. "I mean, I'm grateful to him for being there and for helping. And he was so wonderful today, making me an honorary little sister – that was such a kind gesture. But …" She gave Jane a shy smile. "He's not like Wade."

"No. He isn't. And don't worry. I know what you mean. He's a good guy, but he's tougher. We joke that there's a divide in the family; the dark side and the light side. Ford is undoubtedly darker."

"That's what I thought when I first saw him. Not dark in a bad way, just dark and brooding. While Wade, he's more like … sunshine."

Jane laughed. "Yep. You've got the two of them figured. Anyway. Instead of standing here figuring out the men in the family, we need to find you some clothes. If we take too long, Wade will be over here to check you're okay. I'm sure."

Sierra couldn't hide her smile as she followed Jane to her bedroom. She loved the idea of Wade wanting to check on her. She already missed him, and it had only been a few minutes since it had been decided that Jane could bring her to find some clothes to borrow.

Jane opened her closet and looked back at Sierra. "I wasn't joking when I said that you might prefer to keep Wade's things on than wear any of mine, you know."

"Well, since we're being so honest with each other, I'll admit that I do like wearing his things. It feels like just one more way that he's taking care of me."

Jane chuckled. "I thought as much. It's like in high school, wearing your boyfriend's jacket, right?"

"I suppose so, but I wouldn't know. I was never allowed to have boyfriends. Is that what you did?"

Jane laughed out loud. "I never had a boyfriend in high school and not because I wasn't allowed. Just that no one was interested. I've always been the frumpy dumpy one."

"I wish you wouldn't say that about yourself. You're pretty."

"Oh, please! I know how I look. I'm okay with me."

Sierra sat down on the bed, while Jane rifled through her closet. "Do you mind if I ask why?"

"Why what?"

"Why you don't … ugh. I don't want this to come out wrong. You call yourself frumpy dumpy and say you know how you look. Why don't you do something about it? Gosh! That sounded awful! I don't mean that you need to or that you should or anything. I'm so sorry. I don't mean to be rude. I just …"

"It's okay. I'm not offended. I know what you mean. I could make more of myself if I tried. I know that. But no matter how much I did, it wouldn't be enough. I tried when I was younger, but it was like fighting a losing battle. So, I gave up."

Sierra wanted to ask her to explain, but she'd already been rude enough.

Jane smiled. "I wish you were going to stick around. I think we'd become good friends, you and me. We're comfortable enough with each other to share our secrets already. You told me about Wade, and for some reason, I'm going to tell you what most of my family doesn't even know."

"I hope we will become friends. You can come and visit me. I'll come back and see you." Sierra reached out and touched Jane's arm. "I'd love for us to become real friends."

Jane squeezed her hand. "I hope so. I'd like that. And maybe if I come and see you in San Francisco, I'll make the effort to look nicer."

"No! You don't need to do that. You're lovely just the way you are. I wasn't trying to change you. I was only curious."

"I know. Most people try to give me advice about what I could and should do. Hair, makeup, clothes. As if they think I'm stupid and don't realize it. You didn't do that. You asked me why – like you actually want to know."

"I do." Sierra smiled. "I want to know what makes my new friend tick."

Jane blew out a sigh. "I'm a twin. Did you know that?"

"No! One of the boys?"

"No. I have a twin sister, Laney. We're not identical."

"Oh, she lives in Kentucky? Is that right?"

"Yeah. She works with horses."

"Are the two of you close?"

"We are …"

"But?"

"I love her dearly. She loves me, too. But our personalities are as different as our looks. She's beautiful. And she's outgoing and feisty and …" Jane shrugged. "Laney got the personality and the looks."

Sierra frowned but didn't dare interrupt.

"I know you want to speak up in my defense and I love you for it. But it is what it is. When we were born, my mom named us Laney and Janey. But it was obvious even when we were small that Laney was the pretty one and I was plain. My dad stopped calling me Janey. He used to tell people that I was plain Jane. And it stuck."

"Oh. That's awful. I'm so sorry."

"I'm used to it. I went through a stage in my early teens when I thought I'd be like the ugly duckling and turn out to be a swan. I tried makeup and saved up to buy nice clothes. But no one noticed me. The boys were all after Laney. And I got along with animals better than I got along with boys anyway." She reached up and scratched Achilles' ears. He rewarded her by rubbing his head against her cheek and purring loudly.

"But Laney moved away?"

"Yeah. She had some stuff of her own going on. But I think she might have stayed if it weren't for me. See, I got friendly with a boy up in town. I really thought he liked me for me. But then he started asking about her. I was just a way for him to get close to her. One night, I saw him drop her off back here and watched from my bedroom window when he kissed her in his truck. I was so jealous. I yelled at her when she came up to our room. It wasn't fair. I hadn't told her that I liked him or that I thought he liked me. She didn't know. But I told her she was selfish. Told her that my life was miserable because of her and I was sick of living in her shadow." She blew out a sigh. "A few weeks after that she had a job lined up in Kentucky. I begged her not to go. Told her I didn't mean any of what I said. She told me that wasn't the reason she was leaving, and like I said, she did have some stuff of her own going on. But I know it was part of the reason she went. She never meant to hurt me. She can't help it that she's the pretty, outgoing one. I miss her." Jane blew out a sigh. "So, there you go. That's my sad story. I chased my own sister away."

"It doesn't sound that way to me. She would have gone anyway. She had her own life to live. And she does love you."

"I know she does. And I love her, too. I just wish I hadn't screwed things up between us."

"Maybe she'll come home one day, and the two of you will be close again."

Jane let out a bitter laugh. "There's a lot you don't know about this family. Laney swears she'll never set foot on the ranch again until our dad is dead."

"Wow!"

"Yeah. That's a whole other story. But not one for today. To say that he's not a nice man would be the understatement of the century." Jane smiled. "And since we're going to be friends, I'm sure I'll tell you all about him at some point. But for now, we need to find you some clothes. Otherwise, you'll have no choice but to keep wearing Wade's because he'll come back and whisk you away again."

Sierra tried not to smile. She shouldn't like the idea of Wade wanting to whisk her away as much as she did.

When he and Tyler got back to the house, Wade wandered from the kitchen, through the dining room and into the living room, trying not to make it too obvious that he was looking for Sierra. He'd had to go over to the lodge with Tyler and check in with the staff. It was what he always did after Sunday lunch. They all took Sunday off when they could and had lunch as a family. But they each had responsibilities that they needed to get back to, which determined whether they'd get to spend the rest of afternoon hanging out at the house together.

While he and Tyler had gone back to the lodge, Ford had gone to talk to the foreman and Tanner had gone over to the barn. Either everything was peaceful, and no one had any pressing issues to deal with, or they were all more concerned about getting back to the house to figure out what they were going to do about Sierra.

Ford was standing in the living room and raised his eyebrows when Wade got there. "Looking for someone?"

"I … ah …"

He spun around when Tanner laughed behind him. "Don't try to deny it, dude. You swept in here like you were ready to tear the place apart looking for her. They're not back yet."

Ty came to stand beside Tanner and smirked at him. "I told you we didn't need to rush back."

Wade ran a hand through his hair. "Shit. What am I even playing at?"

"I don't know," said Ford. "But you might want to cool it."

"Why?"

Ford rolled his eyes. "So defensive. I'm not trying to tell you what you should do, well I guess I am. But only out of concern. I don't want to see you getting all hung up on her and then have to deal with you moping when she leaves. At the most, she's going to be here for two weeks."

"I know. Sorry. I don't know what's gotten into me."

Tanner shoulder bumped him. "I do. You need to get laid."

Wade scowled at him. "Not funny, bro. She's ... a lady. And you know what she's just been through. I ..." He stopped when he realized that they were all laughing at him. "What?"

"You're the only one in this room who thought he was talking about Sierra," said Ty. "You know what Tan's like. That's his solution to every problem — go out and get laid. He wasn't suggesting that you and the lovely Sierra should get it on. Though we all know how much you want to."

Wade gave them a rueful smile. "Shit! I'm a mess. I don't know what it is about her."

"Then let me tell you," said Tanner. "She's gorgeous. She's got a figure on her that any guy would want to get his hands on, a real pretty face, hair that would feel good wrapped around your fingers, and as if that wasn't enough, she's sweet as pie. She has a big heart and a generous spirit. And she's in trouble and needs protecting. She might has well have been made to order to fit everything that you want in a woman."

Wade just stared at him. It was an accurate assessment, but Wade wouldn't have been able to sum it up so well, and he had no clue what to say.

Ford smiled at him. "He's right. She's your perfect package. She's too ... nice for me. Too delicate for Ty, and too innocent for Tanner."

Wade shook his head. "That may be true. But she's not just some girl who wandered in here, is she? She's a runaway bride, a freaking billionaire, an artist – and from what she said, in a couple of weeks, she's going to be a mom, too."

"Shit! I didn't think," said Tanner. "You're divorced because you wouldn't have kids."

Wade shrugged. This wasn't the time to get into explaining that he didn't want to have kids with Josie. That was very different from not wanting to have kids, period. "As if that even matters. I'm not denying that she's gotten to me. But Ford's right. She's going to be here for two weeks at most. I just need to keep a lid on it."

"Maybe you should stay away from her," said Ford. "That might be best all around. She can stay up here at the house with me and – "

"No!" Wade said it before he could stop himself. "She asked me to …"

He stopped when he realized they were laughing again. "I'm winding you up, bro. It might not a be a bad idea for her to come and stay at the house rather than in the cabin. But only because there are more of us here – in case anything happens. I can't see anyone coming after her. It wouldn't make sense. But it still wouldn't hurt to circle the wagons. But even then, you and she could take the second floor. I don't think she'd come without you. I don't know if you're playing it cool, or if you seriously haven't noticed that she's got it as bad for you as you do for her."

Wade couldn't hide his smile. "She does, doesn't she?"

Tanner laughed. "Yup. So, now that we've got that sorted. What's the plan?"

Wade sobered quickly at the question. "I'm going to call Cash."

Ford raised his eyebrows. "You think we need the big guns?"

"No." He knew he had to tread carefully around Ford when it came to their eldest brother, Cash. He hadn't lived on the ranch in years, and with him gone, Ford had stepped into the role of head of the family. Wade didn't want to piss him off. "We don't need him. I know we've got it covered. I want to ask him if he knows anything – or can find anything out – about her brother and this Dax."

Tanner nodded. "I was thinking I can give the commander a call, too. If her brother was on the teams, and this Dax still is, he should be able to tell me something."

"I'd like to know the story behind these kids," said Ford.

"Yeah," Wade agreed. "I want to think that this guy is taking advantage of her somehow. But he's a SEAL. I can't see that being the case. Though there must be another solution for these kids than for her to take them on."

Tyler raised an eyebrow at him. "You thinking about their best interests or yours?"

"Hers." Wade scowled at him. "As much as I'd like to think it might, her adopting a couple of kids isn't going to affect me. I don't know anything about the kids to know what might be best for them. My concern is for Sierra. Do you think she even knows what she's getting herself into? You heard her. She thinks she can give them a good life. But I'd put money on her knowing nothing about kids or about how much they'll change her life."

"True," said Ford. "But she seemed pretty set on it. And it's none of our business what she chooses to do."

"I know." Wade blew out a sigh. "I'm getting carried away. The first thing to do is talk to Cash. If Dax has been on the teams for a few years, he'll probably know something about him – or be able to find out."

"You might want to call him later," said Tanner. "Janey just pulled up. They're back."

Tyler shook his head. "If no one else is going to do it. I'll take her to town myself tomorrow to buy clothes. Who knows what Janey will have dressed her in."

"Ty!" Ford scowled at him.

Tyler just shrugged. "I'm only saying. And you can't deny the rest of you were thinking it. Anyway, I'm out of here. I said I'd meet Colton at The Mint."

They all turned when Jane came in, followed by Sierra. Wade's breath caught in his chest at the sight of her. She looked amazing. She was wearing a sweater of Jane's that he recognized, but it looked way different on her. She'd fastened a big wide belt around the waist and wore it with a pair of leggings that only looked a little too big for her. The overall effect made him want to go and close his arms around her tiny waist and hold her against him. Shit. He needed to snap out of it.

Ty was already beside her, holding out a phone. It didn't surprise Wade that Ty would just happen to have a prepaid cell phone lying around that he could let Sierra have to replace her own. It looked like he made quick work of transferring her contacts over to it, too.

Jane came to Wade, and he took out his need to hug on her. She laughed and hugged him back. She'd told him once years ago, when she'd been his bridesmaid, that she knew she'd never get married and the only thing she felt like she was missing out on was hugs. He was a hugger anyway and he always made a point to make sure that Janey got more than her fair share.

When he set her down, she smiled up at him. "I really like her, Wade."

"I do, too, Janey."

She squeezed his arm. "I know. Call me crazy but I think there's something there between the two of you. Do me a favor?"

"What's that, honey?"

"Give it a chance?"

He let out a short laugh. "There is no chance. I wish there were, but come on."

"Just don't decide that there isn't a chance. And if you see one, take it, okay?"

She looked so earnest, she had him curious. "Why?"

"Because I like her. And I love you. Okay?"

She was coming toward them now. Ty was on his way out the front door, taking her phone with him. There was no time to question Janey further. She just gave him a meaningful look before turning back to Sierra.

"Doesn't she look great, guys? I know you were all worried that I was going to give her the frumpy dumpy treatment."

Wade felt bad that that was exactly what they'd been thinking.

Jane nodded. "I know. You can't hide it. But Sierra's so beautiful she can even work wonders with my wardrobe."

Wade knew he was starting to fall for Sierra when she went and linked her arm through his sister's and smiled at her. "I've told you, Janey. You're beautiful just the way you are. And if anyone tries to tell you otherwise, they'll have me to answer to."

Wade could tell that both Ford and Tanner liked her response, too. She genuinely cared about Janey, and it showed. Even the fact that she called her Janey rather than Jane, won her brownie points that she couldn't understand.

Ford caught his eye and nodded. It seemed she was capable of softening even the hardest heart.

Chapter Eight

Sierra followed Cassidy out onto the deck. Her house was beautiful. It had an amazing view of the mountains, and the Yellowstone River ran just below the deck. Cassidy had called on her way back from the airport this morning and Sierra had driven up here to see her friend for lunch. While they'd eaten, Sierra had caught Cassidy up on everything that had happened over the last few days. It seemed hard to believe that only forty-eight hours ago she'd been getting ready to get married.

Once they were seated, Cassidy smiled at her. "I don't think you should stay here."

Sierra sat back in her seat. "What do you mean when you say *here?*"

Cassidy laughed. "Don't worry. I'm not trying to banish you from Paradise Valley. I mean that I fully intended to invite you to stay here at the house for as long as you want."

"And now you're not going to?"

"Nope. And don't look like that. You know damned well why."

Sierra tried to hide her smile. "You're going to tell me anyway."

"You're right. I am. I'm going to tell you that you should stay at the MacFarland place. On a practical level, I think Wade's right. You're better off there than anywhere else. But on a more personal note, why would you want to go anywhere else when you have that hot cowboy looking after you?"

Sierra rolled her eyes. "You know why! I shouldn't even be interested. I'd be on my honeymoon right now – except for the fact that Jared wants to kill me. And as if that's not enough reason, I'm about to become a mom. There's no way I should be mooning around after Wade."

Cassidy laughed. "When you put it like that, I'd say that you should be more than mooning after him. You should be making the most of him. You had a narrow escape from a bad marriage and possible death, and you're about to turn your life upside down for a couple of kids you've never even met. I'd say that's more than enough reason to get all the hot sex you can while you can. Celebrate the fact that you got away with your life, and stock up because who knows when you'll ever get any again."

Sierra had to laugh. "You're terrible."

Cassidy shrugged. "You say that, but you don't mean it. What you really mean is that you wish you were brave enough to do it."

She blew out a sigh. "Maybe."

"Definitely!"

"Okay! So, I'm kind of besotted with him. But I shouldn't be. He's been kind and generous and he makes me feel safe and …"

"Horny," Cassidy filled in for her.

Sierra chuckled. "Okay! Yes! I … there's just this pull when I'm around him. The closer I get to him, the closer I want to get. But it's not just that. He's such a good guy and on top of that he's gorgeous, and sexy and …"

"And you should sleep with him."

"Cass! You know I'm not like that."

"Like what?"

"I don't sleep around. To me that's part of a relationship; you need to be dating before you go to bed with a guy."

Cassidy rolled her eyes. "So, stick around then. If you need to be dating him before you can sleep with him, then you'll just have to stay here so that you can date him. Because you *so* should sleep with him."

"You're crazy! I can't do that."

"Why not?"

"Because ... because I can't."

"I don't see why not. You have the next couple of weeks to fill. There's nothing going on in your life. I'm not going to invite you stay here because you need to stay at his place and be around him. I just have a feeling about you and him. Wade's awesome. All those guys are. But Wade's my favorite."

"How well do you know them?"

"Pretty well. They grew up and went to school with Shane and his brothers. And this valley's like that anyway. Everyone knows everyone. They all help each other out."

Sierra took a sip of her drink. "They said I could stay."

"So, stay!"

"I want to."

"What can I do to persuade you? Actually, forget that. First, tell me why you wouldn't? You can't go home. Well, you could but it'd be crazy. Why would you want to go back? That'd just be putting yourself within Jared's reach again."

"I know. I don't want to go back."

"But you don't want to stay?"

"I never said that I don't want to. I do. But ..."

"Go on, give me one valid reason why you shouldn't stay?"

Sierra shrugged. "I don't have one. It just feels wrong to start thinking about Wade that way when I'm supposed to be on my honeymoon right now."

"Nope. Not buying it. You said yourself. You tried to call off the wedding when Jared didn't want to take on the kids. That's one thing I don't hold against him. I think you're nuts taking them on. And I think he was well within his rights to say that he didn't want to. But the fact that they were more important to you than he was, should tell you all you need to know. You're not in love with him."

"No."

"And you don't need to impose some time limit between ending things with him and moving on with someone else."

"It's not as though I'd be moving on with Wade. Just …"

"Why not?"

"Because … how could I? He lives here. I live in San Francisco. He's a cowboy. I'm an artist."

Cassidy laughed. "Apart from the living in San Francisco part, which I haven't done for years, you could be talking about Shane and me."

"That's true. I never thought I'd see you settle down. And much less with a cowboy."

Cassidy pushed her long blonde hair back off her shoulders. "Neither did I. But Shane …" She smiled. "He's amazing. I love him more than I knew it was possible to love someone."

"And did you just decide to go for it with him? Did you just decide to sleep with him because you wanted to?" Sierra fully expected her to say yes. She'd known Cassidy for over ten years, and she'd always gone after what she wanted without a thought to what people might think.

"No. I didn't. I kept him at arms-length for a long time. I'd given up on men. I thought he was going to be just another big ego-ridden asshole. But he didn't give up. He kept asking me out until he finally wore me down. And I'm so glad he did."

Sierra loved the look in her friend's eyes. There was no mistaking that she loved her husband with all her heart. Cassidy had always been a tough cookie, and it seemed that being with Shane hadn't changed that, but it had brought out her softer side.

"So, I guess maybe I'm seeing you and Wade in the same way. Maybe I'm projecting my stuff onto you. I didn't intend to give Shane a chance, and he turned out to be the best thing that's ever happened to me. I don't want you to miss out on discovering that Wade could be the best thing to ever happen to you."

"I wish." She said it before she thought about it, and Cassidy laughed.

"See. Part of you knows that it's worth exploring."

"I do."

"Then roll with it. Who knows what will happen? Maybe you'll find out that he's not what you want or that you're not what he wants. But you can totally have some fun finding out."

Sierra's heart was pounding as she considered the possibility. "What would I even do, though? It's not like I could ask him out."

"Of course you can." Cassidy's smile faded. "Hmm. Or knowing you, maybe not. But from everything you've told me, it sounds like he's into you, too. Just make it obvious that you like him. Something will happen."

"How can you know that?"

Cassidy laughed. "I just do. And if it doesn't, I'll figure something out that'll throw the pair of you together."

"No! You can't do that."

"Then you'd better get on it yourself first, hadn't you?" Cassidy grinned. "In fact, I think I'll invite everyone over this weekend. It's been a while since we all got together."

Sierra raised her eyebrows. "Who's everyone?"

"All Shane's brothers and their wives. And shit … you know Hope, don't you?"

"Hope?"

"Davenport. Well, Malone, now. She lives here. She's married to Shane's brother, Chance."

"She lives here? Oh, wow! I haven't seen Hope in a few years. Not since she was with Drew."

Cassidy made a face. "Yeah. Another asshole he was. But on the bright side, she could maybe teach you by example."

"Teach me what?"

"How to get over being cheated on by an asshole."

Sierra laughed. "Let me guess – by hooking up with a cowboy?"

Cassidy laughed with her. "For starters, yeah. And then going on to marry him."

Sierra's smile faded. She could hardly see that happening.

"Okay. Sorry. I pushed it. I know. But it happens. And if you haven't figured something out for yourself by the time the weekend rolls around, then I'm going to help you out."

"Now I'm worried."

"You should be. I'm going to invite everyone over on Saturday and if you and Wade haven't figured it out by then, we may need to give you a little push."

"No, Cassidy! No pushing."

"Only if you don't figure it out for yourself first."

Wade checked his watch as he ran up the back steps at the lodge, then stopped when he heard laughter behind him.

"She's only been gone a couple hours."

He turned back to see Tyler grinning at him from the bottom of the steps.

"What? Who?"

"You're not fooling me, bro." Tyler shook his head as he trotted up the steps and held the door open for Wade to go through. "You've been useless since the second you watched Sierra drive away. You should have gone with her. You could have claimed you needed to see Shane or something."

Wade took his hat off and ran his hand through his hair. "Can you believe that I actually considered that?"

"Sure, I can. She's got your head turned right around."

"Yeah. But I need to get over it. For all I know she might come back and say that Cassidy's invited her to stay there and she's going."

"Nah. Not going to happen."

"How do you know? It might."

"Nope." Tyler walked into the office and took a seat in one of the easy chairs. Wade walked around his desk and sat opposite. "She's got as much of a thing for you as you do for her."

Wade pressed his lips together, but couldn't quite hold his smile in.

Tyler laughed. "I don't think I've ever seen you like this. You should ask her out."

"I can't! You know what her situation is. She was supposed to get married on Saturday."

Tyler shrugged. "Yeah, but she didn't. She even said that she'd figured out that she didn't love the guy. I say go for it."

"But she's only going to be here until she gets things figured out."

"Exactly. Hurry up before you miss your chance."

Wade turned his pen over and over. "Wouldn't it be an asshole move to ask her out right now, with everything that she has going on? What she needs is a friend. Not some guy making a move on her."

Tyler laughed. "You're not just some guy and you're not making a move on her. You're just going to ask her out. It's obvious that she's into you, too. You're already being a good friend to her – she might appreciate some benefits, too."

"I dunno, dude. It doesn't seem right."

Tyler shrugged. "Up to you. But if it were me ... I'd go there."

Wade scowled at him, but Tyler just laughed. "I don't mean with Sierra. I mean if I were in this situation with a girl that I liked. I'd be all about it. Women love that shit, you know. The hero to the rescue. The big strong guy to keep her safe in his big strong arms." He laughed. "They eat that shit up."

Wade shook his head. "That just seems like preying on her when she's in a difficult situation."

"I see it more like giving her what she wants. I mean, it's not like she's going to be here for long. After everything that happened with her wedding, she's probably going to remember this as one of the worst times of her life. If she gets to spend a few nights with her hero cowboy, it might take some of the sting out of it."

Wade stared at him. Spend a few nights with Sierra? Damn. He'd love to. But he wanted to be there for her as a support, not as some guy swooping in to take advantage of her when she was down. "You reckon?"

Tyler shrugged. "Yeah. If you're asking me, I'd say let her know that you're interested. She'll soon set you straight either way. If she's not, you haven't lost anything. And if she is ..." He grinned. "Well, it's like Tanner said; you need to get laid."

"I ..."

"You need to either go for it or forget about it. Simple as that. Get on it or let it go. But I didn't come to talk to you about that. I wanted to ask you about the big cabin. Have you decided what you want to do about it? I like the idea of using it as an event space. It has the room."

Wade blew out a sigh. The big cabin was supposed to be one of their biggest moneymakers. A family from California had booked it for the entire summer and he'd been thrilled. Until they'd gone and canceled late last week. They'd paid a whole month's rent as a cancelation fee. But that still left him with another couple of months to fill. He hadn't marked it as available on the website again yet because Tyler had suggested that they could rent it out for events – weddings and private parties. Wade liked the idea, but it'd be a lot of work to market it and then to cater any events that came in. He knew Tyler wanted to do them. He was a godsend at the lodge, but he was destined for bigger things.

"I was wondering if we should put it up on a few of the rental sites first. It'd bring in more money and be less hassle if we could get another booking for a couple of months. I was kind of looking forward to it being one less headache. If we get one set of renters in there for the summer, it's guaranteed income and a lot less hassle than short term rentals – or events."

Tyler blew out a sigh. "You're right. I'm just being selfish. I want to try my hand at some big events."

"I know. And I hate taking the possibility away from you. You deserve it. And I feel like if we don't let you challenge yourself here, you'll go off and find somewhere else. And I wouldn't blame you. But we need you."

Tyler shrugged. "I'm not going anywhere. I committed to doing the summer with you and it's great to be back. But I need my own thing. I feel like I'm just tagging along on your thing. You know, the lodge is your baby. Ford's always been the cattleman. Tanner came back and stepped right in at the stud – and that's as it should be. It's taken a load off your plate, and he is the stud anyway."

Wade chuckled. "Yeah. In every sense. I know you need your own thing. And I feel like a shit not just giving you the cabin. But I think even if we go that route, it's not going to be ideal. It's not going to be enough. It's not a purpose-built event space. So, there'd be lots of compromises we'd need to make."

Tyler let out a short laugh. "It's not like we'll ever have a purpose-built space though, is it?"

"Never say never."

"No? What you thinking?"

"Well, I probably shouldn't say anything yet. I don't want to dangle the carrot. But the lodge has done way better than I projected. I've been playing with the numbers, and I think we could build a restaurant."

"A restaurant?" Tyler looked skeptical. "For the number of guests …"

"No. I don't mean just for the guests. I mean separate. There are enough tourists coming through the valley over the summer that every place is crowded. There aren't that many options right around here. I mean, there's Chico and the Valley Lodge, but other than that, if people want anything more than a burger, they have to drive up to Livingston or down to Gardiner."

Tyler grinned. "So, you're talking about something upscale?"

Wade grinned back at him. "Yeah. The kind of place that'd be worthy of having you as the head chef."

"Damn! Well, that'd be worth sticking around for."

"Yeah. If I can swing it. And I don't want to lead you on and tell you that it's a definite until I know for sure."

"That's fair. I know how it goes. How about we give it a couple weeks to see if you can find a seasonal renter for the big cabin? If you can, great. I'll just keep doing my thing at the lodge and bide my time. If not, I'll take it on as an event space – and I mean, I'll take on all the headaches and the marketing and everything else. How about that?"

"Okay. You've got yourself a deal."

"Although, if you think it'll bring in more money as a rental, I might just stick with that plan and try to find you a renter."

Wade cocked an eyebrow.

"I want to do whatever will bring in the most money – to go toward my restaurant."

Wade chuckled. "We'll see what we can do."

They both turned to look when a vehicle passed the office window, heading to the cabins beyond the lodge. Wade's pulse quickened when he recognized Sierra's SUV.

Tyler winked at him. "I don't think there's anything around here that's so important that you couldn't take the afternoon off."

Wade swallowed. He couldn't. That wouldn't be like him.

"I say go for it. Remember, you're doing a good thing – helping her through a tough time."

Wade ran his hand through his hair and then got to his feet. Why not? Tyler was right – she needed a friend. As for the rest – well, he'd just have to play that by ear.

Chapter Nine

Sierra parked the SUV in front of the cabin and sat there for a few moments. She'd stayed at the big house last night and she probably should have gone straight back there now. But it felt weird. They'd all been so good to her. But she didn't feel like she could just waltz into their home.

This cabin had felt like a safe place. She pursed her lips – probably because it was Wade's place. It had felt like a little cocoon of safety that he'd welcomed her into on Saturday night. She wanted that feeling back again. If she were honest, she wanted him back. Wanted to be alone with him again.

Cassidy had told her she should make it obvious that she liked him. But how was she even supposed to do that? She'd never been the kind of girl who knew what she was doing when it came to men. It was easy for Cassidy to say it. She'd always been the girl who guys flocked around, eager to impress her. Sierra supposed that there'd been plenty of guys who tried to impress her, too. But that was different. It wasn't about her as a woman. It was about her being a Hartford.

She jumped when someone tapped on the window. Wade was standing there, smiling at her. Well, wasn't she a fool, sitting there outside the cabin lost in her thoughts?

She opened the door and smiled back at him.

"Are you okay?"

"Yes. Sorry."

He held her gaze as he smiled. "You really don't need to keep apologizing."

"Sorry. I ... Well, shoot!" She let out an embarrassed laugh. "I did it again. Didn't I?"

She loved the way his eyes crinkled when he smiled. There were well worn lines that said he smiled a lot. "It's okay. I came to see what you're doing."

"Oh. Well, I came back from Cassidy's, and I didn't like to just go into the big house. I came back here because ..." If she was going to try out Cassidy's advice, this was the moment to do it. "Well, because I thought you might be here."

His smile grew bigger at that. Okay, so maybe it wasn't such a terrible idea to be honest with him, then.

"And here I am."

"You are. I didn't know if you'd still be working. But I feel more comfortable in your space than anywhere else."

He held her gaze for a moment, as if he wanted to check that he understood what she was saying.

She nodded. As if that might help. "I don't want to bother you, though. Or hold you up if you're busy." Darn! And there went her manners – or possibly her nerves – trying to let him off the hook.

"You're not bothering me." He smiled and held the door open for her. She slid down and when her feet hit the ground, she looked up into his eyes. He put his hand on her shoulder, and this time the feelings it sent coursing through her felt as though they were laced with something more than friendly support. He held her gaze when he spoke. "I was working. But when I saw you come back, I wanted to come see you."

"Thanks. I'm okay. I made it." He was just checking on her after all. She shouldn't let herself get carried away.

"I'm glad. But I didn't just want to check how you were doing. I mean … I wanted to see you."

"Oh." She really didn't know how to do this. She could imagine Cassidy laughing and tossing her hair and saying something flirty. But all Sierra could do was look up into his kind eyes.

"I decided that I'm done for the day. Do you want to do anything?"

She sucked in a deep breath, but there was no way he was suggesting that they should do the kind of things she was thinking about.

One side of his mouth quirked up, and she felt her cheeks flush, hoping that he hadn't read her mind. "Do you want to go up to town? We could buy you some clothes. Or …?" He shrugged. "Whatever you want. Name it. I'm in."

She only just managed not to laugh at the thought of naming what she wanted. "I'm okay for clothes. Thank you. Cassidy gave me a bunch." Cassidy had also taken her to a cute boutique where she'd been able to stock up on underwear, but she didn't see the need to tell him that. She frowned. "I hope Janey won't be offended."

"She won't."

"Okay." She half wished that she'd said yes to going to town with him, instead of shutting him down.

"Well, we have a few options. I can show you around the ranch. We could go for a drive, and I'll show you the valley, or we could go up to town anyway and get whatever else you might need." His smile disappeared. "You are going to stay, aren't you?"

"Yes. Sorry. That should have been the first thing I said. I should have asked if it's still okay. Cassidy said she thought I'd be better here than at her place – since her husband's at work, and she is much of the time, too." She dropped her gaze, not wanting to look him in the eye while she thought about the other reasons Cassidy thought she should stay here – because she thought Sierra should sleep with him!

"Of course it's okay." He looked at her, then glanced at the cabin. "Would you rather stay here than at the house?"

She swallowed. She would. But she wasn't sure that she should say so. After spending last night at the big house, how could she come back here? And how would it be okay for Wade to come back here with her?

She held his gaze, feeling like she'd been caught but unable to tell the truth.

A slow smile spread across his face. Had he read her mind? "How about we take a ride up to town? We can stop at the grocery store and stock up." He chuckled. "You're probably going to want something other than beer and frozen pizza, and that's all I have in."

"Okay. Let's do that. But you must let me buy. If you're going to be kind enough to let me share your space, the least I can do is feed you." She smiled, feeling more relaxed since he seemed to understand her answer even though she hadn't said so. "I can cook for you. It won't be as good as Tyler, but I'm not a bad cook."

"Well, alrighty then. I won't say no to that. Do you want to go right now? Do you need to do anything first?"

"I'm good to go." She turned to get back into the car, but his hand came down on her shoulder again, sending shivers racing down her spine.

"I've got my truck here. We can take that."

"Okay."

He walked her to the passenger door and held it open for her. He could give the guys at the country club lessons in how to treat a lady. She had to grab for the handle inside the door to haul herself up. His hand on her elbow helped. Once she was seated, she turned to smile at him. "I think I might need a rope ladder to get down."

He chuckled. "Nope, you're good. I'll be right here to catch you."

She laughed with him, but her heart melted a little bit at his words. He was the kind of man who would be there to catch his girl and never let her fall. It was just a pity that no matter what little infatuation she had going for him, she wasn't ever going to be his girl. They were from different worlds, and she'd have to go back and face her own world all too soon.

~ ~ ~

Wade paused at the cabin door and took a deep breath. Ford was right. He must be crazy to want to play house with Sierra. But crazy or not, he was doing it. They'd had fun this afternoon. He'd driven up the valley and loved her wide-eyed appreciation of how beautiful it was. She'd fallen in love with the place as he watched.

When they'd gotten to town and gone into the grocery store, she'd commandeered a cart. That moment hadn't been the highlight of his day. It had taken him back to grocery shopping with Josie when they were still married. He'd hated it then. Josie was the kind of person who noticed the negatives in every situation – and liked to bitch about them. The produce was never fresh enough, the canned goods had dents, she liked to gossip with her friend who worked at the deli counter. Grocery shopping with her had been an ordeal, but it was still better than letting her go alone – apparently that was tantamount to marital neglect. He'd even offered to do it alone – anything rather than endure another miserable trudge up and down the aisles with her, but the thought of him getting groceries without her had set her off on another rant – about what people would think of her. With those memories filling his head, Sierra's grab for a shopping cart had filled him with trepidation.

However, it turned out that grocery shopping with her was fun. She flitted around – excited – and it wasn't an act. She was genuinely excited to explore the store. To find familiar items and discover new ones – at least, they were new to her. She made him laugh when she stood in front of the butcher's counter, reading the signs pinned to the wall.

Eldon, who'd been a year behind him in school, came out from the back and watched her. He'd raised an eyebrow at Wade when he realized Sierra was with him and gave an appreciative nod.

"It's amazing that you can get oysters out here. I'd have thought it'd be all beef." She pointed at the sign. "Do they come in frozen or are there special deliveries?" she asked Eldon.

He smirked at Wade. "Do you want to explain?"

"Thanks." Wade chuckled.

"What?" Sierra looked puzzled. "Are they frozen?"

"No. They're fresh, all right. Fresh from the ranch. That's why people have to get their orders in the week before."

"I don't get it."

He chuckled again. "Rocky Mountain oysters are not actually oysters."

"Oh." She looked so cute in her confusion. "What are they then?"

"Bull balls," Eldon said with a laugh.

Her eyes widened as she looked at him and then back at Wade. "Bull balls? As in …?" Her cheeks tinged with pink.

Wade nodded, trying not to laugh at her expression. "Yep. Testicle specials."

Her hand came up to cover her mouth as she giggled. "Wow! I had no idea."

"You wouldn't have unless you spent any time around here. It's a Rocky Mountain thing. Up in Canada they call them prairie oysters."

She'd smiled at Eldon and then turned her cart away. Wade had hurried after her, only to find her still giggling when he caught up.

"I'm sorry. That's funny!"

He'd had to laugh with her. She apologized for so many things that she didn't need to. She sure as hell didn't need to apologize for laughing. The sound of it tugged at his insides.

They'd kept laughing and joking the rest of the way around the store, with Wade pointing out anything he saw that he thought might be new and interesting to her, and Sierra introducing him to a few items that he'd never noticed before.

He shook his head and came back to the moment. No matter what Ford might say, playing house with Sierra had turned out to be a lot of fun so far. And that was only while they were out and about. Now, after going back and checking that everything was okay at the lodge, he was about to find out what it would be like to play house at home – to spend the evening, and the night, under the same roof.

He pushed the cabin door open and took his hat off as he stepped into the hallway. The smell of cooking stopped him. The whole place felt different. It could just be the fact that there was someone here. He was used to the place being empty. But it was more than that. It was the smell – whatever she was cooking smelled great. And the sight of her purse on the table. The sweatshirt that he'd given her earlier was thrown across the back of the sofa. The whole scene struck him as – domestic. And he loved it.

"Hey." She'd turned from the stove but was still holding a spatula. She looked worried. "Is everything okay? You said I could cook. Is it ... do you mind?"

He came to his senses, realizing that he'd been standing there staring and must have freaked her out. "I don't mind. I'm ... amazed." He smiled. "It was a surprise to walk in and have the place feel so ... lived in."

She still looked worried. "I don't want you to think I'm taking over or anything. I ..."

He went to her and took the spatula out of her hand, setting it down on the counter while he talked himself out of telling her that he'd love for her to take over the cabin – and make it a home. He needed to get a grip.

"Relax." He smiled down at her. He was standing too close, but it wasn't close enough. "I said it was a surprise – it's a good one."

His gaze dropped to her lips as she rolled them together. Was Ty right? Would she want him to kiss her? Want him to ... Nope. He shouldn't even be thinking about it. He took a step back. "Have you heard anything more from home?" He needed to remember that though she might be a little lost at the moment, she already had a home. It was back in San Francisco, and it was full of people – people like her friend Amelia, who was no doubt worried about her, and Barney, who ran her family business – and since she had no family left, that meant it was her business and by all accounts it was a billion-dollar corporation. And if that wasn't enough of a reminder that he shouldn't be thinking about offering her anything more than friendship, there was also the small matter of the man she'd almost married just a few days ago.

His question brought a frown to her face. "I have, actually. Barney called me. He said that he's started an investigation into

Jared. It looks as though he's been embezzling from the company."

"Damn!"

She nodded. "Apparently, no one has seen him or Lori since they left Utah. I kind of hope that he stole enough money from the company to disappear to Mexico or somewhere and that'll be the end of it." She blew out a big sigh. "I know that probably makes me pathetic, but I've never been one for lots of drama or to want revenge. I just want it all to go away." She gave him a sad smile. "I talked to Amelia. She thinks I need to hire investigators to hunt him down and ..." She shrugged.

"What do you want?"

Her gray eyes were like liquid silver when she looked up at him. "What I want, what I need more than anything right now, is a hug."

His breath caught in his chest.

"My dad and my brother were both huggers. At least, they were for me. I don't think either of them ever really understood me or knew what to do with me. They were both smart, strong, silent, logical types, and I'm more well ... creative, I guess. They didn't know what to do with me, but they loved me so much. They rarely knew what to say when I was sad, but they both knew that a hug always helped."

Wade held his arms out to his sides and jerked his head to the side in invitation. "I know I can't be a stand in for them, but I'm a bit of a hugger myself. You'll have to ask Janey how good I am." His heart hammered when she stepped closer, and his arms closed around her of their own accord. She rested her cheek against his chest and slid her arms around his waist and relaxed.

He closed his eyes and rested his cheek on top of her head. She fit perfectly. She felt perfect against him. He held her a little closer, and her arms tightened around his waist. Damn!

He was lost. He breathed in the scent of her. It'd driven him nuts yesterday whenever he'd gotten close enough to smell her – she smelled of him. It was only his shower gel, but it'd done something strange to him. Made him feel like she was his. That he'd somehow marked her with his scent. Today she smelled of something prettier, something very feminine. And standing there with his arms around her, she still felt like she was his.

~ ~ ~

Sierra clung to him. He was so big and solid. Yet so gentle. She closed her eyes and nuzzled her cheek against his hard chest. She knew that asking for a hug hadn't exactly been what Cassidy meant when she'd said to tell him what she wanted. But it was a big step for Sierra. She couldn't remember ever asking a man for anything, at least not anything physical. She let them take the lead. This was new, but she was very pleased with herself – and with her reward. She couldn't help smiling when he swayed her from side to side.

"Are you okay down there?"

She chuckled against his chest. "More than okay. I hope you don't mind being my hugging post."

He stiffened at her words, and she wondered what she'd said wrong.

"Post?" He relaxed again and she felt rather than heard him chuckle. "You mean you see me like … say … a scratching post for a cat? I'm your hugging post?"

"No!" She had to lean back to look up into his eyes, but he didn't loosen his arms around her. "I don't mean it that way at all. I chose the wrong words." She smiled. "Hugging buddy?"

The lines around his eyes creased a little deeper, but he didn't look amused. He looked – pained? "Buddy?" He nodded and smiled, but it didn't reach his eyes. "I can be your hug buddy."

Sierra's heart sank. He made it sound like something else. She knew that some of the girls at the office had what they called *fuck buddies*. They didn't want a boyfriend, just someone they hung out with – a friend – who they also had sex with. When she looked up at him again, he was watching her face.

"Is that what you want?" he asked.

"No. I have to tell you." Her heart hammered even faster, but she was going to say it. "I ... I find you very attractive. And not just physically. I feel a draw, a connection to you. I want ..." Her cheeks must be bright red, they felt so hot, but she needed to be honest. "I don't know what I want. I don't think I'm in a position where I should want anything from you. But I do."

Her tummy flipped over when his hand came up to cup the side of her neck. His fingers slid into her hair, sending shivers chasing each other down her spine. His gaze dropped to her lips and then came back up to meet hers. "I feel drawn to you, too, Sierra. I sure as hell shouldn't ask anything from you. But I want to kiss you."

She stared back into his beautiful, green eyes until it hit her that he was waiting for her answer. She nodded and rolled up onto her tiptoes, bringing her lips closer to his. "I want to kiss you, too."

He lowered his head, holding her gaze until his lips brushed over hers, and then her eyes closed, and she sagged against him. Her whole body quivered when his fingers stroked the nape of her neck. His other arm tightened around her, holding her closer against his hard, muscular chest. Then his tongue traced the seam of her lips and she opened up to him. It was a good thing he was holding her up because she felt as though she'd melt into a puddle at his feet if he let her go. She brought her arms up around his shoulders, pulling him closer, needing him to take the kiss deeper, and he did.

His kiss was just like him. Strong but gentle. She couldn't help but compare him to Jared. His kisses were aggressive, as if he were taking what he wanted with no thought for her. Wade kissed her slowly, deeply, gently but oh so thoroughly. He made the world fade away. He made her body melt against him as he held her closer.

His hand slid down her back until it closed around her butt and held her closer against him there, too. She moaned into his mouth. She could feel him through his jeans; he was hot and hard – and big.

He brought his hand back up between her shoulder blades. Her breasts were pressed against his chest, and she pressed closer and rocked her hips, wanting to feel him closer there again.

His tongue swept deeper and then he lifted his head and looked down into her eyes. His breath was coming hard and fast – matching hers.

"Sorry. I …"

"No! Please don't say you're sorry." She reached up and traced her finger down his cheek.

"I thought I could keep it … low key? I thought I could kiss you in a way that'd make you feel better. But that connection between you and me? It's quicksand, darlin'. Once we're in it, it's going to be tough to get out. And I don't want to take more than you want to give."

Sierra's heart hammered. Was he talking about kissing her so thoroughly – or about taking more?

"You're in a bad place. You've had an emotional time of it. I don't want to take advantage of that, and I don't want you to regret getting carried away by the moment."

He still had his arms around her, and she pressed herself closer against him. "The way you kissed me did make me feel better – better than …" she probably shouldn't say it, but she was going to, "better than Jared ever did. I won't deny that I'm in a state. But I want to go wherever this takes us. I won't regret it. I promise you."

He dropped his head and brushed his lips over hers again, making her cling to him and hope that he was going to take her back to where they'd been. But he lifted his head and shook it. "I want you to think about it, Sierra." He gave her a rueful smile. "It smells like you've made us a great dinner. We should get to that first."

She stepped away from him and blew out a big shaky breath. "You're right. But I'm not going to change my mind. I understand if you want to, though."

His arms snaked back around her and pulled her against him before she even knew what was happening. She was crushed against his chest, looking up into his eyes. They seemed to dance as he smiled down at her. "I'm not going to change my mind darlin'. I'm trying to look out for you, that's all."

She had to smile back at him. "And I appreciate it. You're a good man, Wade. I know you don't want to take advantage of me. But please don't hold back on me. It's taking everything I have to be this … brazen and tell you what I want."

He chuckled and tucked his fingers under her chin, tilting her head back and dropping a kiss on her lips. "You are far from brazen, Sierra."

She chuckled with him. "I'm trying my best, darn it."

"You don't even curse, do you?"

She shrugged. "I don't. I tried it out when I was a teenager, but Seb and Dax teased me mercilessly. They thought it was hilarious. So, I stopped. And the circles I move in, it's just not seemly for a young lady, you know?"

He chuckled again as he shook his head. "I can't say as I do know." His smile faded. "We don't exactly move in the same circles, do we?"

Sierra's heart sank. He was right. And it was a reminder that she'd only be here for a couple of weeks at the most. Then she'd go back to her world, and he'd stay here in his. She didn't want to get bogged down in thinking about that. What she needed to do was make the most of the time she had with him. "Well, I'm in your circle for now. So, maybe I should learn to curse a little, dammit."

He stroked his hand over her hair, and the look in his eyes sent a rush of warmth spreading through her chest. "Nah. Don't do that. It wouldn't suit you. You're perfect just the way you are. My world's a rough and busy place; you're like a soft, sweet breeze blowing through. Don't try to change to fit in. Be yourself and let your sweetness soften this place up a bit."

"Aww." She put her hand over her heart. "What a lovely thing to say."

He rolled his eyes and gave her a rueful smile. "Sorry. My brothers tell me I'm the romantic in the family."

"They're right. But now it's my turn to tell you not to apologize. I love it!"

"Okay then. Note to self. She likes the mushy stuff. So, don't hold back."

"It's not mushy!" She stepped away from him and reached for the spatula. "You're right, though. We shouldn't let this dinner spoil." It was safer to get back to making dinner than to tell him how happy she was to discover that he had a romantic side. She'd told Jared early in their relationship that she needed him to give her a little romance. He'd insisted that real men didn't do romance. Wade was a much more real man than Jared would ever be, and he'd just restored her faith.

He came to stand behind her as she stirred the pasta, which was probably going to be too soft by now. She closed her eyes and smiled when he slid his arms around her waist and rested his chin on her shoulder.

"What freaked you out?"

She turned her head and he met her with a peck on her lips. "Yep, I know what you're thinking – can he read my mind? And the answer is yes." He laughed. "Nah. It's not really. But your face gives you away. I'm guessing you don't play poker?"

"No."

"Good. You'd lose a fortune. But go on. Something about me saying that you like the mushy stuff was a problem for you."

"No. Not really. It's just that you're right, and I do. But I'd been told that …"

"Let me guess. Jared told you that romance is bullshit, and you shouldn't expect any."

She let out a short laugh. "Pretty much. Yes. But you also managed to prove him wrong. Because he said that real men don't do romance."

He nuzzled his lips into her neck. "We do."

"So I'm discovering."

He straightened up and put his hands on her shoulders. "You know. I've been second guessing myself. Thinking that we should go back up to the house and stay there and just be friends. But I think Jared has done me a favor."

"How?"

"His take on real men and romance has given me an idea."

"What?"

"I think that while you're here, I'm going to make it my mission to prove to you just how wrong he was."

She turned to look up at him. He was smiling, but he was serious. "And what exactly would that look like?"

He chuckled. "I don't exactly know yet. But I'll make it good. If you like the sound of it?"

This handsome cowboy proving to her that he was a real man and that he did romance? Heck yes! She nodded. What girl wouldn't like the sound of that?

Chapter Ten

Wade opened the bedroom door and peeked out. He was hoping that he'd be able to sneak out without waking Sierra. Not because he didn't want to see her – but because he wanted to see her a little too much. He adjusted his jeans before he opened the door to the not quite finished second bedroom where he'd spent the night.

It would have been all too easy to have kept things on the track they were on last night and to have ended up spending the night in the master bedroom – with Sierra. He sucked in a deep breath and shoved his hands in his pockets. Instead of taking her to bed, he'd sent her off by herself, not because he didn't want her. Not even because he thought she didn't want him. She'd made it all too clear that she did. He wasn't even kidding himself that he thought he should wait because this could be the beginning of something between them – he knew damned well that it wouldn't be. Well, it'd be something, but only something short lived. He was going to be her rebound guy. He'd get her through and past the dark days that were supposed to have been her honeymoon. While he was at it, he planned to teach her how a man should treat her – and hopefully get her to a place where she wouldn't settle for being treated with anything less than the respect she deserved in the future.

But part of treating her with respect meant not rushing her into bed – no matter how much he wanted to, or even how much she tried to make clear that she did. He couldn't help smiling as he tiptoed down the hallway. Her version of making it clear that she wanted him was nothing like any other woman he'd ever known. He'd thought that he was only attracted to assertive women, women who went after what they wanted. He used to find that attractive. Maybe it was the way Josie had proven to be so ruthless in getting what she wanted that had put him off. Or maybe it was just that Sierra was so cute.

He knew that it had taken all her courage to ask him for a hug last night. After that, she'd backed off while they had dinner, and he'd refrained from acting like anything more than a friend. But when they'd sat down to watch a movie later, she'd snuggled right up to him on the sofa, and it'd taken all he had to hold back from stroking anything but her shoulder and her hair.

At one point, she'd rested her hand on his thigh. As it had started to creep higher, he'd almost given in to his need for her, but he'd made do with just a kiss. It was a kiss that had left her in no doubt that he wanted her, but after that he'd sent her to bed.

He made it to the kitchen and was pulling his boots on when the bedroom door opened, and she came out. He let out a groan at the sight of her. How was he supposed to resist? He'd spent most of the night tossing and turning and second guessing his plan to take things slowly. She was only going to be here for two weeks, after all. He'd woken up with a hard on that no baseball stats were going to be able to help him ignore. And now here she was, padding barefoot — bare legged — down the hallway toward him, wearing nothing but one of his T-shirts. Her hair was mussed-up, her eyes were still bleary – and she was the most beautiful thing he'd ever seen.

She stopped a few feet away from him. "Good morning." Her smile hit him right in the chest, catching all his breath.

"Morning, darlin'. Did you sleep?"

She gave him a rueful smile. "I did eventually, but it took me a while to get off."

He closed his eyes. She meant get off to sleep. She had to. But her words sent his mind spinning away to all the ways he wanted to get her off.

She gave him a shy smile. "Not like that!"

He chuckled. He had to.

"You look like you're ready to head out. Do you want me to make you some coffee before you go?"

He blew out a sigh. There was no way he was going to be able to stick with his plan of leaving. She was up now. And even if it were only for a few minutes, he wanted to be around her.

"I'll get it."

"Thank you." She turned around and started back down the hallway again.

The only thing that Wade could think was that she was going to get dressed and that was the last thing he wanted. "Don't I get a hug?" Jesus. He shouldn't have asked her that. Once he got his arms around her, he didn't know how he'd be able to let her go.

She turned back with a smile and came straight to him. "Yes, please." Her arms came up around his neck, and he bent to wrap his around her waist.

She was warm and soft, and she smelled so good. He buried his face in her neck and breathed in deeply. She giggled and shuddered against him, her arms tightening around him.

"Wow! That feels so good."

He didn't need telling twice. He nuzzled closer and this time nibbled the soft skin just beneath her ear.

"Wade." Her voice was barely more than a breathy whisper. The sound of his name on her lips fried his brain. He knew all the reasons why he wasn't going to be anything more than her rebound guy, but the way she said his name made him want to be way more than that.

He tightened his arms around her waist and straightened up. She giggled and clung tighter to his neck as her feet left the floor. "Ooh! I like it. Where are we going?"

He groaned when she wrapped her legs around his waist, pressing her heat against the one part of him that knew exactly where it wanted to go.

He took two steps toward the bedroom before his senses kicked back in and he stopped. He spun around and forced himself back to the kitchen, where he deposited her on the counter.

The disappointment in her eyes when she leaned back to look at him, almost changed his mind. He was crazy enough to deny himself – but disappoint her? No. He got a grip — on his lust, and on her hips. He curled his fingers around them and dropped a kiss on her lips.

"I thought you were going to take me to bed," she breathed.

He nodded before he spoke. When the words came out, his voice sounded low and growly — desperate — even to his own ears. "I am." Her eyes widened, but he shook his head. "There's no question that I'm going to take you to bed, Sierra. But not right now."

"Why not?" She echoed the question that was playing on repeat in his head.

He blew out a sigh. "Because it wouldn't be right. I have to get to the lodge. I have to work today. I don't want to ... actually that's not the truth." He chuckled and pulled her to the edge of the counter, allowing himself to press his cock between her legs, so she could feel just how much he did want. He closed his eyes when she rubbed herself against him.

"I want to."

He shook his head sadly. "You're killing me, Sierra. It'd be so easy to pick you up and take you back to bed and ... go there right now. But it'll be way better if we wait."

"How long?"

He had to laugh at the disappointment in her voice. "Not long. I don't think I could survive for long."

"Tonight?"

He hadn't wanted to give her a timeframe, hoping instead that he might be able to hold out for a while – whatever a while might mean. But the look on her face, the desire in her eyes, the feel of her against him and her legs wrapped around his waist? They all added up to irresistible. He might be a gentleman, but he was no saint. He nodded slowly before giving in and agreeing. "Tonight."

The way she smiled made him feel as though fireworks were exploding in his chest. She was unlike any woman he'd known before. He'd sure as hell never had a woman beg him to tell her when he was going to take her to bed. And he couldn't remember ever wanting a woman as much as he did Sierra.

He closed his hand around the back of her neck and claimed her mouth in a kiss that felt like a promise – a promise that he planned to make good on tonight, no matter what he might have been thinking earlier about taking his time.

~ ~ ~

Sierra had gone back and forth with herself for over half an hour about whether she should wear some of the things that Janey had let her borrow. In the end, she'd decided against it. Jane had called not long after Wade had left the cabin this morning and offered to come pick her up. She'd said that she was going up to the shelter in town to collect a dog that had been brought in and she wanted the company.

Sierra doubted that Jane was the kind of girl who needed company for anything. She seemed to be perfectly at peace with herself — in a way that Sierra envied.

She was waiting by the window when Jane's truck pulled up and she went out to meet her, hoping that she'd made the right decision to wear Cassidy's designer jeans and a gorgeous, light blue sweater that made her eyes seem blue to match it.

Jane grinned at her when she hauled herself up into the passenger seat. "Good morning. I see you went shopping. Maybe I need you to take me on a shopping trip, too. Even when I think I should make an effort, I can never find anything that looks that good around here."

"Oh." Sierra gave her an apologetic smile. "I … I didn't go shopping. I went to see Cassidy and she took charge — she's like that."

She needn't have worried about Jane's reaction. She laughed out loud. "Don't look so worried. I was the one who was worried about you schlepping around in my stuff. It makes much more sense for you to wear Cassidy's stuff. It's much more your style."

Sierra pulled on her seatbelt as Jane pulled the truck away from the cabin. "I'd love to take you on a shopping trip if you want to go?"

"Nah. That's fine. I don't know what I was thinking. What I wear is practical for my work." Jane let out a short laugh. "For my life. It's not as though I go out much."

"Cassidy talked about getting people together this weekend. We should go shopping and get you something to wear for that."

Jane shrugged. "There's no need."

"I'm sorry." Sierra felt bad. "I'm not trying to be … I'm not saying that you need to."

"I know. It's okay." Janey gave her that warm smile that reminded Sierra just what a beautiful person she was. "I don't see the point, I guess. I don't need to look good to do what I do. The animals I work with don't care what I'm wearing. And the people I mix with already know me for who I am. If I were to dress up, it would only be to impress people. And I don't feel the need to do that. If people aren't impressed with who I am and what I do, then I don't really care if they're impressed with how I look or not."

"I understand that. You're so much stronger, much more real than I am. I've always felt that the way I look is important because it determines how people see me. And that really shouldn't matter." She blew out a sigh. "But in the world that I live in, it matters a lot."

Jane looked over at her. "I wouldn't worry about it. You're fine the way you are. And I'm fine the way I am. I'm just glad that the superficial differences don't make a difference between us. It was hard growing up and maybe even harder when I was in vet school. Lots of them looked down on me because I didn't want to play the game. You don't look down on me."

"No! I look up to you! You know what's really important and you don't let yourself be swayed by what people might think."

Jane laughed. "You make me sound so noble. I'm really not. All I did was decide that I don't want to play a game I know that I can't win. Laney's the pretty one, so I stopped trying to compete in a world where I couldn't win. That's all. And I do still care what people think. It's just that I live in a small world where most folks already know me, and it doesn't matter."

Sierra nodded. "What about dating?"

Jane laughed again. "I don't. For all the crap I spout about people taking me for who I am, I'm not stupid. Guys like women who look good – and I don't."

"And you don't want to make an effort – sorry, that sounds wrong, but you know what I mean. You wouldn't want to change who you are for a guy to like you."

"That's the theory. But it's pretty much untested. I haven't met anyone I'd be interested in in a very long time."

While they'd been talking, they'd driven past the lodge and back up the long driveway. Jane brought the truck to a stop when another one pulled in off the road. She let the window down and smiled when the driver of the other truck did the same.

"Hey, Emmett. I have to run up to the shelter. They had a stray mama brought in last night. Sounds like she's due any day, so I said that I'd bring her back down here."

The man driving the other truck nodded. "Okay. My day's looking quiet for now. I should be around when you get back." He glanced past Jane and smiled at Sierra.

She smiled back. It seemed this valley was full of good-looking men, no matter what age they might be. This guy had to be around fifty. There were weathered lines on his face, but his brown eyes were warm and full of life as they looked out at her from under the brim of his cowboy hat.

"Oh, sorry," said Jane. "Sierra, meet my partner, Emmett. Emmett, this is Sierra Hartford. She's staying with us for a little while."

Sierra was grateful that Jane's explanation didn't go into the reasons for her presence here – or the details of just who she was staying with.

The man nodded. "Nice to meet you, Miss Sierra." He chuckled. "Now, I'll be able to tell my girls who the pretty lady at the big house is."

Sierra raised an eyebrow, not understanding.

"Emmett's daughters are into everything," Jane explained. "Nothing gets by them. They'll no doubt be over to investigate you when we get back."

"I'll keep 'em out of the way if that's a problem."

Emmett must have noticed Sierra's expression change. She forced herself to smile again. "No. I'll look forward to meeting them. How old are they?"

"Twelve and fourteen," said Jane.

Emmett laughed. "Going on twenty-five and thirty. Anyway, I'll let you ladies get going. See you later."

"We won't be too long," Jane told him.

Sierra watched the truck in the rearview mirror as Jane pulled out onto the highway.

"Go ahead and ask," Jane said. "I can tell you have questions."

Sierra had to laugh. "Is that a MacFarland thing?"

"What do you mean?"

"I mean, you all seem able to read my mind."

"No. I could tell you had questions. If I could read your mind, I'd know what your questions were."

That was true. It was the same with Wade. He seemed to be able to tell when she had questions, or was hesitant, but he didn't know exactly what she was thinking. She'd do well to remember that.

"I was wondering about Emmett. You said he's your partner?"

Jane laughed. "In the practice. We work together. He's a vet, too. He's awesome. He's one of my brother's best friends. His place burned down a few years ago – the same year that I was finishing vet school. We decided to go in together. I put up the land, he brought in his contacts and between us, we've built a thriving business."

"Wow. That's amazing."

Jane nodded happily. "It is. It's worked out better than either of us could have imagined. The practice has grown. We have more than enough business. And Emmett built himself a house right there so that he could be on site."

"And his wife?"

Jane sighed. "She died when the girls were small. He's by himself."

"Wow. With teenaged girls?"

Jane smiled. "They're good kids. Although, they're not really kids anymore. I do what I can with them. I love them and I know they love me right back. But Alana, that's the older one, she's turning into a girly girl and as we already touched on – I'm no use to her with that stuff. Tanya's still more of a tomboy – but I have a feeling that she'll follow in her sister's footsteps. I hope you won't mind if they glom onto you. They're desperate for a woman in their lives. Like I said, I do what I can, but I'm not the kind of woman they need."

"I'd love to meet them, and I can chat with them about girly stuff – that's right in my wheelhouse. But it sounds as though Emmett needs to find a woman of his own who might be able to come into their lives."

"I'll let you be the one to tell him that. He's a good guy, and there are plenty of women in this valley who'd love to help him out in every sense, but he's not interested. It took him years to get over Emily. But I don't think that's what stops him anymore. He's just not interested."

Sierra jumped when her phone rang and pulled it out of her purse. She smiled when she saw Wade's name on the display.

"Take it," said Jane. "Don't mind me."

"Hello?"

"Hey, darlin'. I heard you were headed up to town with Janey."

"You did? How?"

He chuckled. It was a low deep sound that made her tummy flip over. She glanced sideways at Jane, hoping that she wasn't mind reading. "I crossed paths with Emmett."

"I see." She didn't know what else to say. She was thrilled that he'd called, but she didn't know what he wanted, and she was just the tiniest bit embarrassed to talk to him in front of his sister.

"Anyway. What's your favorite color?"

She frowned, wondering if she'd heard him right. "Excuse me?"

He chuckled again. "I want to know what your favorite color is. And before you ask, the answer is no. I'm not going to tell you why."

She laughed with him. "In that case, I'm not sure that I want to tell you."

"Aww, help a guy out, would ya?"

She laughed again, loving his playful tone. Right from the first moment she'd seen him, he'd felt like sunshine, and the more time she spent around him the more it felt like he was brightening up her life. "Okay, then. Pink."

"Awesome. I should have trusted my gut."

"You guessed pink?"

"I did. But what kind of pink? Pale or deeper?"

She was surprised that he asked. "Deeper. My very favorite is fuchsia."

"That's like purpley-pink, right?"

She laughed. "Yes. Purpley-pink."

"Okay. Thanks."

"That's it?" She so wanted to know why he was asking.

"Yep." He chuckled. "Oh. And I should be done by around five-thirty tonight. If you don't have any other plans, I hope I'll see you at the cabin whenever you're done with your day."

"Okay. I'll be there."

"I'll look forward to it." His voice sounded lower, gravelly. Or maybe it was just her imagination at the thought of what he was looking forward to.

"Me too."

"See you later, darlin'."

"Bye."

She ended the call and put her phone back in her purse, then blushed furiously when Janey laughed. "Oh, my God! That was Wade, wasn't it?"

She nodded.

"Don't look so embarrassed. It's none of my business. And I shouldn't say a thing. But it's what friends do – and I know that we're going to be friends. So, yay! I love the thought of you and him together and you can't tell me there's nothing going on between you."

Sierra smiled through her embarrassment. "Actually, I can."

"What? Are you serious?"

"Sort of. There isn't anything going on yet."

Jane laughed. "But there will be, and we both know it."

Sierra nodded but didn't want to have to spell out what exactly would be going on between her and Wade tonight.

Chapter Eleven

Wade checked his watch. He'd told Sierra that he'd be done by around five-thirty, and it was five-fifteen already. He wanted to leave for the day, but Ford had called him and asked if he could stop by for a word. His brother would only give him shit if he knew why he was so antsy. He stuck his head out of his office, but there was no sign of Ford.

Anita, who ran front of house for the lodge, smiled when she saw him. "I take it you've been busy? Your door's been closed all afternoon."

"Yeah." He ran his hand through his hair. He'd been catching up on his least favorite part of running the lodge – the paperwork. It wasn't his thing, but he knew he had to be the one to do it. The lodge had been his idea. The rest of the family had gotten on board – as long as he was going to be the one to run it. In its first year, it had far exceeded his expectations, but he wasn't one to rest on his laurels. He wanted to keep growing the business.

Anita stopped when she reached him. "Well, I'm happy to report that all's quiet out here. I wouldn't blame you if you want to call it quits for the day. I know being a desk jockey isn't your idea of fun."

He gave her a rueful smile. "I'd love to but I'm waiting for Ford. He's coming over to have a chat about something."

"Oh." Anita nodded. "I'll bet he wants to borrow some of the horses. If he does, I'm sure we'll be able to juggle. Some of this week's group don't ride."

Wade made a face. "Have I told you lately what a gem you are? If Ford had hit me with that, I wouldn't have known what to tell him. I feel as though I lose touch with the day-to-day stuff when I get locked in the office."

"Hey. It's my job to stay on top of the day-to-day details. You're supposed to be the big picture guy."

He shrugged. "I guess. I just ... I dunno. I'm more comfortable being the cowboy."

She laughed. "Soon, you'll be like the guests – only getting to play cowboy for vacation."

He scowled. "No way. I'd be more inclined to bring in a manager and get back in the saddle than get fat and soft like – " He stopped abruptly when one of the guests came wandering into the reception area.

Anita shot him a warning look. "I know, but watch your mouth."

He had to laugh. "Yes, boss! See, you're the one who should be running this place."

"Maybe so. And when you're ready to hire a manager, you can add my name at the top of the interview list."

"Wow! Now, that sounds like an idea worth investigating."

"It does to me, too. But here's your brother." She smiled. "Be nice to him, and tell him that I can handle the details, okay?"

"Gladly." Wade pursed his lips. "Are you serious? About wanting to do more."

"Hell yeah! I'd love to."

"Okay, then. Let me give it some thought. And since you're so smart, why don't you see what you can come up with, too. We should sit down before the end of the week and start working on a plan of what you can take over."

"Great. I'll set us up a meeting – Friday morning?"

"Sure."

"Wade."

He turned to greet Ford. "What can I do you for?"

"Horses. I brought in a couple extra hands, and I need some rides. Can you spare me any?"

Wade grinned at Anita. "You'll have to speak to the boss."

Ford looked puzzled. "Okay. But I need to talk to you about something else, too."

"If it's day-to-day business, Anita probably knows more than I do."

"Nope. Only you can help me with this."

Wade sighed inwardly and headed back into his office.

"I'll find you when I'm done here," Ford told Anita before following Wade inside and closing the door behind him.

"What's up? What is it that only I can help you with?"

"You're the only one who can tell me what you're thinking with Sierra."

"True. But why do you need to know?"

Ford laughed. "I'd rather not know about your love life, if that's where you're planning on taking this. But I talked to Cash."

"About?"

"About her whole situation. The groom who wanted to kill her. The brother's SEAL friend who wants to saddle her with a couple of kids. You know, just little details like that."

Wade made a face. He'd been doing his best not to think about the children.

Ford sighed. "She seems like a sweetheart, but she comes with more baggage than anyone we've ever known – and that's saying a lot."

"And what did big brother have to say about it all? I'm surprised you called him."

"I didn't. Tanner did. Then after he'd done some investigating, Cash called me."

"Uh-oh. So, we're going through official channels of family hierarchy?" None of it mattered to Wade. He didn't need to feel like he was the head of anything, but Ford was different, He saw himself as the head of the family – and he was, at least, of the family still on the ranch. But their eldest brother, Cash was the one who called the shots when it came down to it.

Ford shrugged. "I guess. That's not important. What's important is that Cash knows this Dax guy – the one with the kids. And he knew Sierra's brother. They were on the teams a long time after he was, but I guess that doesn't make much difference. There's a community amongst those guys."

Wade nodded impatiently. Most of his brothers had been in the military. He knew there was a brotherhood amongst them, but he'd never felt the desire to be a part of it. "And?"

"And Cash talked to Dax and they both think that Sierra should stay here."

"She is."

"Not just for a couple weeks. Not just while she would have been on her honeymoon."

Wade's heart hammered in his chest, but why, he didn't know. "How long then?"

"Until Jared's been caught and brought in."

"But she's supposed to go home to start her life with the kids."

Ford held his gaze. "And they're saying that she might be better off doing that here."

Wade didn't know what to say. It was one thing to wish that he could be something more than her rebound guy. It was another thing completely to think that she might stick around long-term – with a couple of kids.

"What's your take?"

Ford shrugged. "I haven't had time to process that yet. I just wanted to let you know. I know you like her. I know I've joked that you maybe shouldn't be playing house with her in your cabin. I don't want to know how far into that you've gotten. But I thought that before you get in over your head, you should know that she might be here a while."

"What about *her*, though? Just because Cash and this Dax guy both think she should stay here it doesn't mean that she'll agree. That she'd want to. She's a woman with her own mind, not just some package to be shunted wherever someone else decides is best."

Ford gave him a rueful smile. "Trust you to see it that way." He held up his hand before Wade could protest. "I'm agreeing with you, bro. I told Cash it was pretty high-handed of him and Dax to be deciding her life for her. But apparently, that's how she rolls. She's spent her life waiting to be told what to do and falls apart when she's left to her own devices. I hate to say it, but I can see her being that way. And it'd explain why Jared was able to manipulate her so easily."

"We don't know how easy it was." Wade felt as though he needed to defend her. He saw her as sweet and gentle, but he didn't think she was weak.

Ford shrugged. "I don't know. All I wanted to do is give you a heads up. I know that you like her. But this situation puts a whole new spin on things."

"Yeah. Does she even know that other people are deciding for her where she should live?"

"Apparently, Dax was going to call her this afternoon."

Wade ran his hand through his hair. He'd been looking forward to the evening – and night – ahead. Now, he had to second-guess all his plans with Sierra.

"You okay?"

"Yeah."

"Sorry, bro."

"I don't know what to think."

"I don't know what to tell you. Seems to me that her sticking around could be a good thing. I like her. I could see her being your ideal woman – except for one small detail. Well, make that two small details."

Wade nodded. "Yeah. Even if it weren't for the kids, though, it's probably a bad idea."

Ford grasped his shoulder. "I don't know what to tell you."

Wade shrugged. "I'm going to head home."

"Home to the cabin or are you going to bring her back up to the house?"

"I don't even know that. I guess what I need to do is talk to her. Perhaps if she's going to be here for longer than a couple weeks, she won't want to complicate things by crossing the line with me."

Ford gave him a sympathetic look. "I didn't like to ask if you'd already crossed it."

"Nope. And now I'm starting to think that maybe we shouldn't."

~ ~ ~

Sierra stroked the little dog's head one more time. She was adorable. She looked more like a teddy bear than a dog. Sierra had asked if she could stay with her while Jane had been busy with a rancher who'd brought one of his cattle dogs in.

That had been a while ago and she was starting to think that perhaps she should leave. Jane popped her head around the door and smiled.

"I had a feeling that you might take a shine to her. How's she doing?"

"She seems worn out."

"I'm sure she is. I don't know how long she's been on the streets, but I'd guess it's been at least a few weeks. I just hope the pups are going to be okay. She's malnourished."

Sierra blew out a big sigh. "How can people be so cruel?"

"Ugh. I'm the wrong person to ask. I have very little faith left in human nature after some of the things I've seen. But fortunately for this little lady, someone found her and brought her into the shelter. We'll do what we can for her and for the pups when they're born."

"What will happen to them then?"

Jane shrugged. "The shelter will no doubt be able to find homes. Everyone loves puppies."

"And this little lady?" Sierra couldn't help stroking her again.

Jane laughed. "Are you asking for yourself?"

"Oh! No! I don't think. Jared doesn't … Well, shoot!" She looked up at Jane. "I was about to automatically say no because he doesn't like animals. But that's not a factor anymore, is it?"

Jane pursed her lips. "I have to say it Sierra, in my mind, it should never have been a factor in the first place. I'm so glad that you're rid of that man. I only just met you and I know that you're better off without him."

Sierra blew out a sigh. "I know. I am. I was so stupid."

"I'm not saying that. I'm saying that I'm happy you're free now. And I hope that going forward you'll make your own decisions in life and never let anyone walk all over you again."

"I hope so, too."

"Jeez, Sierra! You don't have to hope. You get to decide. You're the one in charge of your life."

"I know. I need to get better at it, too. I feel as though I've always been along for the ride on someone else's life. But now it's time for me to figure it out for myself."

"It is. And you know everyone around here will support you in that. So," Jane laughed, "you can decide for yourself right now if you want me to give you a ride back to the cabin, because I have to leave. Or if you want to hang out with this girl for a while longer. You'll have to walk back if you do."

"Oh. I should go. If you don't mind giving me a ride."

"I wouldn't have offered if I did."

When she brought the truck to a stop in front of the cabin, Jane smiled. "You're welcome to come over and see her again tomorrow if you'd like."

"I'd love to. Are you going to give her a name?"

"We should. See if you can think of one."

Sierra narrowed her eyes. "Are you thinking that if I name her, I'll be more likely to want to keep her?"

"Nope. I wouldn't try to manipulate you like that. I just thought you might like to have the honor."

"I would, thank you." She smiled. "And I am thinking about keeping her. If you think that would be okay. Would you teach me? I've never had a dog before."

"If you decide you want her, of course I will. But you'll do fine. Just the fact that you realize you need to learn is a good start. I have to get going, but I'll see you tomorrow. In fact, do you want me to pick you up on my way out in the morning?"

"Where are you going?"

"I'm meeting my cousin, Frankie, at the bakery. Not for long, just for coffee before we start the day. I haven't caught up with her in a while."

"I'd love to."

"Okay. I'll pick you up at seven-thirty."

"Thanks, Janey. I'll see you then."

Sierra let herself into the cabin and looked around. She loved the place. It was so homey. The entire place was only the size of her living room back in San Francisco. But it wasn't the size that mattered. She chuckled at that. At least, not when it came to houses.

She fished her phone out of her purse when it rang. She really needed to do something about buying herself a purse. The little white satin clutch didn't fit here. And it was a constant reminder of Jared and everything that had happened.

Her heart raced when she saw Dax's name on the display. He was away somewhere. She never knew where he was or when he'd come back. It'd always been that way with Seb and him. Usually, she was thrilled when he resurfaced. Today she was less enthusiastic. She was going to have to tell him about the wedding – and about Jared. Hopefully, he would be as relieved as Amelia that she hadn't married him, and everything else would pale next to that.

"Hi, Dax."

"Sierra."

He sounded weird. "What's wrong?"

"You tell me."

"Oh. Did you hear?"

"I did. I'm sorry."

"Don't be. I'm not. I'm relieved. And I'm starting to wake up to how I've been living my life. I always thought you and Seb pushed me because you didn't understand that I'm not as brave as you guys. But now I can see that it wasn't as much about me living scared as living stupid."

"No. You're not stupid. Don't say that. But I'm glad you're starting to look at things differently. What are you thinking you're going to do next?"

"I still want to take the children."

"I wasn't asking about them. I'm asking about you for your own sake. What do you want to do?"

"Well, I don't know how much you know. I never do. You guys are like secret squirrels. You have ways and means of knowing things that I can't even begin to guess at."

"I talked to Barney. He filled me in on what had happened with Jared – with the wedding and with Lori. Shit, Sierra. I'm so sorry. You deserve a guy who's going to treat you right."

"I know that now. If we want to look on the bright side, that's one lesson I learned from it."

Dax chuckled. "Always look on the bright side, right?"

"You know I try to."

"Yes, but in the future, I hope you won't let whatever brightness you can find in a situation blind you to the ugly truth."

She blew out a sigh. "Don't worry. I intend to be more realistic in the future."

"Good. So, what's your realistic plan from here? I have an idea for you, but I want you to tell me what you're thinking first."

"Well. Do you know where I am?"

"I do. And … what the hell. I'm going to tell you. The eldest MacFarland brother is a former SEAL."

"Oh, my gosh! You know him?"

"Until today I only knew him by reputation – and it's an impressive one. He called me."

"Wow!"

"He suggested that you might stay there for a while, and I agree that might be for the best – if you want to."

"I do. In fact, I've already decided that I'm going to stay here for the next couple of weeks – while I would have been away with Jared. Barney thinks it's a good idea, too. Until they find Jared. Do you think they will? I kind of hope that he's skipped the country and that will be the end of him."

"If I find him, he'll wish he had skipped the country. But I was talking about more than the next couple weeks, Sierra."

"What do you mean?"

"I mean. I'll be back then, and I'll have the kids with me. How would you feel about staying up there with them?"

"Why? Wouldn't it be better to get them settled into their new life with me in San Francisco? I have everything ready. I got them clothes and toys and …"

"And you could have all that stuff sent to you right where you are."

"You think it'd be dangerous for me to go back? Is that what you're saying? But why? Since we're obviously not going to get married, there's no way he could get my money by killing me." Her blood ran cold. "Is there? Why don't you want me to go back, Dax?"

"Don't be scared. I don't know anything for sure yet. I just think we're better off safe than sorry."

She swallowed. "Or safe than dead?"

"Not going to happen, Sierra."

"Then why are you so worried that you want me to stay here?"

"Because I can't be around to keep an eye on you. After I drop the kids off, I'm going to be gone again for a little while. When I told Cash that, he suggested that you stay right where you are – on their ranch."

Sierra's heart hammered in her chest. "But I can't just land myself on them."

"You're not. They're happy to have you."

Her mind was reeling. Part of her would love to stay here, to have the chance to be around Wade – and everyone else – for longer. But where would that leave things between the two of them? She had the feeling that Wade was only willing to let her stay with him, only wanted to sleep with her, because he knew that she'd be gone soon. And to be fair, she'd only been as honest as she had with him because she'd been looking at it as a now or never kind of deal.

"You still there?"

"Yes."

"What are you thinking?"

"I don't know, Dax."

"Okay. I don't want to make your decisions for you. How about you have a think and I'll call you again tomorrow – same time."

"Okay. Does that mean that you're still someplace where I can't call you?"

"Yes."

"But Cash was able to get hold of you?"

He chuckled. "Yeah. He's not on the teams anymore, but he's a well-connected guy."

"All right. I'll think about it. But how long are you even thinking that I should stay here?"

"I wish I could say. I'd like to find Jared and get him taken care of before you go home. However long that takes."

She sighed. "Which could be a week or a year, right?"

"I doubt it'd take a year."

"No. But if we're here long enough for the children to start school, then it'd be a year because I wouldn't want to uproot them twice. And …"

"Sierra, I have to go. I'll call you tomorrow at the same time and we'll talk about the children. I want you to be sure about them, too. We can always …"

"No, Dax. You're not going to pack them off somewhere else. Not unless you think that being with me would put them in danger somehow."

"I don't … if you stay there. But I really have to go."

"Bye, Dax."

He didn't reply. He'd already cut the connection.

Sierra sighed. Stay here? What about her life? She made a face. Despite what people thought about the Hartford heiress, she didn't really have much of a life. The social side of it had all been commandeered by Jared since she met him. Her work was fairly solitary. She spent most of her days in her studio painting. Her only friends ... she frowned, her only friend. Apparently, Lori hadn't been a friend after all. Amelia was the only one who would miss her. And Sierra would more than miss her. She couldn't imagine not seeing Amelia every day.

She pulled her phone out to text her. It'd only been a few days and they'd spoken several times, but she missed her.

Sierra: Would you miss me if I didn't come back for a while?

The three little dots that indicated her friend was replying appeared almost immediately.

Amelia: Of course! Why? Do they think you need to stay away?

I'll come to you if you need me. And how long's a while anyway?

Sierra smiled. That was a typical Amelia-type response.

Sierra: I don't know how long yet. Dax thinks I might be safer here.

If it were for a while, would you really want to come? I miss you already.

Amelia: Tell me when you want me, and I'll be there! I can work from anywhere, you know that. Want to talk instead of text?

Sierra: I'll call you tomorrow, okay?

Amelia: Whenever you like.

Sierra: Thanks. Love you bunches!

Amelia: Right back at ya!

Sierra knew how lucky she was to have such a good friend. She was hardly a great friend herself, though, was she? She told

Amelia that she'd talk to her tomorrow instead of now because Wade was due back any minute. She wasn't sure that she wanted to know what he'd think about the possibility of her sticking around longer term.

Was it terrible that she wished that Dax had waited until tomorrow before he called? She had no doubts that she and Wade would have slept together. Now, it was a different proposition. It cast things in a different light for her, and it was only fair that she should tell him. She imagined that he'd reconsider, too.

She looked up when the cabin door opened. Her tummy flipped over at the sight of him. He took off his hat and ran his hand through his hair and then smiled. She really did have to give him the chance to back out. But that smile made her want to know what it'd be like to be with him for something more than just a rebound fling.

She smiled back and went to meet him, leaning against him when he closed his arms around her. She must be crazy, but she could happily imagine this being her life. Welcoming him home at the end of the day. She closed her eyes and pressed her cheek against his chest. And that kind of thinking would no doubt freak the poor man out if he could hear it!

Chapter Twelve

Wade rested his cheek on top of Sierra's head and held her against him. She felt so right. He closed his eyes and breathed in the pretty, flowery smell of her. Damn. He wished that he'd left the lodge before Ford showed up. He'd spent the afternoon looking forward to this evening – and tonight. She'd asked him if he was going to sleep with her. They'd agreed that tonight … But that was before.

Her arms tightened around his waist, and he realized that they'd been standing there for a long few moments, not talking, just holding each other. He hadn't even said hello yet. A shiver ran through him when she nuzzled her cheek against his chest. He loved the way she did that. He wanted to know how it would feel when his chest was bare, when there we no clothes between them. His jeans started to get tighter in front. She was so close he knew she had to feel it. He should back away.

But she let out a little sigh and pressed closer, making his arms tighten around her. It'd be so damned easy to kiss her, to walk her back into the bedroom and give her what he knew she wanted. Easy? Yeah, no question about it. But right? That was a different matter. He gave her a squeeze and then stepped back.

"Hey."

"Hi."

Her lips quivered when she smiled. He couldn't help it; he lowered his head and brushed them with his own. Not a wise move. Her arms came up around his neck and pulled him down to her. What was supposed to be a brief touch of lips turned into a slow, deep exploration. He loved the way she kissed him. Her kisses were as shy as she was, at first. But as they progressed, she showed him trust, letting him in, opening up to him, and then she grew confident, kissing him back, seeking more. She was warm and soft in his arms. He got the feeling that if he let go, she might fall. She was depending on him to keep her upright. And while he used to get squirrelly at the thought of a woman depending on him for anything, it was different with Sierra. He loved the idea of her trusting him enough to lean on – in any and every sense.

By the time he lifted his head, he was hard, and she was making needy little noises that were almost enough to make him forget everything other than getting her into bed. Almost. But not quite.

She blew out a big sigh and her eyes flickered with emotion when they met his. She searched his face, and his heart clenched when the final emotion that settled on her face looked a lot like sadness.

"What's wrong?"

She shook her head with a small smile. "Nothing. It's okay. I just … I wanted you to get so carried away that we just … you know?"

He chuckled. "Oh, believe me, I know, darlin'. And I almost did, but we need to talk."

"You're right, we do." She frowned. "Although, what do you need to talk about?"

He held her gaze, wondering where to even start. How was he supposed to tell her that other people wanted to organize her life for her – and that as much as he disliked it, he knew they only wanted to do what was best for her? "Ford talked to our eldest brother Cash today."

"Oh. Of course."

He cocked an eyebrow.

She shrugged. "I talked to Dax today." She sighed. "He thinks I should stay here."

It made sense that this Dax guy would have spoken to her directly – that she'd already know about the suggestion – or was it really a plan? – that she should stay here for longer than she'd initially intended. What he wanted to know now was how she felt about it. "And what do you think?"

She shrugged. "Do you want a beer?"

He nodded and couldn't help smiling when she took his hand and led him to the kitchen, where she got two bottles from the fridge. She scrabbled in the cutlery drawer for something. Wade popped the tops off the bottles while he waited.

"Oh." She turned around at the sound and smiled. "I was looking for the opener."

That made him laugh. He couldn't think of anyone he knew who used an opener to pop a beer – not even the women. His smile faded when he realized that it was just another reminder of how different Sierra was from anyone he knew. He handed her a bottle and headed for the couch.

She followed and sat beside him, turning and bringing one knee up so that she faced him. He lifted his bottle to her, and she clinked hers against it.

"What are we drinking to?" she asked.

Wade didn't even know. "Just celebrating that you're here I guess."

"Are you glad? That I'm here, I mean."

He reached out and rested his free hand on her leg. "You can't tell?" He smiled through pursed lips. "That kiss didn't say it?"

She smiled. "It did. But that was just being in the moment. When you came in, I wanted to kiss you." She dropped her gaze. "And more. And I know we kind of agreed that tonight there would be more, but ... things are different now, aren't they?" She peeked up at him from under her lashes.

His heart sank. She was right. He'd been thinking the same thing himself. If she was going to stick around for a while, then it was better if they didn't go there. He nodded sadly but didn't take his hand back. Instead, he brushed his thumb back and forth over her thigh. This wasn't about him. It was about her. It was about keeping her safe. He'd been envisioning them enjoying a couple weeks together – enjoying each other for a couple weeks was more like it. But everything looked different with her sticking around for a while. He had to shift his focus back onto what she needed.

"Yeah." He leaned forward and rested his forehead against hers. "I thought I could be the guy who helped set you back on your feet after everything that's happened. I thought maybe we could make a few memories that'd take the sting out of this time for you."

She rested her hand on top of his. "You've already done that."

"Good to know." He gave her a rueful smile. "Then I guess I shouldn't feel so bad about not doing it the way I intended to."

His gaze dropped to watch her breasts rise and fall as she sighed. "I haven't decided for sure that I'm going to stay yet."

That brought his gaze back up to meet hers. She chuckled. "I know it makes sense for me to not go home until things are resolved with Jared. Until he's been found and … well, I don't even know what's going to happen with him. But the children are coming to a whole new life with me. I don't want them to start a new life here and then have to move them to San Francisco after a few months or however long it takes."

"That makes sense."

Her gray eyes bored into his. "Do you want me to stay?"

He closed his eyes. That was a loaded question if ever there was one. "I don't want to tell you what to do, Sierra. It seems to me like you have enough people in your life who do that."

"I do. I always have. I'm not weak – at least, I don't think so. I've just always been … I don't know … like I'm the passenger along for the ride on someone else's life."

"When we first arrived here, when there were no rooms at the lodge and you thought that you were going to have to find somewhere else to stay, you told me you needed to get back in the driver's seat. It seems to me that now might be the time to do that in your life."

"I know. It is."

"So, what do you want? Do you want to stay here, or do you want to go home?" His heart thundered in his chest. At the beginning of this conversation, he'd thought that he wanted her to go home, so that they could spend the next couple of weeks enjoying each other's company – and bodies. But while he waited for her to respond, it hit him that he really didn't want her to leave.

She gave him a sad smile. "I don't have a straightforward answer to that. I think I'd like to stay here. I think it could do the children good to come here rather than to San Francisco." She surprised him by pressing her lips against his. "But I know that if I'm going to be here for longer that I won't get the chance … we won't … you know. You were expecting me to be a quick fling who you could say goodbye to in a couple of weeks."

His hand tightened around her thigh. The way she said it made it sound like he was just looking to get laid. "It's not like that. I … you're right. I thought maybe we could enjoy each other's company for a little while and then that would be it. But only because you don't need anything more than that. You're not in a place where … you're supposed to be on your honeymoon right now." He gave her a rueful smile. "And I'm not …" He was going to say that he wasn't looking for anything serious or long-term either, but the way his heart was still pounding made him wonder if that was true. "I'm not exactly the kind of guy you'd want for the long haul anyway." That much he knew was true.

She brought her hands up to cup his face and planted a sweet kiss on his lips. "I know we come from different worlds, but you're exactly the kind of guy I'd want. I just didn't know that you existed before."

He gave her a wry smile. She was too sweet, trying to make him feel better. He knew the score. She was out of his league and they both knew it. "So, where does it all leave us?"

She shrugged. "Dax said that I should think about it, and he'll call back tomorrow – he didn't want me to feel like everything was already decided for me. I think I probably should stay here."

"But? It sounds like there's a but coming."

"There is. I think I should probably stay here, but if that means that we don't get to … that you don't want to. Then I'm seriously considering going home anyway. Just so that we can spend the next couple of weeks … like we thought we would."

Damn! He hadn't meant for her to have to go all the way out on a limb like that, but he was glad that she had. "Don't go." The words came out before he could stop them.

"Are you saying that you don't want to –?"

"No. I do want to, more than you know. But I don't want you to go home just to make it okay for us to go there." His mind was racing. Sure, the circumstances had changed, but the way he felt about her hadn't. The more time he spent with her, the more he liked her.

"How about …" A little wrinkle furrowed her brow, and she rolled her lips together before she continued. "How about we carry on as we were? We thought we only had two weeks and we were both prepared to make the most of them. When it comes down to it, we still only have two weeks. After that, I'll have to find a place to stay, and I'll have the children. So, even if you wanted to, I wouldn't be able to … spend time with you in the same way."

She had a point. It made sense. Wade smiled. "You might be onto something there."

She smiled back at him.

"What do you mean about needing to find a place to stay, though? I thought that the whole point of you staying is to be here – on the ranch."

She frowned again. "I couldn't ask you to let me stay here in your cabin for who knows how long."

He opened his mouth to protest, but she cut him off.

"Especially not with two children."

Ah. That was true.

She shrugged. "And your whole family has been so kind, but there's no way I would stay at the big house. It wouldn't be right, for your brothers or for the children."

Wade nodded.

"Ideally, I'd like to find a rental. But I'm sure the vacation rentals will be all booked up – we're heading into the summer after all. And I don't know if there are such things as annual leases out here."

"Annual?" The thought of her staying for a whole year had his heart rate picking up again. He just wasn't sure why.

She nodded. "I imagine that's what I'd have to look for. I doubt there's anywhere that would let me rent month to month. It doesn't make sense for the vacation homes to do that."

Wade couldn't help the smile that spread across his face. "I know a place you could have."

"You do?"

"I do. I have a cabin that was supposed to be rented out for the whole summer, but they canceled at the last minute. It's available for the next three months. And if you need it for longer, it doesn't have any bookings for the fall yet anyway."

She looked at him with wide eyes. "Wow! That could work. What's it like? I mean, is it big enough for the children?"

He chuckled. "It's plenty big enough. It has five bedrooms and four bathrooms, and the living areas are huge – I built it to accommodate groups."

"That sounds perfect. How much …"

He held his hand up. "You can have it."

"Wade, no!"

"Yes." He didn't want to take her money. He just wanted her to stick around.

To his surprise, she set her jaw stubbornly and shook her head. "No thank you."

"Huh?" His heart sank. "You don't want to?"

"Of course I do! But if I can't pay you the going rate for it, then I won't take it. I don't want to sound horrible, I do appreciate the thought, it's so kind of you. But it's not as though I can't afford it."

He stared at her for a long moment. She had a point. She could afford it. And it wasn't just about him and his desire to help her. The money from renting out the big cabin was going to go toward helping build Tyler's dream.

She raised her eyebrows. "Please may I rent it from you – for the going rate?"

He loved that she still had that stubborn set to her jaw, even if her eyes were filled with doubt. He nodded. He was happy to help her assert herself and come out on top, too. It was an easy victory, but still, it was a start. "Okay."

She grinned and threw her arms around his neck. "Thank you! I thought you were going to argue with me and tell me all the reasons that I couldn't and everything."

He hugged her tight to his chest. "Nope. I'd rather just let you have the place, but I won't ever undermine you. You're right. I was looking for a longer-term renter to replace the one I lost. This is a win-win for both of us."

She lifted her lips and pressed them to his. "Thank you, Wade. You're awesome." Her smile faded. "But did we figure out the rest? Can we still …?"

He could feel her heart pounding in her ribcage. "Are you propositioning me?" he asked with a smile.

Her cheeks flushed, but she nodded. "I believe I am. Please can we still spend the next couple of weeks the way we thought we were going to? I promise I won't get in your way afterward. I won't be clingy or cramp your style, and you know it's true, because I'll have the children."

"I was never worried about that, Sierra." It was true. He hadn't given it any thought because he hadn't considered that she might be here for more than two weeks. Now that it seemed she would be, he was more concerned that he'd be the one feeling clingy after she'd had her fun with him. He wasn't looking forward to stepping back when she settled into the cabin with the children she was about to adopt. He knew he'd have to, though. And that was all the more reason to make the most of the time they had before that happened.

Chapter Thirteen

Wade's hand tightened around her thigh as he spoke. "Okay."

Sierra's heart leaped into her mouth. "Okay?" She met his gaze. "Do you mean that you want to – that we're going to …?" Why couldn't she just bring herself to say it?

Wade leaned closer until his lips brushed over hers. "Yeah."

Wow! Her heart thundered in her chest. "Well, okay then." She'd gotten what she wanted. She was silly to feel nervous. She needed to just get over that and get on with it. She pushed up from the sofa and got to her feet, holding her hand out. Wade took it with a puzzled frown and let her pull him up to join her.

"Where are we going?"

She could feel the heat in her cheeks. "To bed." She took a step, tugging on his hand to get him moving before she chickened out, but he didn't move. Instead, he tugged back, reeling her back into him until he had his arms closed around her.

His eyes danced with amusement as he looked down into hers.

"But … aren't we … don't you …?" Now she felt even sillier. Had she misunderstood him somehow? Had she only imagined that he'd said yes?

"We are and I do. But we'll get there when we get there. It feels a little too pre-meditated right now. Don't you think?"

She dropped her gaze, feeling embarrassed. "Sorry. Yes. It does. I'm no good at this. I don't know how …"

He tucked his finger under her chin and made her look back up at him. "Relax. It's all good. I'm glad we talked about it. I'm glad we both know where we're up to. And we'll get there." He held her closer, and she could feel his hard length pressed against her. "I doubt it'll take long before we do. But I'd rather it happens naturally." He cocked an eyebrow. "Wouldn't you?"

The way he smiled had her smiling back at him. He was right, of course. "Yes. I would." She pressed closer against him. "As long as you don't intend to make me wait too long."

He chuckled. "Like I said, darlin'. I don't think it'll be long at all." As he brushed his lips over hers, and his fingers closed around the back of her neck, Sierra hoped that not long would be counted in minutes rather than hours.

She jumped, and Wade tensed when his cell phone rang. To her amazement, he didn't pull away. He kept on kissing her, ignoring it, or at least trying to. It was no good, though. She pulled away and gave him a rueful smile.

"You should probably get that."

He ran his fingers through his hair. "Sorry. I can ignore it." He smiled when the ringing stopped, but then it started straight back up again.

"Perhaps you shouldn't. It might be something important."

He pulled his phone out of his back pocket and his smile disappeared when he looked at the display. When he didn't answer, Sierra started to feel uncomfortable. What if it were someone he didn't want to talk to in front of her?

"I can go outside. You know … if it's personal."

He frowned at her and then at the phone again. "Don't do that. It's fine. It won't take a minute." His frown deepened as he answered. "What's up, Josie?"

Sierra rolled her lips together. Josie? Was she a girlfriend?

"I'm busy … I'm at the ranch … No … No! … Listen, Josie, I've already told you … I'm not … Yes, I mean it … No, I really don't want to."

He sounded different. He looked different as he spoke. Sierra thought of him as always having a smile on his face. She'd told Jane that he was like sunshine, and he was. But whoever this Josie person was, she had made the clouds roll in. He didn't look happy at all. Sierra went to the kitchen, wanting to find something to occupy herself with. He didn't need her standing there watching and listening.

To her surprise, Wade followed her. He stuck so close that she could hear a woman's voice coming out of his phone. Not clearly enough to make out the words, but enough to hear that she sounded annoyed.

Wade scowled and ran his hand through his hair. "If you need help, you should ask Harland."

That surprised Sierra; she had him down as the kind of man who would help anyone out if they needed it.

He looked angry when he spoke again. "As a matter of fact, I do … No, I'm not. Her name's Sierra … A little while … Jesus, Josie, no! It's more than that. It's serious … That's none of your business. I'm going to hang up now. You need to call Harland."

His jaw was set as he ended the call and put the phone back in his pocket. He went back and retrieved their drinks from the coffee table. He handed Sierra's to her and then took a long pull of his own. Once he'd set the bottle down on the counter, he wiped his hand across his face and sucked in a deep breath, slowly blowing it out before he met her gaze.

"Sorry about that."

"That's okay." Sierra didn't know what else to say.

Wade took another drink, then set his now empty bottle down on the counter and leaned back against it. He folded his arms across his chest and blew out a sigh. "I should explain."

"There's no need. Not if you don't want to."

"I do want to. Honestly, I didn't think it would matter." He shook his head and blew out another sigh. "It shouldn't matter. It doesn't matter to me – *she* doesn't. But if you're going to be staying here for a while, then there's a good chance that you'll run into her at some point. So, you need to know."

Sierra's heart was pounding, but not in a good way. She was starting to wonder who this Josie was.

"I was married to her."

"Oh." Sierra's breath caught in her chest. She shouldn't be so surprised. Wade was, well, she didn't even know how old he was, but he had to be her age, she'd guess a few years older. It wasn't unusual for someone in their thirties to be divorced. Most of the people she knew were either married or used to be. It was just a shock to think of Wade having been married – married to a woman who still called him and wanted him to help her out. Perhaps he would have gone to help if it weren't for her.

She could feel the frown on her face as she met his gaze. "Don't let me keep you if you want to go and see her."

He pushed away from the counter and came to her. His arms closed around her again and he looked down into her eyes. "I don't want to go and see her. I haven't wanted to see her for years. We were divorced eight years ago. She has a husband who she should be calling. She's not important to me, Sierra. She hasn't been for years." His jaw was set as he looked down at her. "Okay?"

She nodded. What else could she do?

Wade dropped a kiss on her lips and then stepped back. "Do you want to watch while I rustle us up some dinner?"

"Okay."

He smiled and put his hands on her hips, lifting her easily and then spinning her around before setting her down on the counter. She was glad to see his smile return.

"I can help," she suggested.

"You are helping just by sitting up there, looking pretty. I don't usually like to spend much time in the kitchen, but with you there I could stay here all night."

He stepped between her legs and leaned in for a kiss, making her hope that he might have something other than cooking in mind, but a few moments later, he broke away and turned to the stove.

~ ~ ~

After dinner, sitting on the sofa with the TV on even though he wasn't paying any attention to it, Wade ran his hand up and down Sierra's arm again. He should probably stop, but it was addicting. She was addicting. She responded to every touch. Little quivers and shudders when he ran his hand up her arm, her breath catching every time he slid his fingers under her hair. She practically melted into him whenever he kissed her. It was driving him crazy for her. He could only imagine how responsive she'd be to more intimate touch.

After Josie's call, he'd decided that tonight wouldn't be the night – that it'd be better to wait before taking Sierra into his bed. It felt as though Josie had intruded into their space and he didn't want her to able to do that, didn't want the specter of his ex-wife shadowing his new beginning with Sierra.

He pursed his lips. It wasn't a new beginning. Well, it was, but only the beginning of something short and sweet. He was being dumb, and Sierra's soft warm body resting against him on the sofa reminded him just how dumb. Josie could only cast as much of a shadow as he allowed her to. And besides, his nights with Sierra were numbered. Why would he waste a single one of them? As Sierra snuggled closer, he knew the answer to that – he wouldn't. She was making it as plain as she dared in her own shy and reserved way that she wanted him. He wasn't going to make her work or wait for him any longer.

He tightened his arm around her shoulders and drew her closer. Her gaze locked with his and her tongue darted out to moisten her lips. Damn. He swallowed as he watched, then brushed his lips over hers. Her hands came up and clung to his shoulders as he deepened the kiss. He could feel her heart pounding, its rhythm matching his own. Sliding his fingers into her hair with one hand, he ran the other down her side until it rested on her hip. He'd been married to Josie for much of his adult life, and he'd had his share of women since, but this felt different. He could feel his fingers tremble as they slid under the hem of her top. They both tensed when he touched her bare skin for the first time.

He lifted his head and looked down into her eyes. "Are you okay with this?"

She nodded rapidly.

"Are you sure?" She'd told him that she wanted him but talking about it in the abstract was different from being here in the moment, and he wasn't sure that he'd trust her to speak up and tell him if she wanted to change her mind.

Her eyes looked huge as she nodded again, more slowly this time. "I want this, Wade. I want you."

Her words made his heart clench in his chest and his cock grow harder in his pants. "And I want you, Sierra. But I need you to promise me something."

"What?"

"I need you to promise me that if you change your mind, if you want to stop or if anything we do makes you uncomfortable, you'll tell me."

"I will."

"I need you to promise me."

"Okay."

He smiled and brushed his lips over hers, loving the impatient look on her face. "Say it."

She frowned. "I promise."

"Thank you. Now, I'm going to ask you again. Are you sure you're okay with this?"

"Yes. The only thing I'm not okay with is you wanting to stop and talk about it."

He chuckled. "Don't worry, darlin'. We're almost done talking. But I need you to know that you're in control here. We're not going to do anything you don't want to."

"Aww." She reached up and touched his cheek. "I've never known anyone like you."

"That's what I'm worried about. I don't want you thinking that you have to go along with anything you don't want to. Not with me, not ever again."

She dropped her gaze and then looked back into his eyes. "How do you know?"

Her words hit him like a physical blow. They confirmed what he'd suspected – that in the past she had gone along with things she didn't want to. He forced a smile. She didn't need to see his anger at the bastard in her past. She needed him to set her on a path toward a better future.

He kissed her and slid his hand around her back. "I just know you."

She pressed closer against him, grasping his shirt in both her hands. "It's strange, but it feels like you do. It feels like you know me better than anyone ever has."

Her words sent a rush of warmth through his chest again, but he needed to ignore that. He couldn't help her with his heart; that wasn't what she was interested in. He should just be grateful that she was interested in what the rush of heat in his pants could do for her.

They didn't need to be fooling around on the sofa like this. He got to his feet and offered her his hand to pull her up with him. She followed him eagerly into the bedroom. He closed the door behind her and then pressed her back against it. "By morning, darlin', I will."

She raised her eyebrows. "Will what?"

He smiled and leaned all his weight against her, rocking his hips to make sure she'd understand. "Know you better than anyone ever has."

"Oh." Her arms came up around his neck, and he lowered his lips to hers, claiming her mouth in a kiss much deeper than he'd allowed himself before. His hands found their way down to her ass, squeezing it tight, making her moan into his mouth. The sound reverberated through his chest. He straightened up, lifting her off her feet. She dangled there, clinging to him.

"Wrap your legs around me."

He closed his eyes when she did just that, opening herself to him so that he could push into the heat between her legs. She felt so good, but it was nowhere near enough. He walked her over to the bed, intending to set her down, but she kept hold, taking him with her until he was lying on top of her. He didn't want to crush her, but couldn't bring himself to move away, not while she was thrusting her hips up to him, rubbing herself against him.

She pulled him down into another kiss, and his hips started to move in time with hers. Taking most of his weight on one forearm, he slipped his other hand down between them. She didn't stop her rocking, and he didn't want her to. His fingers found their way inside her panties, and he angled his hips to give himself room to touch her.

Her panties were hot and damp, making him want to tear them off and sink himself inside her. But as much as his cock might like to argue with him, it could wait. She held her breath when he circled her clit. Then she went still as he moved his hand in time with his hips. Shit.

He stopped, hoping he hadn't scared her, hadn't gone too fast. He needn't have worried.

Her hands scrabbled at his back and her hips rocked frantically underneath him. "Don't stop! Please, don't stop."

The last came out on a moan when he started back up. He had to bite down on his lip as he watched her face. She was lost, moving with him eagerly, her breath coming faster.

"Wade," she breathed.

The way she spoke his name made him smile. He lowered his head to kiss her again, then froze when she put a hand to his shoulder.

"Stop!"

Shit! He held still and brought his hand back. "Are you okay?"

She pressed her lips together and nodded, a frown wrinkling her brow. "I'm so sorry. But you're going to make me … you know."

"You don't want to?"

"Yes! Oh, my gosh, Wade. I want to so much. But I want to save it."

It was his turn to frown. "Save it?"

"You were about to make me … get there. And I want to do that *with* you."

He couldn't help his smile. "You've got no worries there. You'll get there with me."

Her cheeks flushed and she looked away. "You don't understand."

He obviously didn't. "What? What's wrong."

Her gaze met his and then flickered away again. "This is embarrassing."

"It doesn't have to be. You can tell me anything."

"I know. It's not you. It's just … I don't always get there. Not very often in fact. And I was almost there. I didn't want to do it by myself. You make me feel so good that I think I can … with you." Her cheeks were bright red by the time she finished. "I'm not very good at this, am I? I know I shouldn't talk so much. But … you asked."

He dropped a kiss on her forehead. "Talking's good. How are we going to get to know each other and what we like and want if we don't talk about it?"

Her eyes widened. "Don't you need to concentrate?"

He squeezed his eyes shut. He could only imagine what made her think that – who might have told her that. "No. I don't. For me, this isn't about concentrating. It's about enjoying, getting lost in it, in the moment, in each other. Whether that's with touches or kisses or words. I like you talking. I want to know what you think, how you feel, what you want."

"Okay."

"And Sierra?"

"Yes?"

"You don't need to save it. You can enjoy it. You can get there now, that's what I was aiming for."

"But …"

He couldn't help chuckling. "I'm telling you, darlin'. You don't need to save 'em up. You'll get there again."

"But what if I don't?"

"Don't worry about it. There's no pressure, no expectation. All you need to do is relax and enjoy it, okay?"

She still looked doubtful, so he slid his hand back inside her panties and circled her clit. Her legs opened wider, and she pressed against him. His cock was still hard enough to drive nails, despite having stopped for a chat, and pressed eagerly into her heat. There was still way too much fabric between them, but the night was still young, and he needed her first orgasm to be all about her.

"Hold my ass, Sierra. Move me how you want me."

She didn't need telling twice. She grasped him tight and rocked him faster and harder. She was closer than he'd realized. There wasn't enough space for his fingers to work, so he rested his thumb against her clit, circling as they moved faster.

Her eyes squeezed shut and she let out a little moan. He felt the moment she let go, her fingers dug into his ass, and her whole body quivered. He rocked his hips faster and pressed harder, his cock throbbing to be inside her. He claimed her mouth, kissing her deep and hard as she came apart under him. Her hands left his ass and came up to hold his head as she kissed him back hungrily.

When she finally stilled, he shifted his weight to the side, without breaking the kiss. With room to move, he slid two fingers inside and pressed the heel of his palm against her. She gasped as she clenched him tight, and another wave took her.

"Wade!"

"Yes?" he asked with a smile as he watched her come down.

She let out a big shuddering breath. "What did you do to me?" Her eyes were wide, and her smile was huge.

"I got you warmed up."

"That was just the warmup?"

"Yeah." He rolled to the side and caught her hand, bringing it to cover the erection that was straining his pants.

"Ooh!" She licked her lips. "After the way you just made me feel while we were both fully clothed, I can't wait to see what happens once we're naked."

"That's good because you don't have to wait. You're about to find out."

Chapter Fourteen

Sierra lay back against the pillows and watched Wade get up from the bed. Her brain was still a little fuzzy and her entire body felt boneless. Of course, she'd had orgasms before, but never one like that. Nothing like that! And they hadn't even ... Wade had been fully dressed. So, had she for that matter. Who knew that she was capable of coming apart like that just from being touched the right way, from the feel of a man moving against her, moving with her?

Hmm. She pursed her lips. Perhaps it wasn't simply from the feel of *a* man but from the feel of *this* man. He was quite a man. She licked her lips as she watched him pull his shirt over his head. He was all muscle. She'd been able to feel it through his shirt whenever he'd hugged her, whenever she'd rested her cheek against his chest. But seeing it — literally in the flesh — did strange things to her insides. He turned around and winked at her.

"You okay?"

She smiled. "I think I may be more than okay than I've ever been."

He chuckled. "I told you. That was just the warmup." He came and sat on the edge of the bed and pulled off first one boot and then the other.

Sierra watched them drop to the floor. How could that seem so sexy? Was it because they were cowboy boots? Was it because she was used to a man who undressed in the dressing room before coming to bed wearing pajamas – silk pajamas at that? She'd never liked Jared's pajamas. They didn't seem very masculine to her, and she used to hate the way the fabric slid against her when they had sex. He rarely ever took them off for that. He just pushed them down over his hips before rolling on top of her, grunting his way to an orgasm and then rolling off again. She shuddered at the memories. She used to think that he just wasn't a very passionate or sexual kind of man. What she'd seen in the bathroom of his hotel room at the St Regis had told a different story. The way he'd had Lori bent over and was looking down watching himself thrust in and out of her as he stood between her legs, his fingers digging tight into her hip and his other hand twisted in her hair pulling her head back; that had looked very passionate and very sexual.

"Hey." Wade's gentle voice snapped her back to the present. "Are you sure you're okay?"

Why on earth had she let her mind take her back to the horrors of that hotel room? Why would she visit such an awful memory of such a horrible man when she had such a wonderful man right here with her?

"I'm sorry. I'm …" What could she say? She could hardly tell him that she'd been thinking about Jared.

Wade smiled his gorgeous smile and brushed his fingers over her cheek. "Please don't say you're sorry, darlin'. I'm sorry. Was that too much? I can put my shirt back on and …"

He made to move off the bed, but she grabbed his hand to stop him. "No! It wasn't too much. It was amazing! You're amazing. And I don't want you to put your shirt back on. I want you to keep going and get undressed. I want to get undressed with you and ..." She reached for the hem of her shirt and started to pull it up.

"You don't have to." He was frowning, and that so wasn't what she wanted. "I told you. I don't want you to feel like you have to do anything you don't want to."

"But I *do* want to."

He cocked his head to one side and gave her a stern look. "The look on your face just now was more like disgust than desire."

She grabbed both his hands and shook her head rapidly. "I'm sorry. I hate that my face gave me away, but I wasn't thinking about you. Shoot. I know that sounds even worse. But I don't mean it like that. I was thinking about you. I was thinking how wonderful you are and how wonderful what we just did was, even though we didn't really even do it yet. You made me ... feel so good. And I couldn't help thinking about the way Jared used to make me feel and how he didn't seem to even like sex with me – but that reminded me of how much he seemed to be enjoying it with Lori." She blew out a sigh. "And remembering seeing what he was doing to her is what put that look on my face. You can't imagine seeing the man you thought you loved and who you thought loved you – and were supposed to marry in a couple of hours – seeing him ... *fucking* a woman you thought was your friend. A woman who was supposed to be standing by your side as your bridesmaid, a woman who you'd called family, since you had no real family of your own left."

She stopped and sucked in a shaky breath. "And I know you said it was okay for us to talk, but you don't need to hear about this."

He squeezed her hands. "I hate it for you, Sierra. I hate everything that you've been through. I hate that you saw what you did, but in a way, I'm glad, too. If you'd found out any other way, you might still have had doubts, still have wanted to believe his lies, and I'm sure he would have kept telling you lies."

"I know. You're right. I just wish those images hadn't chosen to flash through my mind right now."

"It's okay." He gave her another reassuring smile. "I reckon I've got you for two weeks. We don't need to rush anything."

She held his hands tighter. "Don't think you can back out and leave me wanting now."

He cocked an eyebrow. "I thought …"

"I know, you thought that I'd put myself off by thinking about Jared. Well, I haven't. Thinking about that and how awful it was only makes me want you more. You gave me a taste of how wonderful it can be with you, and I want the whole thing. I want you … I want you to …" She didn't want to say have sex with me. That sounded too clinical and impersonal. But she knew she shouldn't say the words that came into her mind instead. They felt very personal and although she might not mind their meaning, she doubted that Wade would …

Apparently, she'd hesitated for too long and he filled the silence for her, with the very words she hadn't dared to speak. "You want me to make love to you?"

She rolled her lips together as she nodded. "If you still want to."

He wrapped his arms around her and hugged her close against his chest. "I want to. I want to very much."

All she could do was breathe him in. His arms seemed even bigger as they pressed her closer to him. His hard chest was dusted with fair hair that tickled her cheek. His warm skin felt like an invitation to press hers against it.

She reached for the hem of her shirt again and this time, he didn't stop her. He helped pull it off and over her head.

She closed her eyes when his hands cupped her breasts, then they slid around her back and unhooked her bra. When it was gone, the feel of his roughened fingers against her skin made her whimper.

He closed his mouth over hers and kissed her deeply. All she could do was cling to his shoulders while he cupped her breasts in his hands, teasing her nipples between his fingers and thumbs until she thought he might take her over the edge again. She wanted him to do that so badly, but the next time he did, she wanted to take him with her. She reached for the buckle on his belt and managed to unfasten it, then she undid his button and zipper, eager to touch him.

His hands mirrored hers and before she'd managed to work her hand inside his jeans, he was pushing hers down over her hips. Without breaking the kiss, he moved forward, until she lay back on the pillows. She lifted her hips, and he tugged her jeans and panties down together. Then he sat back and tossed them across the room, and she lay naked before him.

Just the way he looked at her made her feel sexier than she ever had before. There was a hunger in his eyes as he let his gaze rove over her. She didn't think that she'd ever inspired that in a man before. Jared had certainly never looked at her that way. But there was no way she was going to spare *him* another thought right now.

Wade stood and pushed his jeans and boxers down and off before climbing back onto the bed beside her. She only got a couple of seconds to take in all his naked beauty, but from what she saw he was all man. And from the way one large part of him pointed eagerly at her, she'd guess that he was a very sexual, very passionate man.

She held her breath as she waited for him to roll on top of her. Then let it out when he didn't. Instead, he propped himself up on one elbow and smiled down at her. "You're so freaking beautiful."

Her breath caught in her chest, and she wasn't sure if it was because of the look in his eyes or the way he ran his hand down over her ribcage then brought it back up to cup her breast. He lowered his head and pressed a kiss to her nipple that sent a sharp shock of desire zinging straight to the place between her legs where she wanted to feel him next. He moved over to her other breast, but she cupped his face between her hands and brought him up to look at her.

"Please, Wade." She didn't need to say all the words. He knew what she wanted, and the look in his eyes when he nodded told her how badly he wanted it, too.

He reached over to the nightstand and grabbed a condom from the drawer. She wasn't going to allow herself to wonder about who he usually used them with. It didn't matter. She watched as he rolled it over himself. He was about to use this one with her, and that was all she needed or wanted to know.

He leaned over her, and just when she expected him to climb onto her, he rolled over instead. Flipping onto his back and holding her hips so that she went with him. She put her hands on either side of his shoulders and pushed up to look down at him. "What are you doing?"

She was already used to seeing his eyes shine with amusement, now seeing desire mixed in with it made her tummy and points lower tighten in anticipation.

"I'm doing whatever you want me to." He rested his hands lightly on her hips, and she felt herself get wetter when his hard length pressed against her.

Sierra just stared at him. She didn't know what to do. She wasn't used to this. Of course, she'd been on top before. Not very often, but she had. She knew what to do. But being in charge – having a man ready to do whatever she wanted? It sounded like a nice idea, but she had no clue what she was supposed to want. "I don't …" Was she really going to tell him that she didn't know?

His smile disappeared. "That's okay, we don't have to …"

Ugh. He was ready to back out again? That was about the only thing she knew that she didn't want to happen. "Yes, we do! I want to." The strength in her voice surprised her. She hadn't meant to be bossy.

The way Wade grinned told her that he didn't mind. "That's it, darlin'. You do know what you want. You're just not used to it mattering, so you stopped talking about it. We're going to change that. I think you already know that what you want matters an awful lot to me. And I'm going to need you to talk about it, to tell me. Okay?"

"Wow!"

"What?"

She chuckled. "When you found me, that first night. I told you that you were an angel sent to help me in my *hour* of need. Now it feels like you were sent to me for my *time* of need, to help me with so much more than getting out of a ditch at the side of the road."

He nodded happily. "I plan to help you in a whole lot of ways, darlin'. But I told you then and I'll remind you as often as you need me to; I'm no angel." He rocked his hips underneath her, and the heat of him pressing into her core didn't feel very angelic.

She rubbed herself against him, wishing that he'd roll them back over and take charge, plunge himself deep inside her and …

"It's up to you."

She met his gaze.

"Do what you want with me. Or tell me what you want me to do."

She rolled her lips together. She'd never had an invitation like that before. It would be rude – and crazy – to turn it down. She pushed back until she was sitting upright over him. His cock stood proud, pointing up at her. She curled her fingers around him and swallowed when she found that she couldn't close them. He was big. And hot. And so hard. She moved her hand up and down his length. She didn't think she was very good at that but …

"Is that what you want to do, or what you think I want?"

She looked up at him from under her lashes. It sounded like he already knew the answer.

"What do you want for yourself?"

She shrugged. His hand trailed down over her hip to slide between her legs. One fingertip entered her, making her moan.

"Is this what you want?"

She nodded. "It feels so good."

"And you can't think of anything that would feel better – anything that you might want more?"

Her gaze dropped to where she could feel him throbbing in her hand. "I think this would feel even better."

"Then take it. Or tell me what you want me to do."

She closed her eyes. She'd never been in this position. And after she left here, she probably never would be again. Wade was trying to give her a beautiful gift. She had to take it.

She lifted up on her knees and hovered over him. His hand fell to the bed as she stroked herself with the very tip of him.

"Touch me." The words came out as a breathy whisper, but they acted as a command. She didn't even need to be more specific. He knew what she wanted. As she lowered herself just enough that he breached her entrance, he stroked her clit, circling and teasing, taking her straight to the edge.

"Stop!"

He stopped, but his hand hovered only an inch away. "Why?"

Her eyelids drifted down as she continued to tease herself with his cock, which she could feel straining to be inside her. "I want to take you now and if you keep doing that, I'll get there again."

His lips twitched up into a smile. "And that would be a bad thing?"

"No."

"Let yourself go, darlin'. You sure you want me to stop?"

"No." Her eyes drifted shut when he touched her again. "God, no. Please don't stop." She slowly lowered herself onto him. He was big and so hard. She could feel him stretching her. His fingers teased her mercilessly, circling, touching, squeezing just the right way while he slowly but surely entered and filled her.

"Please?" Her voice didn't sound like her own. It was needy and desperate. She'd lowered herself as far as she could, but he wasn't … and she needed …

He knew exactly what she needed, and he gave it to her. His hand tightened on her hip and pulled her down onto him at the same time that his hips thrust up and he drove deep inside her. In a perfectly coordinated assault of sensations, his finger and thumb closed around her clit and squeezed. It all combined to leave her clenching around him. Two more deep thrusts drove her over the edge. She arched her back, pushing herself against his fingers. Her hands came up of their own accord and closed around her breasts, her fingers pinching her nipples and making her gasp and moan as intense waves of pleasure crashed over her.

Wade kept working her with his fingers until she had to pull away. She couldn't take any more.

She collapsed forward onto his chest, aware that he was still hard and ready to go while she was spent. He stroked her hair away from her face as she lay there gasping. "That was incredible, darlin'."

"But it wasn't … you didn't …"

"No, but I got to watch you. That was the sexiest thing I've ever seen."

She pressed her face into his shoulder. "How?"

He ran his hand down her back and closed it around her butt to rock her against him. He was still so very hard inside her that it sent aftershocks – or maybe they were the next wave of pre-shocks – tingling through her. "You let yourself go. You were on my cock, riding me, taking me deep inside you. You touched yourself and let me touch you, let me stroke where we're joined, and you ask me how that can be sexy?"

"Well." She dared to lift her head and look down at him. "Since you put it like that, it does sound kind of sexy."

"Incredibly sexy. Fucking hot."

For some reason, hearing him put it so crudely made her hot again. She propped her elbows on his chest and smiled down at him. "You want to know what I think would be hot now?"

His lips twitched up into a smile. "Tell me."

She ran her tongue over her bottom lip. "I think it'd be hot if you were on top."

Before she knew what was happening, Wade had flipped them, and he was kneeling over her. "Okay. I'm on top. What else?"

She smiled. "I meant if you were on top and … inside."

His eyes closed and he sucked in a ragged breath as he nodded and lowered himself onto her. He felt so right. His weight was on her, but he didn't crush her. He spread her legs wider with his knees and then ran his hand down the inside of her thigh before hooking her knee over his elbow. That opened her up wide and she could feel him pushing at her entrance.

"You sure?"

"How about you stop asking that, and I promise I'll tell you if I'm not?"

He grinned. "I probably shouldn't agree to that, but right now I'll take it because I need to take you."

His head pushed inside her, then pressed deeper, filling her, stretching her. He reached that point again where it felt like he couldn't go any farther, but then he thrust his hips, and she gasped as he filled her completely.

He took her at her word and didn't ask again if she was okay, but his eyes held hers in a silent command that she should tell him if she wasn't. She nodded breathlessly, and he set a steady rhythm thrusting deep and hard and then slowly pulling back before plunging deep again. With one leg hooked over his arm, Sierra was held wide open and trapped, vulnerable to whatever he wanted to do to her– and she'd never felt safer or more ... loved. He'd been the one who called it making love. Not her. And the way their bodies were moving together, becoming one, she could only think of it that way; he was loving her. And she was loving him right back.

His hand underneath her closed around her butt and squeezed; it made her inner muscles flutter and tighten around him, which in turn made him grow harder still and push deeper. She gasped when his fingers slid between her butt cheeks and one fingertip stroked her back there.

She clenched tighter still and was rewarded by Wade gasping her name. She gasped his when his fingertip stopped circling and pressed a little way in. It was a new one on her. She was glad he'd stopped seeking permission because she would have said no. But it felt so good. Both the thrill of the unknown and unexpected, and the physical sensation sent her hurtling over the edge into an orgasm even stronger than before.

"Oh God, Sierra!" Wade gasped and she felt him tense, thrusting deep and hard twice more before rearing up over her, his release throbbing inside her as she came apart around him.

He slowly lowered her leg back down and slumped over her, holding his weight to one side.

It took a few moments for them to catch their breaths and in that time, Sierra wanted nothing more than to melt into him. She'd known the man for less than a week, and yet she felt like she now knew him, and he knew her, more intimately than anyone else ever had. Of course, in bed, but through sharing that and because of the way they'd shared it, it felt like they knew each other in every important sense, too.

He nuzzled his lips against her neck, making her shiver and cling to him. She turned and pressed a kiss to his cheek. "Thank you."

He lifted his head and smiled down at her through pursed lips. "No. You don't get to say thank you." He leaned down until his forehead rested against hers and looked deep into her eyes. "That was amazing. You were amazing. We are amazing together. There are so many words running through my head right now. Things I want to say to you. But damn, Sierra. Not thank you." He ran his knuckles down her cheek and pressed a kiss to her lips. "I have to go take care of this, but don't move. I'll be right back."

She couldn't help smiling as she watched his bare butt disappear into the bathroom to dispose of the condom. He was right, thank you was such a small thing to say about what they'd just shared.

When he returned, Wade pulled the covers back and gestured for her to get in. Her heart sank. Now that they'd had sex, was he going to tuck her in and wish her goodnight? She'd been hoping that ...

And she needn't have worried. Once she was under the covers, he climbed in behind her and wrapped her up in his arms. "Is it okay if I stay?"

She smiled and snuggled closer. "I was hoping you might." Her smile grew wider as she felt him press against her butt. She wriggled against him. He wasn't as hard as before, but his interest hadn't waned completely.

"Yeah. Sorry about that. He'll go to sleep after a while."

She chuckled. "Aww. I was hoping he might want to stay up and play some more."

Wade's arm tightened around her waist. His other hand brushed her hair away, and her whole body lit up when he nibbled the back of her neck and muttered, "I'm sure he'd be happy to oblige."

Chapter Fifteen

Wade checked his watch. He needed to get up and take a shower and get to work. He tightened his arm around Sierra. He didn't want to go, didn't want to bring an end to what had without question been the best night of his life. Sierra snuggled back against him, making his cock ache for a repeat of last night. But he couldn't do it. He wouldn't mind being late getting to the lodge, but he hated the thought of making love to her again and then hurrying away from her. She deserved more than that. She needed more than that. He knew he should be second-guessing himself on sleeping with her at all. But he couldn't. It had been too good, she felt so right. Sure, losing himself inside her, the way she gave herself up to him, was the best sex he'd ever had, but it was more than that. She felt right in his arms, in his bed.

He made himself stop. He wasn't the kind of guy who was happy to have a woman in his arms and his bed when he knew that he couldn't have her in his life. Not for real. That wasn't who he was. Sure, he'd dated around some since his divorce, but he'd only dated women he'd been able to see a possible future with. Maybe he'd stretched that, none of them had worked out, so apparently, none of those possibilities had been that great, but still. He wasn't like Tanner. He didn't sleep with women just for the sake of it.

He blew out a sigh and regretfully rolled out of bed. He had to go, had to get up and leave her here. And in a couple of weeks, less than that now, Sierra would have to go. She'd still be around – still be in the big cabin, right here on the ranch. But she wouldn't be in his bed anymore, or in his life, not in the way he wanted. Shit! He wasn't supposed to want that. He'd known from the get-go that it just wasn't an option. He wasn't supposed to be getting involved this deep. He was supposed to be helping her recover and move on from the disaster that was supposed to have been her wedding and the asshole who wanted to kill her. He shook his head as he scooped his clothes up from the floor and headed for the shower. The best he could hope to do was to help her find her strength and build some confidence in herself. Wade knew that it wasn't realistic to think that he could be the man for her, but he could still help her learn to stand up for herself and make her see that she deserved the world and shouldn't settle for anything less.

Once he was showered and dressed and the coffee was brewed, he stuck his head back around the bedroom door. She was still sleeping. He went in, he couldn't have stayed away if he wanted to. He squatted down beside the bed and brushed her hair away from her cheek.

Her eyes didn't open but her hand came up and cupped his against her face. "Morning."

He smiled as she slowly opened her eyes. "Good morning, beautiful."

She gave him a sleepy smile that made him want to figure out a way he could see it every morning for the rest of his life. "Hello, handsome." Her eyes opened wider. "Oh. You're up. I'm sorry. You should have woken me I …" She started to sit up, but Wade couldn't help it. He climbed up beside her and closed his arms around her.

"It's okay. It's early. I should have let you sleep in. But I didn't want you to wake up and find me gone." Jesus, it was sappy, and he knew it, but it was the truth, so he had to say it. "I didn't want you to wake up alone after last night."

"Aww," her eyes shone with tears, "that's the sweetest thing anyone's ever said to me. Ever done for me."

He tightened his arms around her, hating to think that no one had ever cared about her that much before. "I did it for me, too. I didn't want to start the day without talking to you." He pressed a kiss to her lips. "Without kissing you."

She waggled her eyebrows. "Without anything else?" she asked as she pressed closer to him.

Damn. He'd love to stay and give her what she wanted but he couldn't. He closed his hand around her ass, pulling her leg up over his hip so that he could press his aching cock between her legs. Even through his jeans and the covers it was enough to make his resolve waver. "You know I want you."

She nodded. "I do. And I know I shouldn't pester you for more." She pressed another kiss to his lips. "But I'm glad I did because even this feels so good." He closed his eyes as she rubbed herself against him, but then opened them when she pulled back. "But I can be good. I can let you get on with your day. I should really get on with mine, too." She met his gaze and held it. "Will I see you tonight?"

"Of course." He hated that she even felt the need to ask. "I'll be home as soon as I can when I get done with work. If you need anything in the meantime, you call me and I'll be here, okay?"

"That's okay. I'll be fine. I'm going for coffee with Jane and her cousin – wait, your cousin, Frankie – this morning. And then I said I'd call Cassidy. You don't need to worry about me. I have lots to do."

He closed his fingers around the back of her neck and looked deep into her eyes. "I'm glad you have things to do, friends to see. I'm glad you're going to be busy. But please don't tell me not to worry about you." He swallowed, trying to stop the words from coming out, but he couldn't. "I always will."

Shit! He shouldn't have said it. He needed to put a lid on it. Just because he was getting in over his head with feelings for her, didn't mean that he needed to burden her with them. Her eyes widened, and he held his breath. He didn't know how she'd react. They were both clear that whatever they were doing here would have to be over by the time her children arrived. It wasn't fair of him to use words like always.

He relaxed when she gave him a small smile. "Thank you. I hope we'll always be friends."

"Yeah." That was sweet of her. She'd let him off lightly without making it an embarrassing moment for either of them. And since she'd given him an open door, he couldn't stop himself from reinforcing his point. "We will, and I'd like to think that you'll always know that you can call me whenever you need someone." He stroked her cheek. "I'll be there for you."

She pressed a kiss to his lips and tempted as he was to take it deeper and crawl back under the covers with her, he lifted his head and made himself smile and wink at her instead. "I was going to save this for later, but I got you something." He hadn't planned to give it to her yet, but since he'd just told her that he'd always be there for her, he wanted her to understand that it wasn't just words. He rolled off the bed and went and grabbed the bag that he'd left in the smaller bedroom. He'd been second-guessing himself on the color, but all he could do was hope that she liked it.

She'd sat up and was leaning against the headboard when he returned. He sat down beside her and put his arm around her shoulders. "I hope you like it."

She took the bag and pulled out the box with a smile. When she took out the gaudy looking purply pink plastic watch, she gave him a puzzled smile. "A watch? Thank you. It's ... lovely."

He chuckled. "I know it's not lovely and I'm sure you're more used to stuff that's studded with diamonds but let me explain before you go thinking that I'm a cheap ass with very bad taste."

She laughed. "You don't have bad taste. It is my favorite color."

"Yeah. That's why I asked about that. I got this the other day, and I've kind of been putting off giving it to you. It's not just a watch. And ... I don't want to freak you out. It's a safety device."

She looked so skeptical, he had to laugh.

"Seriously. It is. They make them for kids. You know, for parents who are worried, so that they can check where they are." Her smile faded so he hurried on. "I don't mean I want to track you. I'm not trying to be creepy here. The thing is, the reason I got it is that it has an SOS button, too." He reached for the watch and pointed at the button on the side. "If you press that three times, it will email your GPS location to up to five people – you can decide who you want to program in there. And it'll alert 911 as well."

He met her gaze, wondering if this was a horrible idea. Was she going to freak out thinking that he wanted to track her – or worse, wondering why he thought she needed it. She probably didn't need it, but he'd been talking to his cousin Frankie and she'd told him about one of the kids she used to look after who wore a watch like this and how she thought it was a great idea.

When Sierra's eyes filled with tears, he was afraid that he'd screwed up big time. Then she leaned in and kissed him. "Thank you, Wade. This is – it's the best gift anyone's ever given me." She took it out of the box and fastened it onto her wrist. "I love it. Thank you. Will you help me set it up when you get home tonight?"

"I'll be happy to. You don't think it's weird or too tacky to wear?"

She chuckled. "I do not. It looks like one of those fitness tracker things. I love it." Her smile faded. "I hope that I'll never need it. That Jared's gone and won't ever be coming back. But I love that you thought of this. And I'll feel safer wearing it. It'll be like you're with me, even when you're not."

He pursed his lips. "That sounds kind of creepy, and that's the last thing I want to do. I want you to feel safe, not stalked."

She nodded and cupped his face between her hands. "I do. It doesn't feel creepy. It feels special."

"That's because you are special." He smiled. "But for now, I really need to get my ass to work. There's coffee in the pot when you're ready."

"Thank you. And Wade?"

His heart thundered in his chest as he wondered what she was about to say. "Yeah?"

"Have a good day."

Her eyes seemed to say so much more than her words. But he couldn't let himself read too much into it.

"Thanks. You, too."

~ ~ ~

Sierra hurried outside as soon as she saw Jane's truck approaching. Jane smiled at her when she hauled herself up into the passenger seat.

"Morning. You look great. You're all wide awake and bright eyed and … oh my God! Sierra, you're glowing!"

Sierra smiled and did her best to look anywhere except at Jane. As she got dressed, she chuckled to herself at the thought that she looked different. That making love to Wade must suit her. But she'd thought it was just her and her imagination. Apparently, Jane could see a difference in her too.

Jane chuckled. "Sorry. That wasn't nice. I just … I want to say I'm shocked, but I'm not shocked at all. And I'm not wrong, am I?"

Sierra could feel her cheeks burning. "About what? I don't know what you mean."

"Yes, you do. And if we're really going to be friends then this shouldn't be embarrassing. I know he's my brother, but I think it's awesome. I'm stunned by how different you look this morning, and I'm thinking I know what made that difference.

You're all glowing because you slept with Wade last night, right?"

Sierra looked up at her from under her lashes. Her cheeks were still hot, but she couldn't hide her smile. "Yes."

Jane reached across and squeezed her arm. "Sorry. I didn't mean to embarrass you. But if it's any consolation, I think it's awesome. I think the two of you are perfect for each other, and the way you look this morning only confirms that. And now I'll shut up and we can change the subject."

"Thanks."

Jane pulled away from the cabin and they rode up the long driveway in silence. Sierra wanted to break it, but she didn't know what to say. Jane glanced over at her before she pulled out onto the road.

"Are you okay? You're not mad at me for being so nosey, are you?"

"No! I'm not mad at you at all. I am a little bit embarrassed."

"Why?"

"Well, because he's your brother for one thing. And also, because I don't want you to think that I'm the kind of person who just jumps into bed with a guy."

"I don't."

"But that's what I did. We've only known each other for a few days, and I'm supposed to be on my honeymoon right now."

Jane shot another glance at her before turning her focus back to the road. "And you think that I'm going to judge you? Or is it more about you feeling guilty?"

"No! I don't feel guilty. Not one bit. At first, I thought I was wrong to feel so drawn to Wade, you know because it's so fast after I was supposed to get married. But now I don't feel guilty."

"What do you feel?"

She drew in a deep breath and blew it out. "I feel incredibly lucky to have met him. But at the same time, I feel like I have the worst timing in the world."

"Why?"

"Because I wish I could have met Wade at some other time than in the two weeks between the day I was supposed to get married and the day I take on two small children. At any other point in my life, I'd think there was a possibility to pursue this, to hope that something ... something big might happen between us. But with the way everything stands, it's just not possible."

Jane nodded and blew out a sigh. And if Sierra was honest, that was not the reaction she'd been hoping for. She'd hoped that Jane might tell her that it *was* possible, that she believed there was a way for her and Wade to be together for something more than a quick fling. Her heart sat heavy in her chest when Jane sighed. "I want to argue with you, but I know you're right."

Well, there was her answer. She knew that Jane was in her corner, that she liked her and wanted her to explore what she could with Wade. But if Jane wasn't encouraging her to try for more then she had to accept that these next couple of weeks were all she was going to get.

When they got to the bakery, Sierra slid down from the truck and trotted after Jane. As soon as they were inside, she stopped to breathe it all in. She loved the place immediately. It assaulted her senses in the best possible way. The sound of people talking blended in with low music playing in the background. The smell of coffee and pastries made her mouth water. The atmosphere felt homey and welcoming.

Jane looked back at her and smiled. "Are you ready to meet Frankie and her fiancé, Spider?"

"Yes."

"Come on then."

When they reached the counter, a girl who looked to be about the same age as Sierra slid down from one of the stools and greeted Jane with a hug.

When she stepped back, Jane gestured to Sierra. "Sierra, this is my cousin, Frankie. Frankie, this is Sierra." She stopped and frowned, and Sierra guessed that she didn't know how to describe her.

It didn't matter. Frankie stepped forward with a smile and instead of shaking hands, she leaned down to give Sierra a quick hug. "Hey. It's good to meet you."

"Thanks, you too."

"Do you want to sit up here, or should we grab a booth?"

"Let's grab a booth," Jane said.

Once they were all seated, Frankie grinned at Sierra. "So, you ran out on your wedding, huh?"

Sierra just stared at her. How did she even know? She looked at Jane. She wouldn't have expected her to go telling people her business.

Jane gave her a warm smile. "Sorry. I should have warned you. There are no secrets in this valley."

Frankie's smile was gone. "Shit. I'm sorry. I didn't even think. I guess I'm so used to the way things work here it didn't occur to me that you wouldn't be. Sorry. I didn't mean to upset you."

"That's okay." Sierra forced a small smile. "I'd be more upset if you'd told me that I was stupid for running out on my wedding. At least you were on my side."

Frankie grinned. "Hell yeah, I am, girl. Good for you. Do you know what you're going to do now?"

Sierra shrugged. "I think I'm going to be staying here for a while."

Jane gave her a puzzled look, but at that moment a tall muscular man who was covered in tattoos came and loomed over the table. Sierra could feel her eyes widening. She felt like she should be scared of him, but for some reason she wasn't. He wasn't trouble, she could just tell. He was a good guy. Her instincts were proved right when both Jane and Frankie smiled at him, and Frankie caught hold of his hand and pulled him down to sit beside her.

"Sierra, meet Spider."

She smiled at him, and he nodded and smiled back. "It's good to meet you."

"You too. What can I get you, ladies?"

That surprised Sierra; she wouldn't have thought that he worked here, but that seemed to be the case as he took their orders. He dropped a kiss on Frankie's lips before he left the table, telling them that he'd be right back.

She loved the smile on Frankie's face as she watched him go back behind the counter. She looked like a genuine cowgirl and the last person who'd be with someone like Spider – all tattoos and mohawk, but it was obvious that the two of them were together and very much in love.

Sierra bit down on her bottom lip when another man joined Spider behind the counter. He must have come out from the back. He hadn't been there before – she would have noticed him if he were. He was even taller than Spider, his shoulders were even broader, and he was covered in even more ink. He was a handsome devil though.

Frankie glanced at her and winked before turning to Jane. "Did I tell you that Rocket's here?"

Sierra watched in fascination as Jane's cheeks turned bright red and she dropped her chin before saying, "No."

Frankie winked at Sierra again. "I think Spider's going to have him bring our order over."

Sierra looked at Jane and then back over at the big man, Rocket? Was that really his name? He was talking to Spider and smiled when he glanced over in their direction. Well, no, he wasn't looking in their direction, he was looking directly at Janey, and his smile turned into a grin when she lifted her head and met his gaze. Her cheeks turned from red to crimson before she grabbed her purse.

"I have to run to the bathroom. I'll be back."

Sierra watched her scurry away. Frankie laughed beside her. "Don't worry. I'm not being cruel. She's besotted with him, and he feels the same way. But our Janey's stubborn and doesn't believe that he's actually interested in her. I've tried everything I can think of to talk sense into her, but she won't have it. So, now I just stand back and see what happens."

"Is he really interested in her?"

Frankie's smile disappeared and she scowled at Sierra. "Yes. He is. I know that might be hard for someone like you to believe. But not everyone is all about looks and the superficial."

Sierra sat back in her seat, the force of Frankie's words hitting her hard. She was glad that she wasn't that kind of person, she had no doubt that Frankie would beat her down if she were. It was still a little scary, even knowing that they were of the same mind, but instead of being offended or cowering from Frankie's words, she smiled and nodded. "Sorry, that must have come out wrong. I was trying to look out for Janey, not put her down. I wasn't doubting that he should be interested in her, I was more checking whether he has good intentions. That's all."

Frankie held her gaze for a long moment. "Why?" she asked eventually.

"Well, because Janey's my friend. We haven't known each other very long, but I know who she is and how she sees herself and I'd hate for anyone to hurt her – in any way."

Frankie smiled at that. "Okay. I'll let you off then."

Sierra smiled back. "What, you'll let me off for not being as mean and superficial as you decided I was?"

Frankie chuckled. "Yeah. I guess that about sums it up. I did jump to the wrong conclusion. But I'm not going to apologize for it. I did it for Janey's sake, to protect her. I'm glad I was wrong, but I think it's more important to drive away the wrong kind of people. The right kind of people can take a little misunderstanding." She grinned. "As you just proved."

Sierra smiled back at her. She was proud of herself for not backing down. She liked Frankie and now it seemed that Frankie liked her. And they were both united in their determination to look out for Janey.

"Do you think Janey likes him?" she asked.

Frankie snorted. "Err, yeah. Just a lot! I just don't know how to convince her that he's for real about being interested in her. You up for helping me?"

"Absolutely. What do you want me to do?"

Frankie laughed. "Help me figure out what the hell we *can* do."

Sierra watched Rocket make his way over to their table. He was huge! He must be six-foot four at least. And he must be one of those guys who lived in the gym. He was like a wall of muscle. A very broad wall.

He grinned at Frankie when he reached them and then smiled at her. "Where'd she go?" he asked.

Frankie rolled her eyes. "She ran to hide in the bathroom."

Aww. Sierra wanted to pat his hand when she saw the disappointment in his eyes. He was a good guy and there was no question that his interest in Janey was genuine.

He set the tray down on the table and then sat down next to Sierra. "Sorry. It's good to meet you, little lady. You're Sierra, right?" He held his hand out.

As Sierra shook with him, her own hand was engulfed by his. "That's right. It's nice to meet you, too."

He grinned. "Thanks. So, you don't think I'm scary? I don't make you want to run away and hide?"

"No!"

Frankie laughed beside her. "I've told you before. Janey doesn't hide from you because she's scared of you."

To be fair, when he scowled, he did look scary. "I know. She's just not interested, right?"

Frankie sighed. "She is interested."

Rocket shook his head. "But I have to be patient."

"Yup."

Rocket shrugged and smiled through pursed lips at Sierra. "Do you have any tips for me?"

She smiled. "I'm not too good at that kind of thing myself, but I promise I'll put in a good word for you."

"Aww, thanks. And I thought you were going to be one of them who'd look down their noses at me."

She laughed as she looked at Frankie. "It seems to me that we should all give people a fair go at showing us who they are before we judge them based on their appearances."

Frankie just laughed. "Touché. You win that one, and I'm glad."

"You are?"

"I am. I'm glad to be wrong. I'm glad that you're not a snooty bitch."

"Frankie!" Rocket scowled at her, but she just shrugged.

"What? We're being honest here, aren't we?"

Sierra smiled and answered before Rocket could. "We are. It's all good. But do you think I should go and bring Janey back?"

Frankie shook her head. "I'll go."

Rocket didn't move and they both watched Frankie make her way to the restrooms at the back. Sierra jumped when he spoke beside her.

"I haven't been here long myself. But I already know how fast gossip travels. I've heard your story."

Her heart pounded, and she swung her head to look at him. "You have?"

"Yeah. 'Fraid so, sweetheart. I don't mean to embarrass you. I'm not bringing it up for any reason other than to say that if you ever need a bit of extra muscle ..." He smiled. "If you need a scary looking dude to wheel out either for show or for real, you can count on me, okay?"

It felt quite surreal. She was sitting here in a crowded bakery in the middle of an empty landscape, next to a man whom honestly, yes, she'd be scared enough of to cross the street from normally. Yet, his words made her smile, gave her a warm feeling, and made her feel … at home.

She looked up into his eyes. "Thank you."

He grinned. "Of course."

"Do you mind if I ask why?"

He chuckled. "I don't mind, but it makes me sad that you need to."

She raised her eyebrows.

"I'm offering you help if you need it because that's the right and decent thing to do. It's just unfortunate that doing the right and decent thing is so uncommon these days that it comes as a surprise."

"Wow. You're right."

"Yup." He'd diverted his attention from her and was now watching Frankie and Janey make their way back to the table. Sierra could feel him tense beside her and could see him twisting his big hands together; even his fingers were covered in ink.

"Just be yourself," she said quietly.

"You reckon I stand a chance?"

"I honestly don't know. But Frankie said that Janey likes you, so I have to guess that you do." If she hadn't seen it with her own eyes, she wouldn't have believed that a guy who looked the way he did would ever be so nervous about whether a woman liked him.

Frankie reached the table first and sat down, leaving the only empty space next to Rocket. Janey mumbled something that might have been hello as she perched beside him.

Sierra watched with interest as he turned to Janey with a smile.

"Hey, beautiful. It's good to see you."

Jane didn't even meet his gaze. She stared at a point somewhere over his shoulder as she mumbled, "You, too."

Oh, she was interested. She was definitely interested. Sierra snuck a glance at Frankie, who grinned back at her and nodded.

Sierra wanted to say something to break the tension, but she didn't know what. She wanted to pull Janey aside and attempt to reassure her. But all she could do was sit there in the uncomfortable silence that descended.

Jane snatched up her coffee cup, spilling some of it in her haste. "We should be quick, Sierra. We need to get back."

"You got a busy day lined up, beautiful?" Rocket sat back and stretched his arm along the back of the seat behind Janey.

Sierra was silently cheering him on until Jane sat forward, looking uncomfortable.

"Come on, Sierra," said Frankie. "If Janey's going to steal you away so fast, I'd better get you those cookies for Wade."

Sierra leapt to her feet. "Thanks, that'd be great." She turned to Janey. "I'll only be a minute if you can hang on?"

Frankie didn't even give her time to answer, she just took Sierra's arm and the two of them practically ran to the counter, where Spider opened a door and let them both through.

When Sierra looked back, Rocket was leaning toward Jane, smiling, and saying something while Jane just sat frozen.

"Is she really okay?"

"She is. Don't worry. Watch."

She did, and as Rocket continued talking, Jane visibly relaxed. She laughed at something he said and the way she looked at him gave her away. She was very much interested in him.

Sierra grinned at Frankie. "I promise I'll do whatever I can to help."

"What are you scheming, sweetheart?" Spider gave Frankie a stern look.

She laughed. "Nothing yet. But I'm working on it."

Spider looked over at Rocket and Jane and then back at Frankie and Sierra. "Don't you think we should leave them to figure it out for themselves?"

Frankie shrugged. "We have and they're not getting anywhere." When Rocket and Jane got to their feet, she looked around wildly.

"What's up?" Spider asked.

"I need cookies for Sierra. That was our cover story."

Spider laughed and fetched a bag which he proceeded to fill with cookies from the display before handing it to her. He must have put two dozen in there at least.

She chuckled and reached for her purse. "How much …"

Spider waved a hand at her. "No way. You don't need to pay. I bet you had no idea you needed cookies till Frankie dragged you over here."

She chuckled. "That's not the point. I'm still going to enjoy them."

Frankie grinned at her. "Don't forget I told Janey that they're for Wade."

"Don't worry. I'll make sure he gets most of them."

Frankie raised an eyebrow at her. "Since we're friends now. Are you going to tell me that I was right to assume that you're happy to share your cookies with Wade?"

Sierra wished she didn't embarrass so easily, but the way Frankie said it sounded … dirty and very appealing. She laughed, even though she knew her cheeks were red. There was no point denying it. "More than happy."

"Can I get a coffee here or what?"

The woman's angry voice made them all turn. Sierra felt bad for keeping Spider from his customers, and Jane and Rocket were at the counter now. She took the bag from Spider and let herself back out with a murmured sorry, for holding them up.

"Are you ready?" Jane grabbed her arm and towed her toward the door before she could thank any of them.

But not before she heard Spider ask the impatient woman, "What can I get you, Josie?"

Her heart pounded in her chest as she looked back over her shoulder. Was that Wade's Josie? The woman he'd been married to? The woman who'd called him last night, wanting him to go over and help her? She was pretty. She had shoulder length dark hair and was way taller than Sierra. Just before Jane dragged her out the door, Frankie caught Sierra's gaze and smiled. She jerked her chin toward Josie and shook her head.

What did that mean? Sierra wanted to think that Frankie was reassuring her somehow. Was she telling her that Josie was nothing to worry about? Or was she saying that she shouldn't be sharing her cookies with Wade because of her? No. That wasn't it. She was being ridiculous. She didn't even know if that woman was Wade's Josie. And even if she were, she was his *ex,* Josie, and he'd told Sierra himself that she wasn't important to him and hadn't been for a long time.

She pulled herself together and scampered after Janey, who was already climbing into her truck and still looking flustered. As soon as Sierra closed the passenger door behind her, Janey pulled away in a hurry.

"Are you okay?" Sierra asked.

"Of course. I just need to get to work. I'll drop you off at the cabin."

"Oh. I thought I was coming with you to see the little mama dog."

Jane glanced over at her. "Yeah. Right. Sorry."

Sierra wondered whether she should keep quiet about Rocket, but Janey looked so stressed, she decided that she couldn't. "Are you going to go out with him?" she asked quietly.

"What? With who?"

"Rocket."

Jane blew out a sigh. "Come on, Sierra. I don't know what he's playing at. I mean, I know he acts all charming with all the women who go in there, but he doesn't need to bother doing that crap with me. I know better and I've told him so."

"What crap?"

"Pretending that he's interested."

"He is."

Jane shot a look at her before turning back to the road. "Don't you start. Frankie's bad enough. Wait. Did she put you up to this? Is that what the cookies are for?"

"She didn't put me up to anything. Rocket likes you. What's the problem?"

Jane let out a big sigh. "There is no problem. Sorry. I didn't mean to snap at you. But don't be ridiculous. He doesn't like me. It's just his personality. He's a charmer. He charms all the women."

"He is a charmer, but I didn't see him deliberately trying to charm anyone but you. You like him, don't you?"

Jane made a face. "As if I could hide it. But come on, Sierra. I'm not stupid enough to set myself up for that kind of fall."

"I don't understand."

"Have you seen him? He's gorgeous, right?"

"He is a good-looking guy."

"Right. And have you seen me?"

Sierra scowled. "Of course, I have. And you're —"

"Don't! Don't even go there. I'm nothing to look at is the nicest, most honest thing that you could say, so I'd rather you didn't say anything."

"I wasn't going to say that."

"I know. And I'd hate to hear you lie to me. I'd rather we just dropped this."

Sierra blew out a sigh of her own. "If you don't want to talk about it, I'll respect that, but I need to say one thing first."

"What?"

"You've been busy encouraging me about Wade. I want to encourage you about Rocket. He is interested in you. He said so. And Frankie knows it too. I have my hang-ups that I shouldn't like Wade because I'm supposed to be on my honeymoon right now. You told me I was wrong. You have your hang-ups about the way you look, meaning that Rocket wouldn't be interested in you. I'm telling you that you're wrong, and I think it would be a real shame to let your hang-ups stop you from exploring something that could turn out to be something wonderful."

Jane shook her head sadly. "Thanks. I know you're only saying it because you care. But … I just can't, okay? It'd hurt too much to let myself hope and then find out that … You've said your piece. Let's drop it."

"Okay."

They drove in silence for a while. It was only when Jane turned onto the driveway at the ranch that she spoke again.

"I do believe him that he wants to get to know me better. I'd love that. But I know that it would be short-lived. I'd rather keep him at a distance and slowly turn him into a friend than try for something more than that and get my heart broken when he's the one putting me in the friend-zone when he meets someone better."

Sierra shook her head sadly. "It's your choice to make. And I'll respect whatever you want. I won't push you or bug you. But Janey, you only get one life; isn't it better to reach for something good even if you might not get it, even if you fall and get hurt? Isn't that better than never even hoping – than telling yourself that good things just aren't meant for you?"

Jane looked over at her but didn't say anything. Sierra just hoped that she might decide to take a chance. Although her words had been meant for Jane, she mulled them over herself. Should she try to reach for something good with Wade? Should she let herself hope that if she stayed here … It'd be too easy to tell herself that he wasn't meant for her. That there couldn't be anything between them because she was about to change her whole life for two little children she'd never met. Would it be better to hope or to lock herself down to the reality that in less than ten days from now whatever there was between them would have to end?

Chapter Sixteen

Wade shut his computer down and grabbed his hat from the rack. He wanted to get home, back to the cabin and to Sierra. He was surprised at how quickly he'd come to think of it as home. Until she'd moved in with him, he'd only ever called it the cabin. He shook his head as he headed out of his office. He'd have to get used to thinking of it that way again in just another short week. After that, she'd be moving into the big cabin, and he'd be going back to the house with his brothers. He could get the last of the work done and put the cabin on the books for guests. That had been the plan from the beginning; he needed the extra beds. He might be sentimental and want to keep living in the space that he'd shared with Sierra, but he wouldn't do it. He crammed his hat on his head as he strode down the hallway to the conference room. He might want to go home to Sierra but before he could, he had to meet with his brothers.

Ford was already there, standing with his back to the room staring out the window at the mountains. He turned when Wade entered.

"Sorry I'm late."

"You're not. The others aren't here yet anyway."

"Yeah." Wade stuck his head back out the door, hoping that Tanner and Tyler were on their way and that they wouldn't hold him up too long.

"What's up?" asked Ford.

"Nothing."

His brother smirked. "Yeah, right. I'm guessing you're in a hurry to head home?"

Wade gave him a sheepish smile. "You got me."

"Seems to me that you've got *her* if you want her."

"What do you mean?"

"That in the space of a week, you and Sierra have gotten real close. That if you wanted her to stay, I believe she would."

Wade blew out a big sigh. "Nah. I mean, she is going to stay. You know that. In the big cabin. Which is awesome, really. We thought we'd lost that income when the original renters canceled, so to have Sierra —"

"Stop!"

"What?"

"It's me you're talking to. Don't bullshit me. I'm not talking about cabins and income; I'm talking about you and that sweet little lady who seems to me like she's fallen head over heels in love with you."

Wade closed his eyes. He couldn't allow himself to go there. "Shit, Ford. I've only known her a week. We have a good thing going, I'm not going to deny that. But it's not going anywhere. Next weekend she'll move out of the cabin. I'll come back to the house."

"How can you say it's not going anywhere? Yeah, you've only known her a week, but you're already living with her."

"We're not … it's not." He struggled with what to say to that. How could he deny that he was living with Sierra when that was exactly how it felt to him? But he wasn't, not really. They'd even talked about it. He hadn't wanted her to feel like she was under any kind of pressure, or to feel weird about things moving so fast between them. Somehow, they'd ended up agreeing that what they were doing was like some kind of vacation fling. It was intense and moving so damned fast it made his head spin, but it was okay to roll with it because it had a predetermined end date.

Ford raised his eyebrows and waited.

"We're not living together."

Ford looked toward the door at the sound of Tanner and Tyler's voices as they came down the hallway. "Whatever you say. I'll let it go if you want, but I think you're a fool if you let it end next weekend."

Wade frowned at him. "I thought you'd be the one to call me a fool to try and keep it going."

"So did I. But you and Sierra, you just seem right together. I know you never wanted kids, so that'd be a tough one. But I like seeing you with her. You're the happiest I've seen you."

Wade held his gaze for a long moment.

Ford shrugged. "I know I'm the last one you'd expect to be encouraging you, but I am. Okay?" He gave a small chuckle. "Believe me, I know. You don't find the truth of a relationship in months or years; you find the truth in moments. The moments that light you up, the ones that take your breath away and the ones that set your heart on fire, that's where you find it. You going to tell me you don't know what I'm talking about?"

Wade just stared at him. He knew damned well what he was talking about. So many moments with Sierra had done all of those things – lit him up, taken his breath away, set his heart on fire. And his heart knew the truth. He might have only known Sierra for a week, but he'd had more of those moments with her than he'd ever had with Josie, the woman he'd known through high school and married not long after.

As if reading his mind, Ford continued. "Maybe you're making up for the fact that it took you years to figure out that you were with the wrong woman by figuring out in less than a week that this time you found the right woman."

Wade opened his mouth, but before he could say anything, Tanner and Tyler came in.

"Is everyone going to Shane and Cassidy's tonight?" asked Tanner.

Ford held Wade's gaze for a moment before turning to answer. "Yep. Everyone except you, since you won't give up your shifts behind the bar at Chico."

Tyler laughed. "Why would he do that? You know he only works there so that he gets his pick of the tourist chicks every weekend – and he doesn't even have to buy them drinks."

"Hey!" Tanner shrugged. "It works out well. I'm great behind the bar. The ladies love me. Everyone goes home happy."

"Well. Not everyone," said Tyler. "You leave a lot of lovely ladies disappointed when you choose the one that you're going home with."

"What can I say? I can't please 'em all. I mean I wouldn't mind trying, but …"

Ford laughed. "You're a dog."

"Nope. I'm just doing my part for the local economy."

"What?" Wade couldn't help laughing as he asked.

"I am! I show the tourists a good time, they go home and tell their girlfriends about the hot cowboy they got to sleep with and when they come back, more friends come with them looking for a cowboy of their own."

Wade shook his head.

"Yeah, well, never mind that," said Ford. "How about we get on with it since we all have somewhere else we want to be tonight. While you go off and choose the next willing victim to succumb to your charms, the rest of us want to go home and get ready to go over to Shane's place to hang out with friends."

Tanner made a face at him. "You really do think I'm a dog, don't you? As a matter of fact, I have a call in to Andy to see if he wants to switch with me tonight. I'd rather come over to Shane's and hang out with you guys."

Ford raised an eyebrow. "There won't be any single women there."

"Jeez. I'm not constantly looking to get laid."

Tyler laughed. "No, just most of the time."

Tanner turned to Wade for sympathy, but he just shrugged. "I don't know what to tell you."

"Well, it's not like you have to worry about it, is it? I always thought you should have been my hunting buddy, but Josie got her claws into you young and now that you're finally recovered from that, you got yourself Sierra."

Wade didn't know what to say. If even Tanner thought that he and Sierra were … something, then it must be blatantly obvious.

Tyler grinned at him. "Yeah. I'm glad she's taking the cabin. Are you going to move in there with her?"

"No!" Jesus. He wanted to. He'd thought about it enough. They'd only had a few nights together, but he was already dreading the time when he'd have to sleep without her by his side again. "She's moving in there so that she has room for the kids, remember?"

"What, and that means there's no room for you?" asked Tyler.

Ford blew out a sigh. "Jesus, Ty! Remember why he's not married to Josie anymore?"

"Oh. Shit. Sorry."

Wade just shrugged. They all seemed to think that Josie wanting kids when he didn't was the only reason that they'd gotten divorced. He'd tried when he first moved back home to explain that the reason he didn't want to have kids with her was because of all the other underlying flaws in their relationship. But Josie had fed the rumor mill that he didn't want kids and that part of the story was the only part that had stuck – even with his own family. After eight years, he didn't see the point in trying to enlighten them now. Especially not when he was hoping to get out of here sooner rather than later.

"Anyway," said Ford. "Let's run through everything and get out of here, can we?"

"Gladly," said Wade. He knew he'd probably look forward to these end of the week roundup meetings with his brothers again soon enough. But tonight, he just wanted this one over with.

~ ~ ~

Sierra eyed herself in the mirror over the dresser as she applied a coat of lip gloss. She had to smile at the way she looked – she looked good. She was dressed more casually and wearing less makeup than she ever normally did, but she looked better. Living out here suited her in so many ways.

Wade came out of the bathroom and stood behind her, wrapping his arms around her waist and meeting her gaze in the mirror. Have I told you today how beautiful you are, little lady?"

She leaned back against him, loving the feel of the warm skin of his chest naked against her back, still damp from the shower. "You have, thank you. I'd say you're the beautiful one, though." She turned within the circle of his arms and rolled up on her tiptoes to press a kiss to his lips. "Have I told you that you're the most handsome man I've ever known?"

He batted his eyelashes at her, making her giggle. "Aww, shucks. You can't go saying stuff like that, it'll go straight to my head."

"It won't. You're not like that. You're not just the most handsome man I've ever known, you're also one of the most decent and ..."

He chuckled as he caught her hand in his and pressed it to the front of his boxers. He was hot and hard. She sucked in a deep breath.

"When I said it'd go straight to my head, I meant that one." He cupped his hand, still holding hers so that she could feel him twitch and grow.

"Oh." She was getting used to him, getting used to the way he was so open and sexy, but she still didn't know what to say most of the time. "I could help you out," she suggested.

The lines around his eyes crinkled as he closed them. "I'd like nothing more. But we should save it until we get back."

"Of, course. Sorry." She tried to step away from him, but he put his hands on her shoulders.

"Hey. Don't think it's because I don't want to. I always want you. You have to know that. But if I get you into bed right now, we won't be getting out for a while. And if we're late tonight, everyone will know why, or at least, they'll assume they do. They'll tease us mercilessly." He held her gaze. "And I don't mind that. I don't mind one bit if they all know that I can't keep my hands off you. Or if they figure out that I'd rather be alone with you than there with all of them. I don't mind if they know the truth. The only thing I'm worried about is how you'll feel. I'm guessing that you'd be uncomfortable with that kind of teasing." He raised an eyebrow. "Am I right?"

She nodded slowly. "Yes. You're right. I'd be embarrassed. I'm not …I don't …" She shrugged.

Wade let go of her and went to get a shirt from the closet. He kept his back to her as he pulled it on. "Do you know when your stuff is supposed to arrive from home yet? I was thinking, I should take you to look at the cabin tomorrow. It didn't even occur to me that you haven't seen it yet. I can be a real dumbass – "

He stopped abruptly when she put her hand on his shoulder.

"What's up?" The fact that he didn't turn around to ask, told her that she was right. He was uncomfortable and moving the conversation on from where they'd been.

She didn't want to make him more uncomfortable, so she rested her cheek against his back and slipped her arms around his waist instead of making him turn around to look at her. "Yes, I'm excited to see the cabin. But before you change the subject, I need you to understand what I meant about being embarrassed if everyone starts teasing us."

All his muscles tensed. "It's okay. I know – "

"It's not okay. You don't understand. You think that I'd be embarrassed about them knowing that we're, what we're …" Ugh, she couldn't even find the right words. But it didn't matter. "I'm not embarrassed about being with you. I could never be. I'm proud to be with you. It makes me feel special that someone as wonderful as you wants to be with me. What I'm embarrassed about, or I would be if they teased us about it, is that … well, I'm not the kind of girl who does this normally. Who sleeps with a guy without it being … being part of something bigger. I'm embarrassed that they'll think I am."

He spun around within her arms. "They don't think that."

She shrugged. "Whether they think it or not, it's kind of true, isn't it? I haven't wanted to examine it too closely, because you're too wonderful and I want to make the most of the time that we have. But no matter how nice we try to make it seem, we're just two people who are sleeping together for a couple of weeks while we can – knowing that it's not going to go anywhere."

His lips pressed together, and a muscle ticked in his jaw. "I guess we are."

Her heart sank. She'd hoped to make him feel better, but instead she'd made things worse. "But only because that's the way it has to be."

His eyebrows drew down and he looked deep into her eyes. For a moment she thought he was going to ask her why it had to be that way, why they couldn't have more than a couple of weeks. Or better yet, that he might tell her that they could have more and that he wanted more. But the moment passed. He pressed a kiss to her forehead and stepped away to button up his shirt. "Don't worry. We'll be there on time. No one will tease you about what we've been up to." She watched him heave in a big breath and slowly let it out before he added, "And you're right of course, this is the way it has to be."

By the time they got to Shane and Cassidy's place, Wade wasn't really in the mood for it. He normally looked forward to getting together with the Remingtons. It was always a good time. He and his brothers had grown up with them, gone to school with them. They'd all helped on each other's family ranches over the years. They were more like family than friends. But the Remingtons really were a family. Their parents were awesome. That was the big difference. While the MacFarlands had dragged themselves up and become decent human beings in spite of their father, the Remingtons had been raised by a loving father who'd taught them by example how to be good men, and how to treat a woman.

He blew out a sigh as he brought his truck to a stop in the driveway in front of Cassidy's place. It had tickled him to think that Shane had been living in a cabin much like his when he met Cassidy, and she'd moved him into this place – which was more like a mansion. He didn't feel like laughing about it tonight, though. He glanced over at Sierra. He wouldn't be moving in with her. He'd only get to see her move in with her new children, and once it was safe for her to leave, he'd get to see her move back to San Francisco with them.

She reached across and rested her hand on his arm with a sad smile. "Are you okay? I feel like I messed everything up with what I said earlier."

He covered her hand with his and gave it a squeeze. She was just too damned sweet. None of this was her fault. He was the one who'd gone and gotten in too deep with feelings for her, and he hated to see her sad.

He forced himself to smile and to wink. "I'm okay, darlin'. Just having a moment of regret that I didn't keep you at home in bed instead."

She smiled back at him, then waggled her eyebrows. "There's still time to change our minds. We could go back and – "

He shook his head rapidly before he agreed with her. He'd love nothing more. But she was right. What they had would be over in another week. But she needed to find her place here in the valley. For however long she was going to stay, she'd need friends and connections and he knew that she'd find them with good people here tonight.

He squeezed her hand again. "Don't tempt me, darlin'. This is where you need to be. I can't keep you for myself."

She opened her mouth, looking as though she was about to argue, but he turned and opened the door before running around to open hers. If he let her argue, he might let her win, and much as he wanted her all to himself, he knew he had to let her go.

Chapter Seventeen

Sierra laughed as she tried to disentangle baby Penny's chubby little fingers from her watch. The little girl was adorable, and she'd taken an immediate liking to the bright pink plastic. Her mom, Summer, scooped her up from Sierra's knee and expertly released her grip on the watch.

"I'm sorry." Summer looked at the watch. "It's the same color as one of her toys. I think she thinks it's hers. Wait! I'm sorry. I didn't mean that to sound wrong."

Sierra laughed. "No. It's fine. I know what you mean; it is a bit bright, but I love it. Penny and I have the same taste." She waggled her fingers at the little girl, who smiled and waved back. "She's gorgeous. And she's so good."

Summer smiled proudly, and Cassidy laughed beside her. "That's because she has the perfect mother and is doted on by her father."

From what Sierra had seen tonight, Cassidy was right. She'd been shocked when she realized that Cassidy's sister-in-law was none other than the country singer, Summer Breese. Although she didn't sing anymore, she'd still written some of country's biggest hits of the last few years, even while she lived out here in Montana – with a sexy cowboy of her own. She was married to Carter Remington, Shane's brother. He was another one who was so big and muscly that he should look scary, but he was more like the definition of a gentle giant. Especially around his wife and daughter. It made Sierra's heart melt in her chest to watch him with them.

She'd loved every minute of this evening. If anyone had told her ten days ago that she'd be hanging out in Montana with a bunch of cowboys and their women, who ranged from cowgirls to artists to celebrities, she would have laughed. Even if she'd believed it, she never would have believed that she would feel comfortable. And yet, here she was. And not only did she feel comfortable, she felt … at home.

She watched Summer and Carter take little Penny inside. She hadn't expected there to be any children here tonight. But there had been a few. Cassidy's other sister-in-law, Corinne, had left with her husband, Beau, a little while ago. Their daughter, Ruby, had been the star of the evening. She was a precocious little madam, and it was obvious that all the cowboys adored her. Sierra did, too. She almost envied her. Ruby was growing up surrounded by people who loved her and who encouraged her to be herself. She was going to grow up to be a strong, independent woman who knew her own mind. She was strong-willed, but she was also gentle and loving with her baby brother and with little Penny.

Cassidy nudged her with her elbow, almost making her spill her drink. "What's got you looking so maudlin, chica?"

"Me? Nothing!"

Cassidy laughed. "Yeah, right. You were lost in your own little world there. I just want to know if seeing all the kidlets tonight has you looking forward to the children coming next

week or if it has you wishing that you could just stick with
Wade and make your own. I have to tell you; you two would
make beautiful babies."

"Cassidy!"

"What? It's true. You're beautiful. He's gorgeous."

Sierra shook her head. "That's neither here nor there." She
looked around to make sure no one else was listening. They
were sitting by the fire pit and everyone else was standing
around in small groups. "You know what the deal is. We're
only ... together for this week and then the children are
coming and ... that'll be it."

"Why, though?"

"Why what?"

"Why does that have to be it?"

Sierra sighed. "Because it has to be. I'm going to be a mom. I
... Wade didn't sign up for that. He didn't sign up for anything
really. We just ... we were attracted to each other. I wouldn't
have even done anything about that, but you encouraged me
to. We agreed that we were going to make the most of the two
weeks I'm here before we knew that I was going to be here for
longer. It was only ever going to be a rebound thing."

Cassidy frowned. "But why? I mean, I get why that's all it
was going to be. But why can't it be something more now?"

Sierra sucked in a deep breath. She'd been asking herself that
question a lot. But she knew the answer. "Because Wade's not
interested in me like that."

Cassidy threw her head back and laughed out loud. "You're
kidding me, right? We are talking about the same guy? The one
who right now is standing with Chance at the bottom of the
stairs, pretending that he's glad to see his old buddy, even
while he can't take his eyes off you?"

Sierra couldn't help looking over to the stairs that led down from the deck. And Cassidy was right. She assumed that the cowboy in the black hat must be Chance – did they breed them for their looks and muscles out here? He was a good-looking guy, but he didn't do it for her in the same way Wade did. As if he felt her looking, Wade turned his head and caught her gaze. His smile melted her heart a little bit. It had right from the first time she saw it, but tonight it seemed to be tinged with sadness, and she felt it, too. All the couples here tonight seemed to be living their happily-ever-after. Her heart ached at the knowledge that she and Wade weren't going to get one of those.

Cassidy nudged her with her elbow again. "I rest my case. He's not just interested in you, he's a goner. And from the sappy look on your face, you are, too. The question is, what are you going to do about it?"

Sierra looked back at her friend. "There's nothing I can do, is there?"

"Hmph! Bullshit. Of course, there is."

"No, Cass." Even though Sierra wanted to agree with her, she knew better. She'd already made a commitment to two little children – to Mateo and Maya. And even though she hadn't even met them yet, she was determined to give them the best life she possibly could. She wouldn't turn them away. And there was no way she could expect Wade to take them on. He'd said that he admired what she was doing, but from a few snippets his brothers had said, she had a sneaking suspicion that part of the reason that he wasn't married to Josie anymore was because she'd wanted children and he hadn't.

"Hope!"

Cassidy's shout made Sierra jump. She got to her feet with a smile when she saw Hope Davenport hurrying toward them. No. She was Hope Malone now. She, like Cassidy, had married a cowboy; Chance, the one who was talking to Wade.

Hope greeted Cassidy with a high-five and then turned to Sierra. "Hey! I couldn't believe it when I heard you were here! Sorry I haven't made it down to see you. And sorry I wasn't here for dinner." She wrapped Sierra in a hug.

"That's okay, I …" Sierra stopped and laughed when Hope let her go. Chance had appeared at her side and was mock scowling at her, but the twinkle in his eyes gave him away.

"I thought you were going to call me to come get you. You know I don't like you driving – " Hope cut him off with a kiss, then stole his hat and put it on her own head with a smile.

"I'm here. I'm safe. The kids are down for the night. Dad and Chris were so eager to get rid of me that I decided to drive instead of waiting for you to come get me. Are you going to bitch about it or kiss me?"

Sierra chuckled as Chance's frown turned into a smile just before he drew his wife in for a kiss that made Sierra blush and turn away.

Turning brought her face to face with Wade, who must have come over with Chance. She wished for a second that he would kiss her like that. But that was hardly fair. She'd told him that she'd be embarrassed for people to know that they were together that way.

Instead of a kiss, he greeted her with a wink and a smile, a gesture that was just so very … Wade. It sent a rush of warmth through her chest. She couldn't help it. She went to him and slipped her arms around his waist.

He looked surprised, but didn't miss a beat, closing his arms around her and dropping a kiss on the top of her head. "Is this a stealth hug? Do I need to let go and hope that no one noticed?"

She shook her head and pressed her cheek against his chest. "No. I don't want you to let go." It was hard to stop herself from adding the word *ever* at the end. But she managed it. "Do you want to go home?"

He looked down into her eyes. "Have you had enough?"

She smiled. "I've had a great time, but I'd rather be with you."

"Well, alrighty, then." He tightened one arm around her waist and guided her toward Cassidy, who was now standing with Shane. "Thanks for having us over, guys. This was great. We should get everyone down to our place one night."

Shane raised an eyebrow at him. "You're leaving?"

Sierra felt him tense at her side and wondered what he'd say. She needn't have worried. Cassidy slapped Shane's arm.

"That's what it usually means when people say thanks for having us. Let them go."

"Oh!" Shane's eyes widened and he glanced at Sierra before grinning and nodding at Wade. "Sure. Thanks for coming. See you again soon." He smiled at Sierra. "I'm glad you're here and I hope you're going to stay."

"Thank you." Sierra didn't know how else to answer him.

He chuckled. "You'll make two of my favorite people happy if you do. Cass has always talked about you. I mean you know her, she has loads of friends, but not another artist. From what she says, nobody gets her like you do."

Sierra smiled at her friend, hoping to let the moment slide. Cassidy wasn't big on expressing emotions if she didn't have to. She preferred to laugh them off. So, it surprised Sierra when she gave her a serious look and nodded. Of course, she soon turned it around with a laugh. "And you know damned well *I'm* not going to beg you to stick around."

Shane laughed and looked at Wade. "And neither will he." He looked back at Sierra. "That's why *I'm* begging you. I have no pride and no shame when it comes to making my wife and my buddy happy."

Sierra's heart thumped in her chest. It was quite the revelation to think that it'd make Cassidy happy if she stayed. But that was nothing compared to thinking about Wade. He stood stiffly beside her now, but somehow, she knew that he wasn't mad at Shane. He was nervous. She could just tell – and that must mean that Shane was right, and he wanted her to stay! She swallowed. Wow. But she *was* staying, just not with him. She risked a glance up at him. He only met her gaze for a moment, but what she saw in his eyes shocked her. Perhaps whatever they had going between them could last longer than a couple of weeks after all.

Wade pulled his truck into the garage and cut the engine before turning to Sierra. He'd come into the garage because he wanted her to see how it felt. While she'd been staying in his cabin with him, they just parked out front. But when she moved in here, he wouldn't be with her. She'd be by herself. Except she wouldn't – she'd have two small children to take care of. Either way, he wanted her to feel safe. He hit the remote and waited for the door to roll shut behind them.

She gave him a puzzled look. "Is everything okay? I thought we were going home. I thought you were going to bring me here tomorrow."

"I was going to, but then I though you should see it in the dark. See what it's like to come home at the end of the day." He jerked his thumb over his shoulder. "I wanted to tell you. I mean, it's not my place. You can do what you want, of course. But I thought I should suggest that whenever you come home, you should come and park in here and make sure that the door's closed behind you before you get out."

She glanced back at the doors, then at him again. "Okay."

He forced a smile. "Come on. I'll show you around." He let himself out of his truck and went around to her door. He'd always loved his truck, but since he'd met her, he loved it even more. It was a long way for her to get down and she usually waited for him to come help her. When he reached her, she'd opened the door but was sitting there sideways.

He put his hands on her hips ready to lift her out, but she wrapped her arms around his neck and looked into his eyes. "Thank you, Wade."

He straightened up. "You're welcome ... but what for?"

"For everything. For being you. For making me feel better about being me. For being so kind. And so sexy." He felt like he grew two feet taller at that. "For being the best, most decent, kindest man I've ever known."

He wrapped his arms around her and drew her to the edge of the seat. "I'm not sure I'm any of those things, darlin'. But thank you, for bringing out the best in me."

She nuzzled her face into his neck, making him step closer and press her legs apart so that he could stand between them. "You bring out the best in me, too. I wish ..."

His heart thundered in his chest as he waited. What did she wish? Did she wish all the same things that he did? The silence drew on. She didn't finish her thought, and he didn't dare to. At least, not with specifics. Instead, he kissed her forehead and murmured, "I do, too."

As he gave her a tour of the cabin, he could imagine it transformed by her presence. Just like she'd made his cabin feel like a home for the first time, she'd do the same with this place. He knew it. He closed his eyes as he imagined her sitting at the big, oak kitchen table with two small, dark-haired children doing homework. She was going to make a great mom. He knew that, too. And for the first time in his life, he wished that he was going to get to be a dad.

He hadn't wanted to have children with Josie because their relationship hadn't been solid. That was what he'd always told himself. But there was another deeper reason. It wasn't so much about the relationship as it was about the person. Josie wasn't warm and loving. And there was no way that Wade wanted to bring a child into a home that wasn't warm and loving and upbeat. He knew all too well how it felt to grow up with a parent who was cold and distant on a good day, and cruel and vindictive the rest of the time. Not that Josie was like his dad. Far from it. But she wasn't the person he'd trust enough to love his children.

When they came back to the great room, he flopped down on the sofa and held his arms up to Sierra. She was someone he'd trust that much. But she was already on the way to building a family of her own – and there was no room in that for him. He knew it. He needed to stop getting carried away. She was going to stay here for a while. She wouldn't leave until her scuzzy ex had been found and brought to justice in one way or another. Best case scenario, she'd stay for the whole of the school year to come. He'd already promised her that he'd always be her friend and he planned to keep that promise. He might not be able to have her in his life in the way he wished, but he just needed to go with being grateful that she was in it at all. He needed to make the most of the week they had left and then make the most of any moments he got to share with her after that.

She came to him and nestled into his side when he wrapped his arms around her.

"What do you think of the place?"

"I love it, Wade. It's perfect."

"Good. Do you think Mateo and Maya will like it?"

She shrugged and looked up at him. "I have no idea. I don't know them. I know a little bit about their background – and it's not good. The poor little things, Wade. I'm afraid it's all going to be overwhelming for them. I mean, their mom died last year. Their dad was killed a couple of months ago. They've been staying with some friends of Dax's while all the paperwork gets sorted out for them to be able to come here and stay. From what Dax says they haven't had any stability in over a year. Mateo's very protective of his little sister, and she doesn't talk much – in fact, I don't think she talks at all."

Wade's heart clenched in his chest. He hated to think what they'd been through. He'd called Cash and gotten Dax's number so that he could get a better handle on the whole situation. Even though he'd wanted to dislike the guy, he hadn't been able to. Dax was good people. He wasn't forcing the children onto Sierra. He was concerned about her. But he was also determined to do what was best for Mateo and Maya, and Wade couldn't argue that a life with Sierra was a wonderful option for them. He just hoped that it would turn out to be wonderful for her.

And he couldn't help but wonder if there was a contribution he could make. If he could be a part of giving them a better life, he wanted to do it.

"We'll have to see if they want to ride."

Sierra looked up at him.

"You haven't met Libby yet; she's family – kind of. She runs a riding program. She gives regular lessons, but she also does equine therapy. She works with vets and kids. Maybe ..." He let his words trail off, unable to decipher the look on Sierra's face. "What? Did I say something wrong?"

"No." Her voice was barely more than a whisper.

"What then?"

"You want to help them?"

"Of course, I do. The poor little mites have had a tough life by the sounds of it. I want to do anything – everything – I can to help them build a new life."

"You meant what you said, then?"

He raised an eyebrow.

"That we're still going to be friends after ... when they come?"

"Jesus, Sierra. Of course, I meant it. I mean it. I want to be there for you. I want to be there for them. I want – " He managed to stop himself before he told her that he wanted to be with her. He didn't know for sure that that was true. Well, he knew he wanted to be with her. But he didn't know if he was what was right for her. He couldn't be with her if her life was going to take her back to San Francisco and more importantly than that, he didn't know if he could be what two little children needed. And without knowing that, there was nothing more he could say. "I'm always going to be there for you, darlin'."

She looked up at him and he could see her swallow. The deeper he got, the more signs he saw that she was feeling it, too. But talking wasn't going to help them figure anything out. Not yet. Not until the kids arrived and they figured out what life was going to look like. For now, words would only complicate things. So, instead he took her hand and led her to the master bedroom. He might never get to sleep with her there once she moved in, and all of a sudden it was important to him that when she lay down in that big bed at night, he wanted her to remember him there with her – and maybe want him there again.

Chapter Eighteen

On Monday morning, Sierra stood in the kitchen sipping her coffee as she watched Wade gather his things and get ready to go to work. He'd suggested that she could move into the big cabin as soon as she wanted, but she didn't want to go yet. She'd come to love Wade's cabin, to love sharing it with him. And although they'd slept at the big cabin on Saturday night, it didn't feel the same. It wasn't his place, not like this was. And when she moved in there it would be her place, hers and the children's – and he wasn't going to be part of it. He kept reassuring her that he'd always be there for her, and she knew that he would and that he meant well, but every time he said it made her sad because she knew that being *there for* her wasn't the same as being *with* her.

He finished pulling his boots on and came to stand in front of her, putting his hands on her shoulders and looking down into her eyes. "You okay?"

"Yes."

He cocked an eyebrow.

"I am, honestly. Why?"

He drew her closer and she went willingly until her cheek was pressed against his chest and his arms were wrapped around her. This had come to be her favorite place on Earth.

He blew out a sigh before he spoke. "You looked sad. But maybe I was just imagining it. Projecting it."

She leaned back to look up at him, but he didn't loosen his arms around her. "Projecting it? Are you sad? Why?"

He shrugged. "I dunno. Maybe it's just the Monday morning blues." He gave her a rueful smile. "I was thinking about what I need to do today and about what time I can finish and what you might want to do tonight. And then it hit me that next Monday morning everything will be different. I mean, I'll still have to get up, go to work, take care of business at the lodge, but when I come back here, it won't be home anymore because you won't be here. It'll just be the cabin again. And I'll get on with finishing the second bedroom, then I'll put it on the books for guests and I'll move back into the big house with the guys."

She tightened her arms around his waist. "You weren't projecting."

He cocked his head to one side.

"I was sad thinking about the same things. It's hard to believe that we've only known each other for a week. But in such a short time I've gotten to know you and come to trust you more than any man I've ever been with before."

He held her gaze for a long moment. "I feel the same way about you, darlin'. I was with Josie for thirteen years, married to her for eight. But I feel like I know you better and I trust you a million times more than I ever did her."

Sierra stared up into his eyes. "Do you think that maybe we're wrong? That we're only seeing the best in each other because we want to?"

"Nah. I think we're seeing the truth in each other."

"Do you think we …" Her heart was hammering in her chest. Was she really about to ask him if he could see a future? If he'd be interested in trying to make things last? No. She wasn't. She couldn't. He was watching her face, waiting for her to continue when his ringtone shattered the moment.

She stepped away from him with a sad smile. "You should get that."

He frowned, looking as though he'd rather wait for it to stop, but she turned away from him to top up her coffee and fill a travel mug for him. He didn't exactly have a long drive to work; it only took a few minutes to get from here to the lodge, but she liked to do whatever little things she could to take care of him.

"What's up, Anita? … No. I told them we'd get back to them with a proposal by the end of this week … shit, really?" Sierra watched him run his hand through his hair. She loved the way he did that, it made her want to do the same. "Okay. I'll be there in a few."

She turned around as he ended the call and held the travel mug out to him. "Here you go."

"Thanks." He took it with a sad smile. "Before my phone rang you were asking me if I thought that we … something. Are you going to finish that question?"

"No." There was no point. She already knew the answer. They couldn't keep things going between them. She was going to have Mateo and Maya to take care of. He was divorced because he didn't want children. Well, she didn't know that for sure, but she'd heard enough hints about it to have a good idea. Even if that weren't true, she was only here for a while – for the school year at the most. She shouldn't be getting so caught up in him, in them. It was one thing to follow her feelings when the repercussions would only last for a couple of weeks. It was an entirely different matter to think about her whole future – and his, and the children's.

He searched her face and then nodded. He didn't push her, even if part of her wished that he would. He must know it, too. "Okay." He curled his fingers around the back of her neck and drew her closer for an all too brief kiss. "I'll see you tonight. Call me if you need anything."

She clung to him for a moment before letting go and forcing a smile. "I won't, but thanks. I'll see you later."

After he'd gone, she'd paced the cabin trying to decide what to do. He'd given her the keys to the big cabin so that she could go over there and get used to the place. She should probably go and check out what was there and see what she needed to buy; she wanted to make it feel as homey as possible for Mateo and Maya when they arrived.

She startled when her phone rang and scurried to get it from the counter.

"Amelia! Hey! It's so good to hear your voice."

"You can hear it any time you like. All you have to do is pick up the phone and call," her friend said with a laugh.

"Oh, my gosh! I'm so sorry. I've been neglecting you, haven't I?"

"No. I was only joking. I'm just surprised I suppose, and a little worried. I kind of expected you to call and ask me to come. But the fact that you haven't tells me that you're doing okay. You are doing okay, aren't you?"

"I am."

The silence lengthened. Amelia was her best friend, her only real friend. Sierra wanted to tell her all about Wade. She'd wanted to tell her all week, but she hadn't, and she wasn't sure why.

"Are you keeping a good secret or a bad secret?" Amelia asked eventually.

Sierra had to smile. "A good one. And I didn't mean to keep it secret from you. I just … I don't know what I'm doing, Lia!"

"Just tell me it's not about a man."

Her heart sank. "Why?"

Amelia blew out a sigh. "I'm not trying to be mean. You have to forgive me if I don't exactly trust your judgment when it comes to men."

"I forgive you. I get it. I totally do. And I know you're only trying to look out for me. But Amelia, he's wonderful." When her friend didn't say anything, she chuckled. "Did I just hear you roll your eyes?"

Amelia laughed with her. "Very possibly. And you know I'm only looking out for you. But I seem to remember you telling me that Jared was wonderful at first."

"Shoot. I did, didn't I?"

"Yup. And you totally believed it, too."

"I did. And I couldn't have been more wrong. But honestly, Lia. Wade's not like that. He truly is a decent man. I like everything about him. He's kind and generous and he gets me. He thinks about me … I mean, he's considerate and …"

"Wade? You mean one of your cowboys?"

"Yes. He really is a good guy. They all are. And Dax knows them; well, he knows their brother. And he thinks it's a good idea for me to stay here. And you know Dax is normally skeptical about anyone I meet."

"True. But I think I need to see for myself before I'll believe it. I believed you that Jared was a good guy until I met him."

"So, come then! You said you would if I was going to be here a while and it looks like I'm going to be here for a long while. So, come."

Amelia laughed. "I will. That's what I was calling about. I miss you already. I'm worried about you. We'd already planned that I'd be with you as much as possible when the children first arrived. But I know everything's different now. Do you want me there?"

"I do."

"But? You don't sound thrilled."

"Of course, I am. I'd love to have you here." It was true. She missed her friend. It'd be wonderful to spend time with her. Her lack of enthusiasm was due to the fact that she wouldn't be spending time with Wade in the same way anymore.

"Are you all caught up in your cowboy? Are you thinking I'll cramp your style?" Amelia knew her so well.

"I am all caught up in him, but come, please. You won't be cramping anything. Once the children come, I won't be seeing him much anyway."

"I see."

"No! I don't mean that in a bad way. He really is a good guy. It's just that we thought that whatever we were getting into would only last a couple of weeks. He wasn't looking for anyone to come into his life, let alone someone who comes with two kids."

"Hmm."

"What?"

"I don't know. I don't know what to say because I don't know what I think."

Sierra let out a little laugh. "Then that makes three of us. But please come. You might have to listen to me pining for him, but I'm going to have my hands full with Mateo and Maya; I could use the help."

"Then I'll be there. And maybe if he really is a good guy, it'll be handy for you to have a babysitter so that the two of you can continue exploring."

"Maybe. But whatever might happen with him, the children come first, they have to."

"I know. When do you want me? When do they arrive?"

"Dax is bringing them on Saturday."

"Do you want me to get there before them?"

"Can you?"

"I can be there as soon as I can get a flight."

Sierra hesitated. Of course, she wanted Amelia to come but …

Her friend laughed. "How about I get myself up there when I'm ready. I've always wanted to see Yellowstone. I can find myself a place to stay and do some sightseeing while you make the most of your time with your cowboy. Then whenever you want me, I'll be on your doorstep – but not a minute before."

"Aww, Lia. I've told you before, but I'll say it again. You're the best bestie in the world."

"It's a two-way street, lady. Listen, I have to go. But I'll let you know what I'm up to. And if you want to talk, call me anytime, okay? I hope your cowboy is as wonderful as you think he is, but if you want to talk about anything, I'm here for you."

"Thanks."

"I'll see you soon."

"See you."

After she ended the call, Sierra drained the rest of her coffee, then grabbed her keys and her purse. She might as well go over to the big cabin and start getting it ready.

~ ~ ~

Wade took one of the stools at the counter in the bakery and sat down heavily. He shouldn't be here. He should have let one of the guys come over to collect the bread order, but he'd needed to get out. He'd managed to keep himself busy most of the week. That wasn't hard to do at the lodge; there were always fires that needed putting out, guests that wanted a few minutes of his time, staff who had questions. But no matter how busy he'd been, he hadn't been able to keep his mind off the fact that his time with Sierra was coming to an end. It was crazy and he knew it.

Two weeks ago – less than that – he hadn't even known that she existed. When he'd first met her, he'd thought that she was way out of his league for a whole host of reasons. A week ago, he'd justified to himself that it was okay to spend time with her because she wasn't going to be around for long, and that in the short time she was here he could help her. He blew out a short breath. His intentions really had been good; he'd wanted to show her how a guy should treat her – and hopefully to teach her not to settle for anything less in the future. He really believed that. He didn't think it was all just bullshit that he'd told himself so that he didn't feel bad about taking advantage of her before she left. But right now, it felt like bullshit. All he'd done was get himself hopelessly caught up in her and he wasn't even going to have to watch her walk away. She wasn't leaving. And that might be even harder to deal with. Even that first night when he and Ford had found her by the side of the road, he'd known that he didn't want to say goodbye to her. Now, he didn't have to say goodbye, but he didn't get to keep her either.

Come Saturday he was going to have to step back. He was going to have to go from waking up with her every morning and coming home to her every night, to ... what? How was it going to work? He didn't even know. She'd still be right there on the ranch, but realistically there would be no reason for their paths to cross from one day – one week – to the next. She was going to have her hands full with two kids, and he ...? Well, he was going to have to just get back to life as normal, even though he wasn't sure that his life would ever feel normal again unless she was in it.

"Wade!"

He almost fell of his stool when someone shoved his shoulder. He spun around to find Chance standing there giving him a puzzled smile.

"Damn. Where the hell were you? I've been standing here for two minutes trying to get through to you."

Wade smiled through pursed lips. "Sorry. I was thinking."

Chance narrowed his eyes at him. "Let me guess; you were thinking about a certain cute little blonde?"

Wade blew out a sigh. "Yeah. For all the good it'll do me. I should just put her out of my mind and let it go."

Chance laughed. "Yeah, right. Because it's that easy?"

"Easy or not, I don't have any choice in the matter."

"Bullshit."

"Really? What do you even know? Actually, forget I asked that. Knowing this valley, you probably know as much as I do about the whole deal. So, why don't you go ahead and enlighten me?"

Chance pulled up a seat next to him and nodded at Spider when he held up a carafe of regular coffee. Once they each had a mug, Chance turned to Wade. "From what I hear, you've been shacked up with her since she ran away from her wedding. But that's all about to end this weekend because she's adopting a couple of kids. When the kids come, she's buying the big cabin, and you're out on your ear. The part where I get fuzzy on it all is when the rumors diverge."

Wade raised an eyebrow and waited for him to explain.

Chance shrugged. "You know what it's like. Listening to rumors is like playing the telephone game around here. Some parts get left out, and other parts get changed by whoever's doing the telling. One version has it that you were just making the most of a hot single chick while she was here, but everyone knows how you feel about kids so once they come, you're out. The other version has it that she was just using you to fulfill a cowboy fantasy until her kids get here."

Wade let out a short laugh. "God, I hate this place sometimes."

Chance gave him a wry smile. "It's not this place. It's people – they're the same everywhere. So, I'm guessing that neither of those two versions is the real truth. You want to tell me what is? Or do you want me to keep my nose out and talk horses and cattle instead? I can do that, too."

"I dunno, Chance. Honestly, it's kind of both and neither. First of all, she's not buying the big cabin. She's renting it."

"That makes more sense. I couldn't see your dad allowing a sale like that to go through."

Wade made a face. Neither could he. But he didn't want to get started on the subject of his dad – that would only piss him off. "No. He wouldn't. And as for Sierra and me." He shrugged. "I thought I could show her a good time before she had to go back to her real life. She's a sweetheart, and she needed someone to remind her that she's awesome."

"And that's all you wanted?"

"That's all I thought was possible."

"And now?"

"It's still all that's possible. Yeah, she has the kids coming. But even if …" He didn't continue with that train of thought. It didn't matter. Even if she wanted him to be part of their lives? Was that where he'd been going? Even if he wanted to? Hell, he didn't know, and he didn't need to. "She's a freaking billionaire who has a life of her own in California and a big ass company and who knows what else. I am what I am. My life's here. How the hell could anything work between us even if we both wanted it to?"

Chance took a sip of his coffee and smirked.

"What?" Wade was pissed. He hadn't expected Chance of all people to laugh at him.

"Think about it, dude! This is me you're talking to."

"I know! And I thought you'd be a bit more … I dunno, understanding."

Chance chuckled. "That's exactly what I am. You're just a bit slow on the uptake. You're trying to tell me that things can't work out between a cowboy and a sweet, smart, beautiful billionaire heiress?" He pushed his hat back and raised his eyebrows. "You're telling me that her living in California and you living here is some insurmountable obstacle?"

Wade continued glaring at him until realization dawned. "Shit."

"Yeah. You could be describing Hope and me, and we made it work." Chance chuckled again. "You're talking to the wrong guy if you want a pity party about the circumstances you and Sierra are facing. Well, all except one thing."

"What's that?"

"The kids. You don't want any and she's about become to a mother of two, right?"

"Wrong."

Chance frowned.

Wade looked all around before he spoke again. He wasn't sure why he wanted to tell Chance when he'd never bothered to correct his own family's assumptions about his views on kids, and he sure as hell didn't want anyone else overhearing what he had to say. "It's not that I don't want kids."

Chance narrowed his eyes. "But that was why …"

"That was just a rumor that I never bothered to correct."

Chance sat back. "Damn. So why have you always let everyone believe that you and Josie broke up because she wanted kids and you didn't?"

Wade blew out a sigh and looked around again. "Because it was easier to let people believe that than to explain that I just didn't see her as the mother of my kids."

Chance nodded slowly. "I can't say as I blame you. I never did like her."

Wade let out a short laugh. "Yeah. I've heard that a lot over the last few years."

"But she's the past. What are you going to do about your future?"

"Hell if I know. You got any suggestions for me?"

Chance held his gaze for a few moments. "I do, but I don't know if you'll like it."

"Fire away."

"Be honest with her. Tell her everything. Tell her how you feel about her, about kids, about the future – but more than that, tell her everything you don't know, too. That's just as important, maybe even more so. At least, it was for me and Hope. I knew I loved her, but I didn't know if I could make it work. She knew she wanted to be with me, but she didn't know if she could move here and leave her whole life behind.

Loving someone is powerful but knowing all their fears and faults and working with them is even more powerful."

"I guess."

Chance took another sip of his coffee. "You keep guessing if you want. But if you're for real about Sierra – and I think you are or I wouldn't be sitting here spouting all this deep and meaningful shit – then you're going to have to take me at my word and try it."

"Be honest about what I know and about what I don't know?"

"Yup." Chance shrugged, the gesture indicating that the time for deep and meaningful shit was over.

Wade gave him a rueful smile. "You realize you sound like fucking Yoda, right?"

"Follow these lessons you must," Chance said with a laugh and in the worst Yoda impression that Wade had ever heard.

Chapter Nineteen

"I talked to Barney today." It was the last thing that Sierra wanted to talk about with Wade, but it was all she could think of. Conversation between them had gotten more difficult over the last couple of days. Not that they were having difficult conversations, but they weren't having many at all. At least, not about anything that mattered. They'd spent the last couple of evenings here in the cabin watching movies mostly in silence. When they talked it was about the movie, or about little things that had happened during the day. It felt as though they were trying to avoid the future, so they kept their focus narrowed in on the present moment. Tonight was going to be their last night together here like this and she couldn't stand the thought of letting it go by without really talking – without really being together.

Wade came back from the kitchen where he'd been putting the dishes away. He sat down beside her on the sofa, not wrapping his arm around her but sitting sideways to face her. It felt like just another way he was distancing himself from her, and it made her heart hurt.

"What did he have to say? Is there any news on Jared?"

She blew out a sigh. "No. They have a team of investigators working on it, but they haven't been able to find anything. It's like he and Lori just disappeared off the face of the Earth when they left Park City."

"Are you scared?" He rested his hand on her leg, and it reminded her of her first few evenings here, before they'd made love.

She covered his hand with hers and took a deep breath. The children were arriving tomorrow. Amelia was already here. She'd been staying in a hotel near the entrance to Yellowstone, but she was coming up tomorrow, to meet the children and possibly to stay at the big cabin. Everything was about to change, and Sierra had decided that she wanted and needed to be honest with Wade before it did. "I am scared."

His hand tightened around her leg, but she pressed on before he could speak.

"I'm not scared of Jared. I don't think that he'll come after me now. Why would he? What would be the point? But I am scared ..." She stopped and swallowed. "I'm scared about what's going to happen between you and me."

His Adam's apple bobbed up and down before he spoke. "What are you scared of?"

"I'm going to miss you." She looked around the cabin. "I'm going to miss this. I don't want to say goodbye to you."

The lines around his eyes deepened, and he looked almost as though he was in pain. "It's not goodbye, Sierra. We'll still see each other. Anything you want, anything you need." He smiled, but it looked forced. "It's like I said at the beginning, whatever you want, tell me and I'm on it."

"I know. I don't think that you're going to abandon me. But it won't be the same, will it? And I don't want things to change."

He nodded sadly. "I don't either. But let's be honest, darlin'; things were always going to have to change for us."

"What do you mean?"

"That what we've had this last couple weeks, it couldn't ever have been anything else."

"It couldn't?" Her heart felt as though it was trying to beat out of her chest. Had she been stupid? Had she gotten so caught up in him and the way she felt about him that she'd missed the fact that he was only in it for two weeks? No. She hadn't. She didn't believe that.

He gave her a sad smile. "I'm not saying that I didn't want it to be something more. But you're … well, you're you, and I'm me. And …" He shrugged. "Your life is in San Francisco. Mine's here. You're a beautiful, talented artist. I'm just a cowboy." He blew out a sigh. "And even though we've never talked about it, you're kinda wealthy, and I'm kinda not."

"But that doesn't matter!"

He blew out a sigh. "It does, though, doesn't it? You're used to a life that I can't give you."

She could feel tears pricking behind her eyes. "But that life can't give me the kind of happiness I've found with you." She sucked in a deep breath to steady herself. "So, even if it weren't for the children, you wouldn't want … you don't …" She didn't even know how to ask. She'd been so caught up in the fact that he didn't want children that she'd blinded herself to everything else. She was stupid. She must be.

"Sierra, come here, darlin'. Don't cry."

He wrapped her up in his arms and she burrowed into him. She might be stupid. He might not want her, but she couldn't help wanting to get as close to him as she could. A sob escaped from her lips as she realized that this would probably be the last time.

"I'm going to tell you the truth. I should have done it before now. Chance told me that I should tell you earlier this week, but I didn't. I didn't want you to feel like I was pressuring you, and I'm not. It's just … seeing you cry … knowing that you think I don't want you? It kills me. I do want you. The truth is, and you have to remember that I'm not asking you for anything, the truth is …"

She held her breath as she waited. What was he going to say? Was he going to tell her that he cared about her? That he couldn't be with her because of the children? That he was going back to Josie? All those possibilities seemed equally likely and equally ridiculous at the same time.

"I don't know if I can be what you need."

Her heart leapt with hope before it sank again. "Are you talking about the children?"

She felt him nod. "Yeah."

That was the one thing she couldn't fight. It broke her heart, but she knew she had to let him go. She had to. It didn't matter if she'd gone and fallen in love with him. That was her burden to bear. It had happened way too fast, and she knew that it would take a heck of a lot longer to get over him – if she ever did. But there was no way around what he was saying. No way she would ever ask him to be part of the children's lives if he didn't want to be. It just wouldn't be fair to them or to him.

She tightened her arms around him and nodded against his chest. "Okay." She wanted to scream that it wasn't okay. She wanted to cry and beg him to see things differently, to meet them first and at least give them a chance. But she wouldn't do that to him, or to them.

"What's okay?"

She buried her face deeper in his chest. She couldn't look at him. "I can't be what you need either. You're right. We're too different. Our lives are too different. It's better this way. I really do hope that we'll always be friends. But I suppose, after tonight, this is it for us."

She felt him stiffen beside her. It was hard to say the words, and she imagined it would be hard for him to hear them, too. But they both knew it was for the best. Even if she could feel her heart breaking. She tightened her arms around him. "Take me to bed, Wade. Make love to me one last time?"

He hesitated for a moment, and then stood before scooping her up off the sofa and carrying her through to the bedroom. It just made her cry harder. She'd never even allowed herself to daydream about having a man who would treat her the way he did, and now that she'd found him, she had to let him go.

~ ~ ~

Wade's head was spinning. He wasn't even sure how they'd ended up at goodbye. He'd been struggling ever since his chat with Chance earlier in the week. He'd wanted to just come out and tell her that he'd fallen in love with her, and that he wanted to see if they could make something work – something that would include the children. He'd kept putting it off, not wanting her to feel like he was pressuring her for something that she didn't want to give. He wanted her to be able to make her own decisions, and if he was honest, he'd been hoping that she'd be honest with him about how she felt – maybe even tell him that she felt the same way he did.

He shouldn't have left it until tonight. He knew that. But he'd hoped that she'd like the idea of him wanting to be a part of the kids' lives, too. He'd thought long and hard about it, and he'd reached the conclusion that he could maybe be good for them. He knew he'd gone about it the wrong way. He'd wanted to tell her that he loved her and that he was going to love the kids, too. That if she'd let him, he'd do everything in his power to make sure they had a good life. But he'd started out with being honest – with saying that he didn't know for sure if he could be what she needed – and that was all it had taken for her to finally be honest with him.

He was still reeling as he laid her down on the bed. Instead of the conversation he'd hoped to start about how neither of them knew for sure what they could and couldn't be and do, she'd gone right ahead and told him that she couldn't be what he needed either. And now here they were at goodbye. She wanted him to make love to her, and his heart felt like it cracked in two as he remembered the look on her face when she said *one last time.* He kicked his boots off before climbing onto the bed beside her. He couldn't deal with his emotions right now, but he could give her what she'd asked him for. He'd make it good for her. He'd make it good for himself, too. He had to – it was going to have to last him a lifetime.

As soon as he was next to her, she wrapped herself around him. Her lips sought his and the kiss tasted of tears. He would have stayed there, content to hold her close and lose himself in that kiss, but she struggled with his shirt and then with his buckle and the zipper on his jeans. She showed none of the hesitation and uncertainty that she had when he first met her. She didn't wait for his lead. Her cheeks didn't even color up when she broke away and pulled her shirt off. It was bittersweet to know that he'd been able to do that much for her.

"I want to be naked with you," she breathed.

He wanted to be naked with her, too. He forced himself to narrow his focus down to this moment. There'd be plenty of time for regrets and for sadness over what might have been – he had the rest of his life for that. If this was his only night left with her, he wasn't going to waste a moment of it by not being fully present.

He got rid of his clothes and then tugged her jeans and panties down over her hips before pulling them off and throwing them across the room. She'd already taken care of her top and bra, so when he was done, she lay beautifully naked before him.

Her eyes shone with tears as she looked up at him. Flashes of emotion shone in the deep dark gray. He ran his finger down her cheek and then on down between her breasts. He rested his hand on the curve of her stomach and leaned down to brush a kiss over her lips. "You're beautiful."

"Thank you."

He had to tear his gaze away from hers. He could feel the sting of tears behind his eyes. She didn't need to see that. He was proud of her for knowing what she wanted, even though it wasn't him. He didn't want to make her feel bad by letting her see how much it hurt.

He dropped his head, and closing both hands around her breasts, he took one taut peak into his mouth. He worked her with his lips and tongue, lavishing attention on one breast then the other until she was moaning and writhing underneath him.

"Please, Wade. I want you."

He closed his eyes. He'd planned to work his way down her body using his hands and mouth to take her there over and over before he finally sank himself inside her. But the need in her voice tugged at his insides. He reached over to the nightstand for a condom and rolled it on.

"Do you want to ride me?" He wanted this last time to be whatever she wanted it to be. Yeah, the memory would have to last him a lifetime, but what he would cherish most about it was knowing how far she'd come in the short time they'd shared. The first time they'd been together she hadn't wanted to *get there* before him – hadn't been sure if she'd be able to come more than once. Since then, her confidence had grown and she'd gotten adventurous, climbing on and riding him when she wanted to. He closed his eyes when he remembered looking up from rolling on a condom and finding her on all fours, ass in the air, looking back at him with flushed cheeks and a smile – asking if they could try it that way.

She shook her head and held her arms up to him. "No. I want you to love me."

He closed his eyes again, and bit down on his bottom lip to stop himself from telling her that he did. His head wanted to deny that thought, wanted to list out all the reasons why this wasn't really love, but his heart knew better – it wasn't about reasons, it was a feeling, and it wouldn't be denied. Come tomorrow, he'd have to bury it, but he wouldn't deny it.

Still, he couldn't burden Sierra with it. So, he propped himself up on one elbow and curled his other arm around her, drawing her closer until he leaned over her and brushed his lips over hers. She traced her fingers down his chest and kept going until they curled around him, but he caught her hand and pinned it to the bed beside her head as he covered her body with his.

She spread her legs wider, rocking her hips, trying to position him at her entrance. He had to smile. "Are you trying to rush me?"

She smiled back, but her eyes still shone with tears. "I am. I want you, Wade. I want you inside me. I want you to make love to me all night long, and the sooner we get started, the better."

He let go of her hand and slid his hand under her ass, opening her wider and lifting her hips to receive him as he pressed inside. He wanted to take it slowly, wanted to savor every moment of the way her body yielded to him. How she tensed at first, making it feel impossible that she'd ever accommodate him and then how with one final push he was seated deep inside, and her body welcomed him home. Shit. She wasn't home. She just felt like it.

Her arms came up around his neck and she pulled him down into a kiss. Her mouth mirrored the movements of her body – opening up to him, welcoming him inside, claiming him. That's how it felt. But she wasn't. He kissed her deeper and thrust his way deeper inside her, loving the way her legs curled around him and she moaned his name.

He shut his mind down and got lost in the feel of her, got lost in the need to drive her toward pleasure. He pushed harder and deeper, loving the desperate noises she made. He recognized his own voice mingling with hers, speaking her name and over and over as they drove each other higher and higher. They pushed each other closer and closer to the edge, until she gasped and her whole body quivered beneath him, her inner muscles clamping around him, drawing him deeper and demanding his release. One more thrust and he froze, holding himself deep as waves of pleasure swept through him and into her. It felt like an eternity that her muscles fluttered around him, milking him for all he had to give – and he gave it all. When he finally slumped down over her, he was spent.

She pressed a kiss to his cheek, and he turned and captured her lips in a tender kiss that he wished could tell her how he felt. It couldn't though; he couldn't tell her, because she didn't need to know. And that thought brought him back to reality. And reality meant taking care of practical details once the magic of the moment was gone. The magic of the last couple weeks would leave plenty of details to take care of tomorrow. But right now, the practical detail he had to see to was the condom. He stroked her cheek and kissed the tip of her nose before muttering, "Be right back."

Chapter Twenty

When Sierra woke the next morning, she snuggled closer into Wade's side. How could she have grown so used to sleeping with him and waking up with him in such a short time? She'd never felt this comfortable with Jared. Even in the beginning, she'd felt like there was an invisible barrier down the middle of the bed, and there had been many mornings that she found herself waking up clinging to the edge on her side. They hadn't slept together every night either. He used to say that it was easier to stay at his place, close to the office because he worked so late. Now, she realized that he probably spent at least some of those nights with Lori.

Yet, in these last couple of weeks with Wade they'd slept together every night, and every morning she woke up pressed into his side. He always held her, his arm around her waist, his leg curled over hers, and she felt like a little creature always trying to burrow deeper into his warmth. She squeezed her eyes tight shut, wishing she could make this moment last. Once they got up this morning, that would be it. She hadn't gotten much sleep. They'd made love two more times, waking up and finding each other, coming together without words, just a desperate need to get as close as two people could. It wasn't just her, either. Wade felt it, too. She knew he did. He might think that he couldn't be what she needed him to be, but in so many ways he already was.

His arm tightened around her, drawing her closer and she went, wrapping her arms around him and wishing that this could have turned out differently.

He greeted her with a kiss and that warm smile of his that she knew she'd never forget. Of course, she'd still get to see him smile. She'd still be here, still see him; she didn't doubt that he'd be there for her like he said he would. But it wouldn't be the same. She had to make a start on her new life – her life as a mom to two children she'd never even met before, and him? Well, he'd be getting on with his life, too. And that smile, the way he looked at her in the mornings like this, the warmth she saw in his eyes for her, that wouldn't be there anymore.

She pressed her face into his neck and kissed him, making him shiver. She pressed closer, hoping that he might want to share that closeness one more time before they got up, but he was tense, and he shifted his hips away from her.

"What's the plan for today, darlin'?"

This was it then. If he wanted to move them onto whatever came next, she wasn't going to beg him to stay in their own little bubble for a little longer. She forced herself to smile and look up at him.

"Dax said that they should be here around two. I thought I should go over to the cabin and make sure everything's ready. I want to bake some cookies. Do you think that's silly? I just … the smell of fresh-baked cookies makes me feel like home. I thought it'd be nice for them …" She stopped. She'd been so caught up in Wade and everything that might or might not happen between them that she was worried she hadn't given enough thought to Mateo and Maya. She wanted to make this move as easy as it could be for them. She wanted them to know that they were safe – and loved. But she wasn't sure that she knew how.

Wade brushed a strand of hair off her cheek and tucked it behind her ear. "I don't think it's silly. I think it's a great idea. And don't worry, Sierra. You're going to do great. They're the luckiest little people on Earth that they get to be with you. You're going to be a wonderful mom to them. They're going to have a great life with you. Don't doubt it for a minute. I don't."

She had to swallow the lump that formed in her throat. She loved that he was reassuring her, but she couldn't help wishing that he wanted to be with her, that he thought he could have a great life with her, too. But he didn't. "Thanks," was all she trusted herself to say.

~ ~ ~

Ford frowned when he came into the kitchen at the big house and found Wade sitting at the table, staring into the bottom of an empty water glass.

"What are you doing here?"

Wade shrugged.

"Where's Sierra? What time are the kids coming?"

"She's at the cabin. Her friend, Amelia, is there with her. They're baking cookies. Dax is supposed to arrive with the kids at about two."

Ford put his hands on his hips and held Wade's gaze but didn't speak.

"What?"

"What are you doing here?"

"I brought my stuff back."

"You're moving back in?"

"Yeah. I'll finish the work on the little cabin and get it on the books as soon as I can. We're booked up at the lodge and all the other cabins for the rest of the summer, and we still get enough inquiries that we should be able to book the cabin out as soon as it's ready, too."

"And what's happening with you and Sierra?"

Wade looked away. It was a simple question, and it had an easy answer. But his throat tightened with emotion, not wanting to say the one word.

"Well?"

"Nothing."

"Nothing?" Ford pulled out a chair and turned it around. He rested his arms on the back and fixed Wade with a stony look. "You're going let her go – just like that?"

Wade blew out a sigh. "I wasn't going to. I thought long and hard about it. I reached the conclusion that maybe I could be good for her."

"Hmph. That doesn't take much figuring out."

"Maybe. But I also figured out that maybe I could be good for those kids, too, you know? I mean, they've lost everything. They've fallen on their feet with Sierra, but I thought maybe I could be good for them. If we were … if she and I were together … it could be good for them to have a man in their lives. I mean, I know they don't need it. I know she doesn't need me, but I thought …"

"So, what went wrong? If you were thinking that way, why are you sitting over here looking like the world just ended while she's over there baking cookies with her friend?"

"I guess I was so caught up in trying to figure out if I could be good for her, that I forgot to take into account what she thought. Last night I told her that I didn't know if I could be what she needs. Ford, I was hedging. I told her I didn't know if I *could* be, and I was about to tell that I *want* to be. But she cut me off and told me that she didn't know if she could be what I need either. That I was right and we're too different. That our lives are too different, and it's better this way."

"Oh, for fuck's sake!"

"What?" Wade stared at his brother. He hadn't exactly been expecting sympathy, but Ford's expression looked like he was pissed.

Ford pressed his fingers to his temples and circled them as if he was trying to rub away a headache. "And you believed her?"

"Why wouldn't I?"

"Jesus, Wade. Think about it. Sierra's been crazy about you since the minute she saw you. I thought she was cute, standing by the side of the road when we found her. But then she turned and looked at you. When you smiled at her, and she smiled back, she went from looking cute to beautiful. I know I'm the last person you'd expect to say this, but the way she reacted to you made me believe in love at first sight."

Wade just stared at him.

"Don't look at me like that. I'm not yanking your chain. I'm deadly serious. I know I gave you shit in the beginning but that was mostly because I couldn't believe myself – that *I* could believe in love at first sight. But damn! You smiled at her, she lit up. She told you what her deal was, and you were a goner. Wrapping her up in your jacket, telling me you wanted to keep her. I've been waiting to see how this would pan out, but I sure as hell didn't expect this."

"And what exactly is this?"

"You screwing it up by being too much of a pussy to tell her how you feel, and then worse than that, believing her when she backs off."

Wade's heart was thudding in his chest. "You think that's what happened?"

"Yup."

"But she said that we're too different. That our lives are too different."

"Uh-huh. And that's true. And if I've got this right, you didn't give her any reason to believe that you'd be interested in living the kind of life that she's going to have, did you?"

"No. I was going to tell her what I'd been thinking about the kids and about wanting to try to keep things going between us. But …"

"But you started out by saying that you don't know if you can be what she needs?"

"Yeah."

"And you wonder why she backed right off? She put herself out there in a big way, spending time with you the way she has since she arrived. It has to have been hard for her. No matter how she feels about you, she has to have been second-guessing herself. I know a lot has happened in the last couple weeks, but even at this minute she's supposed to be on her honeymoon – with a guy who wanted to kill her."

Wade blew out a sigh.

"Do you think that maybe she's a little leery? That hearing you say that you don't think you can be what she wants might be enough to send her back into her shell? That you saying that might make her second guess everything – about herself and her judgment as well as about you and your intentions."

"Shit." Wade rested his elbows on the table and hung his head between his hands. "You think that's what happened?"

"I can't say for sure. I mean, it's possible that she came to her senses and wondered what the hell she was doing wasting her time with an asshole like you." Ford smirked at him. "But I don't think that's it, bro. I think your uncertainty scared her off and she's covering her ass. She probably doesn't want to ask too much of you, doesn't want you to be around the kids if you're not going to be there for them. And I'd guess that you hurt her."

Wade closed his eyes. He hated the thought of hurting Sierra more than anything. "What if I'm right and she's genuinely just not interested in anything more than we already had?"

Ford shrugged. "Then you're no worse off than you are right now. But I seriously think you should talk to her and make sure. Worst case scenario is you make a fool of yourself. You tell her how you really feel, what you want for the two of you, and she repeats what she said last night. Like I said, you'll be no worse off than you are right now – in fact you'll be better off because you'll know for sure. Right?"

"Right. But what do I do? Should I go see her now before the kids arrive – or when? Would it be fair to make her talk about it all when she's focused on Mateo and Maya arriving?"

Ford shrugged. "That's up to you."

Wade made a face at him. "I can't believe you don't have an opinion."

Ford chuckled. "Okay. I do. I think you should wait. Let the kids arrive, let them get settled in. But go over there later today, don't leave it too long. If you're going to be part of their lives, you should meet the kids straight away."

Wade sucked in a deep breath. "Okay. But how am I going to talk to her about all this stuff in front of them?"

"You said her friend's with her?"

"Yeah. Amelia."

"Okay. In that case, I'll come with you."

Wade gave him a puzzled look.

"No way would I offer to be left alone with two small kids while you and Sierra talk. But if her friend's there as well, then I'll play with the kids, and she can supervise."

Wade couldn't help but laugh. "How can you make out that you always need someone else to take care of things? You did the same when we met Sierra; made out like you couldn't deal with it."

Ford shrugged. "I've never said that I can't – just that I don't want to."

"Fair enough. I appreciate it. What time do you think we should go?"

"I'll give her a call about five and ask if it's okay to stop by."

"*You* will?"

"Yup. She won't say no to me, and we don't want you screwing things up before we even get there."

"I guess. Thanks, bro."

"Thank me when it works out."

Wade smiled, liking that he'd said *when* it works out, not *if*.

~ ~ ~

Sierra leaned back against the kitchen counter, her eyes never leaving the two children who sat huddled together on the sofa in the den. "They seem so small; I thought they'd be bigger."

Dax nodded beside her. "I don't know much about kids, but the woman at the orphanage said they were small for their age."

Sierra shuddered. "I hate that they were in an orphanage. That's horrible."

Dax chuckled. "Get over it, Sierra. Don't go imagining they were dressed in rags and covered in coal dust. It was a good place. I made damned sure of it. They had to stay somewhere while we got everything taken care of."

She turned to him; he looked tired and older. "And everything is taken care of now?"

He nodded but didn't meet her gaze. "Yeah. A lot of people called in a lot of favors for those two little guys out there. All the paperwork has been taken care of as far as it can be; they're here legally. Once the adoption goes through, it'll take two years and then they'll automatically be granted citizenship."

She nodded. She knew all of that. She'd done a lot of research and read all about it when Dax had first told her about the children – back when he'd said that he was going to take them himself. She'd known they'd be better off with her. Dax was a good man, but he was a military man. She wasn't convinced that he would have been able to adopt them. He would've had to give up his career just to try.

"Are you sure you're sure about this?" He looked tense. "I can still –"

She smiled. "No, Dax. You can't and you don't need to. They're here. I love them already. I'm going to give them a good life. I promise you."

"I don't doubt it. What worries me is if it will be a good life for you. What will you be giving up?"

She looked away. She couldn't allow herself to think about Wade. Instead, she made herself smile and turn back to him. "In case you've forgotten, I've just had a narrow escape from almost getting into a bad marriage."

He didn't smile back. "And a narrow escape from death. Dammit, Sierra." He shook his head. "You know I'm going to hunt that bastard down."

"Maybe you won't need to. Maybe they'll find him, and he'll go to prison."

"They don't have any leads on him yet."

"Have you talked to Barney?"

Dax nodded. "He has a team of investigators on it, but I'm thinking I might call in some favors and see what I can do."

Sierra didn't like the sound of that. "I don't want you using up your favors for me."

"It's for me, too, Sierra. I'll sleep better knowing that there's no chance of him coming after you."

"You think he might? What about the children?"

Dax sighed. "Honestly? I think he's long gone. I wouldn't leave the kids with you otherwise. But after what he did, what he had planned for you? I'd take great pleasure in making sure that he can't ever come back."

Sierra didn't like to think too hard about what Dax did. She knew in general that he and his team made sure bad guys weren't able to hurt people ever again. But she didn't like to dwell on what that really meant – he killed people. Only bad people, but still. She knew it was his job, it'd been Seb's job, too. But it was hard for her to reconcile that the laughing, joking, caring guys she'd grown up with had gone on to become trained killers.

"How long's Amelia going to stay?"

She was grateful that Dax moved the conversation on. "She hasn't decided yet. She's open to staying as long as I need her."

"That's good. And how are you getting along with the MacFarlands? I didn't know if any of them would be here with you."

Sierra lifted a shoulder. "Janey said that she'd stop by tomorrow. She's the vet. She has a mama dog who's about to give birth. I think I'd like to take the mama in once she's ready, and maybe keep one of the puppies for the children. What do you think?"

"It could be a good idea. They had a dog." Dax shook his head. "The bastards who killed their dad killed the dog, too. It could go either way. It might make them happy to get a new one or make them sad for what they lost."

Sierra sighed. "We'll have to play it by ear then. We should get back in there. How long are you going to stay? I set up one of the guest rooms for you."

"I'm hoping I'll get at least a few days, but you know what it's like. If I get the call, I'll have to go."

Sierra did know, but she was hoping that he wouldn't get any calls, and that he'd be able to stay to help Mateo and Maya settle in. "I guess I'll just have to keep my fingers crossed."

Dax pulled her in for a hug and dropped a kiss on the top of her head. He'd always treated her that way; he was like another big brother and had been for most of her life. All she could think of now though was that his hug didn't feel anything like Wade's did. She missed Wade already and she'd only seen him this morning.

As Dax let her go, her phone rang, and she reached for it. "Oh."

Dax frowned. "Problem?"

"No. Not at all. It's Ford."

"Okay. I'll let you get it. Can I speak to him when you're done?"

"Sure. If you want."

He grinned at her. "Yep, sorry. I'm going to pull the big brother card and make sure that these guys are on the same page about keeping an eye on you."

She rolled her eyes at him, but she was glad that he was still looking out for her.

"Hi, Ford."

"Hey, Sierra. I just wanted to check in on you. How's it going? I saw the SUV out front of the cabin, so I'm assuming Dax and the kids arrived okay?"

"They did, thank you. In fact, Dax asked if he could have a word with you, if that's all right?"

"That'd be great. I was calling to see if we could come over. Of course, we want to meet the kids and to meet Dax and have a chat with him. Would that be all right with you?"

"Yes." Her heart was hammering. She wanted to ask who he meant when he said *we*, but she didn't. If Wade were coming, he would have called her himself – wouldn't he? Or was this how things were going to go between them now? Gosh, she hoped not. She didn't want him to be just one of the brothers. "Of course."

"Is now a good time?"

"Um. That'll be fine." She could have used more time to prepare herself if she was about to see Wade. But then again, she didn't need to waste any time lost in her head about how things might be. It was better to get it over with.

"Okay. We'll see you in a few."

She ended the call and hurried back out to the great room. Mateo and Maya were still huddled together on the sofa. Mateo had his arm around his little sister, and she was nestled as close into his side as she could get.

They looked a little more relaxed now than they had when they first arrived. Mateo was smiling as he watched Dax race a little plastic car around the carpet. Maya's huge brown eyes looked up at Sierra. She didn't look as terrified as she had at first. She hadn't spoken a word, but from what Dax had said, she didn't talk. Sierra's heart melted when the little girl smiled at her. She smiled back and had to stop herself from trying to hug her. Dax said that the orphanage had told him that they should wait and let the children be the ones to initiate physical contact.

It made sense; she didn't want to overwhelm or frighten them, but Sierra ached to hold Maya and reassure her. Instead, she sat down on the sofa beside her and smiled as she spoke. "I just talked to one of my friends and he's coming over to see us. Is that okay with you?"

Maya leaned closer into her brother's side, and Mateo looked at Sierra. "Is he one of the good men?"

"Yes," she gave him what she hoped was a reassuring smile, "his name is Ford, and he's one of the brothers who own this ranch."

Mateo shot a look at Dax. "The good men?"

"Yes. The good men. There are four brothers who live here, remember? Ford, Wade, Tanner, and Tyler."

Mateo nodded. "Okay."

Sierra watched the exchange with interest.

Dax looked at her and then Amelia, who'd been sitting quietly on Mateo's other side the whole time. "I've explained to them that the MacFarlands own the ranch and that they are good men. They will protect all of you if you need it. And Mateo and Maya will never leave the ranch unless one of them is with you."

Sierra did a double take. "Excuse me?"

Dax gave her a stern look. "You heard me, Si." He slid his gaze toward the children and then met hers again. "Mateo and Maya have lived through a lot. They're safe here with you on the ranch. But if they ever need to leave the ranch for anything, one of the MacFarlands will go with you."

She didn't know what to say to that. What about school? It was a little way off yet, but he could hardly expect one of the MacFarlands to make the school run every day. She understood that they'd need to feel safe, but this felt like a bit much.

At that moment, a knock sounded on the front door, and Maya made a little squeak as she ducked for the back of the sofa and Mateo tucked her behind him.

It made Sierra's heart hurt for them. "It's okay. It'll be Ford." She tried to reassure them.

Mateo's eyes were huge when he looked up at her. "You must check."

She nodded rapidly. "Don't worry. I will. There's a peephole in the door."

He watched her warily, and when she reached the door, she made a big show of looking through the peephole carefully. She turned back and nodded, giving Mateo the thumbs up before she opened the door. "It's okay. It is Ford. And I checked. His brother Wade is with him." She added that part so that he'd be prepared for two men to come in instead of one – and because she was both relieved and nervous to see Wade was out there.

Amelia caught her gaze. Amelia had held her while she cried over Wade this morning, so Sierra was a little apprehensive about what kind of welcome she'd give him. But that was the least of her worries right now. It was more important that Mateo and Maya should meet Ford and Wade and hopefully start to trust them. And then she needed to figure out what Dax was thinking, trying to rope them in to chaperoning any trips off the ranch.

Chapter Twenty-One

Wade hadn't known what to expect when he and Ford arrived at the cabin. He didn't know what kind of reception he'd get from Sierra's friend, Amelia. He was curious about Dax; from everything Sierra had said, he'd played a big brother role for most of her life, but Wade couldn't help wondering if there was more to it than that. He knew that was probably dumb, but his mind was skipping around frantically. He was nervous because most of all, he didn't know what to expect from Sierra. He hoped with all his heart that Ford was right, that he'd been the one to chase her away by not being upfront about how he felt. That she really did want to be with him and that she'd backed off because when he'd said that he didn't know if he *could* be what she needed, she thought that he meant he didn't *want* to be.

She'd greeted him with a smile when he and Ford came in, but she hadn't met his gaze. Amelia had been polite, not frosty toward him, but not warm either. Dax seemed like a good guy. But out of all of them, it was the two little people on the sofa who'd caught and held his attention. Mateo was more than wary, he was scared, but he was doing his best to protect his little sister and to speak for both of them.

When Sierra offered to get drinks for everyone, Dax and Ford had followed her into the kitchen. Wade hadn't gone after them. He wanted to talk to Sierra, but he'd have to wait until he could get her alone for that. He looked back at the kids on the sofa, wanting nothing more than to wrap his arms around them both. They looked like they could use all the hugs they could get. But he knew better. Instead, he plonked himself down on the floor in front of them and picked up a little car that was lying on the rug.

"This yours?" he asked Mateo.

The little boy shook his head.

"It is, you know," said Amelia. "All the toys that are here, they're for you. Sierra got them for you."

Mateo slid his gaze toward her and then looked back at Wade and shrugged. Poor little guy was probably just trying to figure what the deal was, and who could blame him?

Wade smiled at him. "Do you like cars?"

Mateo shrugged again.

Wade pursed his lips and rubbed his chin, wanting to let the kid know that he was thinking hard. "Do you like horses?"

Mateo's eyes widened and a hint of a smile touched his lips before he shut it down and shrugged.

That was interesting. It seemed he did like horses, but he didn't want to admit it. Okay, that was something to work with.

Maya looked up at her brother. She didn't speak, but he answered her as if she had. "Horses."

Wade's throat tightened with emotion when the little girl turned big brown eyes on him and smiled. She nodded her head twice and then hid her face behind her brother again.

Well, how about that? They were both interested in the one thing he knew he could help them with. He grinned. "Did Dax tell you that we have horses here?"

Mateo nodded and glanced toward the kitchen. "Yes. This is a ranch. There are horses and cows …" His eyebrows drew together, and he held Wade's gaze. "And good men who will keep us safe."

Wade looked him in the eye and nodded. "That's right. We will. There's me, I'm Wade." He jerked his chin toward the kitchen. "That's Ford, and then there's –"

"Tanner and Tyler. Dax told me."

"That's good. And he's right, you know. All four of us will look out for you. And if you like horses, maybe you want to learn to ride?"

The kid's eyes grew wide again, and Wade could see the longing in them. "You are a cowboy?"

"Yup." Wade pushed the brim of his hat back and smiled. "We all are. And I reckon if you're going to live here, you'll be one too – if you want?"

For the first time, a big smile spread over Mateo's face. Maya peeked up at him and whether she knew what they were talking about or not, it seemed that just seeing happiness on her brother's face was enough to make her feel the same way. She smiled big, too, and in that moment, Wade knew he was a goner. He'd do whatever it took to make them both keep smiling that way.

He looked at Maya. "Do you want to ride horses and be a cowgirl, too?"

She nodded rapidly, her smile growing even bigger.

Amelia cleared her throat. Wade had forgotten that she was even there. When he looked her way, he was relieved to see her smile and give him a slight nod. He was glad she approved, but this wasn't about winning anyone's approval, not even Sierra's. Even if she didn't want to be with him, it wouldn't affect how he felt about these two. He was going to do everything in his power to make sure that their lives got better now that they were here.

He watched Maya wriggle her way to the edge of the sofa and climb down. She stood in front of him for a moment and then tentatively held her arms out. Wade was sitting on the floor cross-legged, still holding the little car. He dropped it and held his arms out to her, inviting her to sit, but not wanting to scare her. She reminded him of a skittish filly, she was curious, wanting to come in for affection, but ready to bolt. She came closer and then sat down on one of his legs, tucking her little arm around his waist and hiding her face in his chest. Mateo sprang after her, and Wade was prepared for him to tear her away. He'd understand if the little guy wanted to keep her safe until he knew Wade better. Instead, Mateo sat on his other leg and threw his arms around his neck.

Wade had to close his eyes and swallow hard as he hugged the two of them to him. It seemed that Mateo took the lead on almost everything, but he was as desperate for affection as Maya was. As he sat there holding them both close, he made them a silent vow that he'd always be there for them. He hadn't thought he believed in love at first sight, even when Ford had talked about him and Sierra earlier. But these two little people had made a believer out of him. He already knew that he loved them, and he'd do anything for them.

"Oh my!"

He opened his eyes in a hurry at Sierra's shocked tone. Shit. He hoped that she didn't mind what she was seeing. If she really didn't want to be with him, they were going to have a problem, because not only did he want to be with her, he now knew that he wanted to be with Mateo and Maya, too.

She'd come out of the kitchen with Ford and Dax just behind her. She was staring at him and the kids, and it didn't look like she had a problem. She had a tender look on her face and her hand had come up to cover her heart. Dax and Ford were grinning at him from behind her. He didn't care if they thought it was funny. He thought it was amazing.

No one spoke for a few moments, then Amelia cleared her throat again. "Dax, I was wondering if you could take me into town? There are a few things I need, and I could use your advice."

Wade's first thought was that maybe she wanted to buy herself a gun. That was the only thing he could think that she'd need Dax's advice for.

"Sure. Do you want to go now?"

"Yes." She got to her feet immediately.

"And I should give you both a tour of the ranch on your way out," said Ford. He winked at Wade. "You can find your way home on your own, right?"

It finally dawned on him that they were all clearing out to leave him and Sierra alone with the kids. He nodded. He wanted to tell his brother that if were up to him, he already was home — his family was complete right here. And now he wanted to get started on building them a good life. But since he could hardly say that in front of the kids, and he didn't even know if Sierra still wanted him, he made do with a nod and a quick, "Sure thing," that sounded gruff, even to his own ears.

Sierra sat and watched the children eat. She'd offered them a sandwich then they first arrived but they'd both refused. She'd kept offering snacks and veggies and fruit, anything that might tempt them, but she didn't want to force them.

After everyone else had left, they'd both stuck close to Wade. Maya had given her a couple more smiles and Mateo looked as though he was starting to trust her a little, maybe. But there was no question that they trusted Wade. And it seemed that he adored them. Her heart had melted at the sight of the three of them sitting on the floor earlier. She was struggling to catch up. She'd thought that he didn't want children – and she supposed that just because he was so good with them, it didn't necessarily mean that he wanted the responsibility of children; that was a different matter. But he certainly seemed to have a way with these two.

They were munching happily on quesadillas that he'd made for them. While she'd been trying to come up with something to tempt them, Wade had taken a different tack. He'd surprised her when he'd asked if he could make himself something to eat. She'd offered to make whatever he wanted but he'd given her a meaningful look and insisted that he could do it himself. She and the children had come into the kitchen with him and sat down at the big farmhouse table and watched.

After poking around in the fridge, he'd taken out onions and green peppers and chopped them up, then stir fried some chicken. Sierra had been a little shocked that he'd just start cooking like that to make himself a snack while the children hadn't eaten. Then he'd gotten out tortillas and cheese and taken the tub of sour cream and the jar of salsa from the fridge and set them right in the middle of the table. He'd made himself a quesadilla, sliced it with the pizza cutter and sat down at the table with them.

Sierra had watched as he'd scooped salsa and sour cream onto his plate and then taken a big bite and actually moaned in appreciation. It had only dawned on her what he was doing when she noticed that Mateo and Maya were both watching him intently. Wade met her gaze for a moment and winked before taking another big bite. When he'd swallowed that down, he pushed his plate a little way toward her.

"Want some?"

She really didn't, but now that she knew what he was up to, she took a piece and bit into it, making an appreciative moan of her own – it was good!

Mateo looked up at her and swallowed. She willed Wade to offer him a piece, but he didn't. He kept on eating and after another few bites, he smiled at Maya and winked. She smiled back at him and held her little hand out.

Wade nudged his plate toward her, and she snatched a piece and ate as though she was starving. Wade pushed the plate toward Mateo, who looked at it and then back at Wade. To Sierra's surprise, Wade grabbed another piece for himself without saying anything. She understood what he was up to when Mateo's eyes widened, and he grabbed a piece as well. Once he had it, Wade smiled.

"That's right. Get a piece while you can. Don't worry, though. I'll make us some more now." He got to his feet and started preparing another.

Sierra followed him to the stove. "Thank you," she said quietly.

He chuckled. "You're welcome. Though for a minute there, I thought you might throw me out for being so damned rude as to start cooking in your kitchen and so damned selfish that I'd pig out in front of them."

She gave him a guilty smile. "I'm sorry. Apparently, you're much smarter than I am. It took me a while to catch on."

He slid his arm around her waist and pulled her into his side. "It's okay. I'm just glad you didn't get mad, and that I was right. It might take a while before they're comfortable admitting that they want anything. I just wanted to show them that it's okay to eat and I figured that letting them think they should get some while they can might make them feel more at home."

"Oh." Sierra's heart sank. "You think they've been going hungry?"

"I don't know about that. But I'd guess that they don't just expect to get three meals a day, no questions asked."

She nodded sadly and rested her cheek against his chest. Then she straightened up and sprang away from him. Shoot! They weren't together like that anymore. "I'm sorry!"

His hand came down on her shoulder in a gesture that was now so familiar, and which sent his warmth spreading through her. "Don't be sorry, darlin'. I'm the one who's sorry."

She tried to blink away the tears that threatened to fall. "You are? What for?" She dreaded hearing him say that he was sorry he couldn't be what she needed. But her heart hammered in the hope that he might say something else, something better, something that might unbreak her heart.

He drew her against him again. "I'm sorry I messed up last night. I was scared. I wanted to tell you how I felt and I messed up."

She leaned back to look up into his eyes; they were such a beautiful green and so full of warmth and tenderness.

"I said I didn't know if I could be what you need."

She nodded sadly. She didn't need reminding of that.

His arm tightened around her. "What I didn't get to finish, what I was about to say, was that I want to be." He glanced at the children and slid the second quesadilla onto another plate. Once he'd set that on the table, he came back and wrapped both arms around her. "I want to be what you need." He tilted his head toward Mateo and Maya, who were eating hungrily. "And now that I've met those two, I've fallen in love with them as well, and not only do I want to be what they need, but I believe that I can be."

She just stared up at him, hoping that she'd heard him right and that she wasn't imagining him saying what she wanted to hear.

His smile faded. "If you want me to be?"

"Oh, my gosh, Wade! I do! I … when you said that last night, I agreed with you because I wanted to let you off the hook. I didn't want to try to tie you into something you don't want."

He dropped his head and brushed his lips over hers. "I do want. I want you. I want them. There's still a lot to figure out. We still have a lot to learn about each other and about our new kids."

She brought her hand up to cover her mouth and tried to blink away the tears. "*Our* kids?"

He nodded happily. "Yeah. That's what I want. I'm not a fool, Sierra. We're going to have a long road ahead of us and it will probably have more than its share of bumps. But I love you and I love them, and I know we can make it work, if you want to."

"I want to." She wrapped her arms around him and hugged him tight. Her heart felt like it might overflow with happiness. "Wait!" She leaned back to look at him. "What did you just say?"

There went that smile of his. "You mean the bit about how I love you and I love them?"

"Yes! That. Oh, Wade." She rolled up on her tiptoes and pressed a kiss to his lips. "I love you, too."

"You do?" He was smiling, but she could tell he was cautious. "You don't have to say it if you're not there yet." He winked. "I'll be happy to work on making you fall for me."

She laughed. "I've already fallen. It might have been that first night that you found me by the side of the road."

His arms tightened around her. "I don't care when it was, I'm just happy that you're there."

"Mr. Wade."

They both turned to Mateo, who was actually smiling at them.

"What's up, son?"

Sierra couldn't help but read too much into his use of that word. It was just a term of endearment, of course. But now she could see it coming true.

"Thank you, Mr. Wade."

Wade let her go but kept hold of her hand and took her with him when he squatted down between the kids' chairs. "You're welcome. Did you get enough? Do you want more?"

"No. Thank you. I will clean the dishes now."

"Oh, no," Sierra began, but Wade shot her a look.

"Thank you, little man. If you can just put them in the sink, that'd be great."

As Mateo headed for the sink, Wade put the lids on the salsa and the sour cream, then smiled at Maya. "Do you want to put these in the fridge for me?"

The little girl smiled at him and slid down from her seat.

Sierra felt like the luckiest girl in the world. She'd been worried that he didn't want kids and that he probably wouldn't know how to treat them. Instead, it was turning out that he was much better at it than she was.

Chapter Twenty-Two

"Mr. Wade, Mr. Wade!"

Wade couldn't help grinning when Mateo came running to greet him the moment he walked through the front door. "Hey, little man. What's all the excitement about? Where's your sister?"

Maya came trotting after her brother and held her arms up to Wade. He scooped her up and sat her on his hip, ruffling Mateo's hair with his other hand. While Maya was openly hungry for all the affection she could get, he knew that Mateo did his best to hide his need, even though he longed for love just as much as she did.

"And don't you think it's time you called me just Wade?" He'd tried to get them to call him that since the first day, but Mr. Wade had stuck. At least, that was what Mateo insisted on calling him. Maya had yet to utter a single word. He believed that she'd get there with time.

Mateo just shrugged. "Can we go to see the horses?"

Wade smiled. He'd promised that he'd take them out to the barn when he finished work. He tapped his watch. "Is it time yet? Are you ready to go?"

Watching Mateo check his own bright blue watch and Maya copy her brother to look at her own yellow one wiped the smile off Wade's face. He'd given them the same tracker watches as he'd given Sierra. And he'd shown them how to press the button three times to send out an alert if ever they needed help. He'd intended to make it seem like nothing out of the ordinary – but the look in Mateo's big, wise eyes had told him that the kid understood. Wade hated what he knew of their past. Their father had worked for one of the big cartels. Their mom had been murdered to teach him a lesson, but apparently, he hadn't learned it well enough, and he'd been shot execution-style to set an example.

Maya smiled and nodded eagerly, bringing Wade back to the moment. He couldn't change their past, but he intended to do everything he could to give them a better future. And right now, that meant taking them out to the barn to see the ponies.

Sierra appeared in the doorway from the kitchen and greeted him with a smile. He went to her and dropped a kiss on her lips. Maya wrapped her arms around them both and Mateo stood close, leaning against Wade's leg.

Wade felt as if his heart might overflow. This right here was his family. This sweet woman whom he'd known for less than a month and these two kids he'd known for less than a week. It should feel wrong. It had all happened way too fast, but it was right, he knew it was. No amount of time would change what he felt for the three of them – well, he knew that with time his love would only grow. He couldn't help but compare what he had now to what he'd had with Josie. He'd been with her since high school. They'd been together for five years before they got married and even on his wedding day, he hadn't felt the way about her that he felt about Sierra. He used to tell himself that it was because they'd been too young. But he knew better than that now. He hadn't felt this away about Josie because she hadn't been the one for him.

Sierra leaned back and smiled at him. "If you're going to the barn now, I'll see you back here in a little while."

"I thought you were going to come?" Mateo and Maya had both fallen in love with the horses, and to Wade's great pleasure, Sierra had, too. She'd been cautious at first; she'd told him that she'd never really been around animals before. But she was making up for lost time. She and the children had been out to the barn every day, and she'd been taking them to Janey's place to see the stray mama dog and her puppies. Wade was a little leery that she might end up bringing the whole litter home when they were ready.

"I was, but I have to go over to the bakery. Spider kept some of the C-O-O-K-I-E-S for me specially, and I haven't had the chance to go over and collect them yet."

Wade grinned. He loved the way she'd taken to spelling out words that she didn't want the kids to hear, but he had the feeling that Mateo understood what she was saying anyway. "So, how about we all go over there first? We can pick those up and then go out to the barn together."

She looked hesitant. "Do you think we should?"

"Yeah. I do." Dax had left after a couple days, and before he'd gone, he taken Wade aside. Not to give him the kind of warning and talking to that Wade had expected – about how he'd better be good to Sierra. Instead, he'd told him that he could see how good he was for Sierra, and for the children, too. Wade had reassured him that he planned to take care of all three of them for as long as Sierra would let him – and that if he got his way, that would mean for the rest of their lives. Dax had simply laughed and told him that he didn't need to say it. That he made it obvious in everything that he said and did. He'd pulled him aside to explain his concerns. He was still worried about Jared. Not that he would harm Sierra, that wouldn't get him anywhere, but that he might try to kidnap the kids and ask for a ransom.

Wade still wasn't sure how he felt about that. He wanted to think that Dax was just looking for worst case scenario because that was what he was used to dealing with – he was a freaking SEAL after all. But whether the threat was real or not, Wade and all his brothers were treating it as if it were. It was why Dax had reassured the kids that whenever they left the ranch, one of the MacFarlands would always be with them.

As he thought about it now, Wade decided that a quick visit to the bakery would be a good way to build their confidence. He wanted them to get used to having as normal a life as possible. And so, he looked down at them. "What do you say? Do you want to all go to the bakery together?"

Two eager smiling faces nodded up at him and burrowed their way even deeper into his heart. Sure, it was still early days yet, but one day soon, he and Sierra needed to sit down and talk about the future, their future as a couple and as a family.

Mateo tugged at his hand. "Let's go."

He chuckled as he caught Sierra's eye and murmured, "I think he knows how to spell."

Mateo grinned at them. "Cookies!"

Sierra held Maya's hand as she pushed open the door to the bakery. Wade followed close behind with Mateo. This should probably feel strange, but it felt good – and right. She and

Wade might both be fair while the children had olive skin and dark hair, but the outward appearances didn't undermine the deep bond that they were all forming. They were becoming a family, and she couldn't be happier.

That first night the children had arrived, when Wade had told her that he loved her, he'd stayed the night at the big cabin with them – with her, in her bed. Dax had said that if they were a couple, then it was better that the children should see them that way from the beginning – and of course, he was right. And so, Wade had stayed that night and every night since. They'd continued as they were before except now, they were living in the big cabin instead of the small one, and they had two children instead of it being just the two of them.

The atmosphere and the smell of the bakery hit her as she walked in; she loved this place. It always made her smile. She stopped halfway to the counter and the smile died on her face. A woman had turned to look at her. It was the same woman who'd been here the first time Sierra had come in – when Spider had given her cookies for Wade. The woman who'd been bitching about getting her coffee and who'd looked at Sierra as if she hated her.

Right now, the woman looked at her as if she wanted to kill her. She looked down at little Maya and then past them to Wade and Mateo, who had come up beside Sierra. She looked back at Sierra with pure venom and then turned and smiled at Wade.

He put his arm around Sierra's shoulders and pulled her into his side before proceeding to the counter. "Josie." He gave her a slight nod before turning away to look at the board.

Spider came to greet them with a smile. "Hey, guys. It's good to see you." He let himself out from behind the counter and came to squat down in front of the children. "You must be Mateo and Maya?"

Sierra was surprised that neither of them seemed to be afraid of him. Perhaps they were used to muscles and mohawks and tattoos. From the little she knew about the life their father had been living, they were probably used to seeing the worst of humanity. Although he might look tough, and she hadn't known him for very long, Sierra knew that Spider was one of the best humans she'd ever met. It seemed that the children could sense that, too.

They both smiled at him, and Maya nodded.

"We live with Sierra and … Wade now," said Mateo.

Sierra glanced at Wade; he looked as thrilled as she felt that Mateo hadn't called him Mr.

"So, I heard," said Spider. "That's awesome. You guys are lucky. They're good people. Kind people. You're going to be okay with them."

Sierra's eyes filled with tears when Mateo looked up at them and nodded. "I know."

Wade squeezed her hand. He'd told her that Spider had spent most of his childhood in foster care but had never found a family to call his own. He'd aged out at eighteen and been homeless for a while before he found his feet. If anyone understood how the children might be feeling right now, she'd guess that he would.

She smiled at him gratefully. "We're doing our best. We might not get it right all the time but," she looked down at Mateo and Maya, "we love you both very much."

She felt as if her heart might explode when Mateo smiled back at her then at Wade and said, "We love you."

"Oh please! That's crazy!"

They all turned to see Josie glowering at them. Maya ducked behind Sierra's legs and Mateo put himself in front of her. Wade put his arm in front of all of them and stepped forward.

"No one asked for your opinion."

Josie let out a bitter laugh. "Maybe not. But I'm giving it anyway." She turned to Sierra. "It won't last, so I wouldn't get too used to it, if I were you. He doesn't want kids. Ask anyone around here. He might be putting up with them for now, but it won't last, you mark my words."

Sierra glared right back at her. "You don't know what you're talking about. He might not have wanted children in the past." She couldn't resist adding, "He might not have wanted them with you. But I can assure you, he's not just putting up with Mateo and Maya. He loves them." She was shaking when she finished. But she was proud of herself for speaking up. She knew Wade wouldn't raise his voice to Josie, but the children needed to know that she was wrong.

Josie laughed again; there was no humor in it, only bitterness and anger. "You keep telling yourself that. Don't say I didn't warn you." She turned and stomped out, leaving them all staring after her.

Wade was shaking as the door slammed shut behind Josie. She could hate him if she wanted, he didn't care about that. But how could she be so damned cruel? How could she talk like that in front of the kids?

He looked down at them. Mateo had wrapped his arm around his sister, and they were huddled together, just like they'd been the first time he saw them. Shit! They needed to know that they were loved; that they were wanted. The last thing they needed was damn Josie – or anyone – casting doubt in their little minds.

He squatted down with them and wrapped his arms around them. "She's wrong, you know. I love you guys, and nothing is ever going to change that."

Mateo looked up at him, and the doubt in his eyes slayed Wade. "Why did she say you don't want children? Who is she?"

Wade took a deep breath and closed his eyes. When he opened them again, Mateo and Maya were both watching him fearfully. He hugged them to him and then leaned back so that they could see his face as he spoke.

"Her name is Josie. I was married to her." He watched surprise register on both their faces. He wondered sometimes how much Maya understood, but she seemed to be following him just fine.

"She was your wife?" asked Mateo.

"Yes. She was. A long time ago."

Mateo's eyebrows drew together. "Do you ... have children with her?"

"No. No, I don't, little man. That's why she said I don't want children. Because I didn't – with her. That's why we're not married anymore. She wanted children, and I didn't want to have children with her."

"Why?"

Wade blew out a sigh. He was going to tell the truth. He had to. He'd let Josie's version of events be the one that people believed all these years because it hadn't mattered to him what people thought. Now, it mattered, it mattered very much; not what people might think, but what these two little people in front of him thought. Still, he wanted to choose his words carefully. "Because … as you just saw, she's not always very kind. What she said just now was mean, it was mean to you guys, and it was mean to Sierra."

"And to you."

"I'm not worried about me. What's important is that I always knew that she could be that way, and I didn't want to have children with her because I wouldn't ever want my children to be treated that way."

They both stood very still watching him carefully, and he was aware that Sierra and Spider were listening closely, too.

"I didn't want to have children unless I knew that I could give them a happy home where they would feel safe and loved by both me and their mom. I knew that I would never be able to give them that with her."

Mateo nodded with way more wisdom than his years.

Wade caught hold of Sierra's hand. "Things are different now. With Sierra I know that we can give you a happy home where you'll always feel safe and loved – by both of us."

"You really love us?"

Wade had to swallow. "I do." He glanced at Sierra. "We do. We haven't known you guys for very long but that doesn't make any difference. We love you and we always will."

He was overcome with emotion, but Mateo still had questions. Wade could see it in his eyes.

"Go ahead. Ask me anything."

"You love Sierra?"

Wade smiled up at her. "Yes, I do."

"But you're not married?"

Wade caught hold of her hand. His heart was hammering in his chest; he'd been working his way up to this. He wanted her to be his wife, but he figured that since he'd only met her when she was running away from her wedding, she'd need some time before she considered marriage again. But this felt like a pivotal moment in their life as a family. "Not yet." He raised his eyebrows.

Sierra's cheeks colored up, but she smiled and nodded.

He let out the breath he hadn't realized he was holding. "Just like we haven't known you guys for very long, but we know that we love you, Sierra and I haven't known each other very long either, but we know that we love each other." He smiled. "I didn't expect to ever meet someone like Sierra, just like I didn't expect that I'd meet kids who I wanted to be mine, but I've discovered that unexpected love is the very best kind. It might happen fast, but it's strong and it's real."

"Unexpected," Mateo nodded. "It's good."

Wade was relieved that he thought so. He'd just spilled his heart to his new family and by the way all three of them were smiling at him, it seemed that they agreed – unexpected love might be the very best kind.

Chapter Twenty-Three

Sierra checked her purse: she had her keys, her cell phone, everything she needed. She already knew she did from the last two times she checked. She should just get going, but for some reason, she was nervous. Wade came and put his hands on her shoulders and looked down into her eyes with a smile.

"We'll be fine. I promise you."

"I know. It's not that I'm doubting you. Don't think that."

He chuckled. "I don't. But if you don't hurry up, you're going to be late. And I don't want Amelia to get mad at me."

"She won't. She thinks you're wonderful."

"She does? Even though she ended up not spending time with you like she thought she would since I elbowed my way back into your life from the first day the kids arrived?"

Sierra had to laugh. "Yes, even in spite of that. I think she fell for you at the exact same moment the kids did. And I can't blame her. If I wasn't already in love with you when they both flung themselves into your arms that first day, I would have fallen for you in that moment, too."

He gave her a bashful shrug, but she knew he loved hearing it. "It was unexpected for all of us, but I know that moment changed all our lives for the better."

"It did."

"But talking about it is only making you later. Go on, have fun with Amelia, and see if you can persuade her to come back with you afterward? I know you say she's all independent, but I feel bad that she's right here in the valley for you and has hardly seen you."

"We've seen each other during the day when you've been at work."

"I know, but I want to include her in our life, too. And all the brothers are coming over for burgers. It'd be good if she came, too."

"Don't worry, I plan to bring her back."

"Good. And don't worry about the kids. We're going to have a busy day of it. We're going to the barn first. I can't believe Tanner bought the ponies."

"Aww." Sierra couldn't hide her smile. "I was worried how your brothers would feel about having children living here, but they've all been amazing."

Wade laughed. "Tell me about it. It's so cool. After Tan shows them how to take care of the ponies, we're going up to the big house so they can bake cookies with Ty."

Sierra chuckled. "I love seeing him with them. I didn't think he'd have any time for them. Now, I'm more worried about having to make sure he doesn't overfeed them."

"He won't. He loves to cook, and they need to eat. I love that he has his own special thing going with them."

"I do, too. And even Ford." Sierra shook her head. "I thought I'd have to do my best to keep them out of his way."

"Nah. He might have a tough exterior, but he's soft on the inside."

"I wouldn't have believed it if I hadn't caught him reading with them."

Wade laughed. "I'm going to see if I can't sneak a photo of him today. Seeing him in that big armchair with them both on his lap while he reads is just …" He shook his head and his smile faded. "You know, at first, I thought it was all about what we could do to make Mateo and Maya's lives better. I had no idea how much better they would make all of ours."

Sierra went and wrapped her arms around him, resting her cheek against his chest. "I'm happier than I've ever been. And it's all thanks to you. I love you, Wade."

"I love you, too, darlin'. But go on. Otherwise, I'll try to keep you and Amelia will really be mad at me."

Sierra reached up for a kiss and then went out to the great room where the children were watching TV. She didn't like them to watch too much, but it was Saturday morning.

"I'm going to see my friend Amelia now. Are you two going to be okay?"

Mateo came and hugged her. "We will be good. See you later." She hugged him back and then turned to catch Maya, who flung herself at her and kissed her cheek. The little girl still hadn't spoken, and they had an appointment to see a child-psychologist over in Bozeman next week. Although, Sierra wasn't too worried. Maya was doing better each day, and Sierra believed that she'd speak again when she was ready.

She gave them both a kiss on the cheek and then went back to give Wade another before she finally made herself leave.

"Sorry I'm late." Amelia was waiting for her outside the bakery.

"You're not. At least, not very. I can't imagine getting ready and getting out of the house with those two adorable little people around. I'd never want to leave them." Amelia greeted her with a hug. "I was thinking, though. Do you want to go in here? After what you told me about Wade's ex, would you rather go somewhere else?"

Sierra shook her head. "No. I hope she won't be here. But even if she is, I can't let her run me off. I live here now. This is about the only place there is to meet up with friends."

Amelia grinned at her. "Yay for you. I'm proud of you."

Sierra shrugged. "I can't say that I'm grateful to Jared, but what he did has taught me a lot. I needed to wise up and toughen up and I'm starting to."

"Yeah. Don't give that ass any of the credit. You're doing it all by yourself. Although, I think Wade might have helped you a little."

"Oh, Lia. You have no idea. He's been so good to me. And he makes me stop and think about what I actually want for myself, too."

"Yeah. I like him, Sierra. It's obvious that he loves you; he's good to you and good for you, and you couldn't have asked for a better dad for those kids."

"I know. I didn't think that he'd want to have anything to do with them, and yet he's a natural. He loves them and he just somehow knows what they need. He's amazing."

"He is. I'm happy for you."

"And you don't mind?"

"Mind? Mind what? That I get to see my friend happy and loved?"

"I mean, you came here to help me out, but since Wade moved in that first day, I've been all caught up in figuring out how things are going to work, how we are together, how we are with the children."

"How the four of you are going to become a family. I don't mind. I'm thrilled. You know me, Sierra. I don't need anything. I'm perfectly fine by myself. I'm happy to stick around as a backup – I know you're busy; I'm still here because I also know that you'll need time for yourself here and there and that when you get it, you'll need a friend to talk to."

"You seriously are the best bestie, you know."

"And you know that it goes both ways. Now are we going to stand out here talking or are we going in?"

Sierra looked at the bakery and then back at her friend. "How would you feel if we went somewhere else? Not because I'm worried about going in here. Just because I've been wanting to go over to Bozeman, and if I don't go now, I don't know when I'll get the chance again."

"Sounds good to me. I've been over there a few times. I like it. I wouldn't trade it for this valley, but it's good when you want a touch of civilization. What do you need?"

Sierra smiled. "There's a gallery I want to check out and an art supply store."

"Yay! I wondered how long it would take you."

"I've had twitchy fingers since the first night I arrived here. I wanted to paint the sunset, but there's always been so much going on that I haven't had the time. Now that things are settling into a new routine, I'm going to carve myself some time out to paint."

Once they were in Amelia's SUV, she pulled out onto the highway. "Now that you're planning on painting, I feel like this is real. That you're really going to make a go of it here."

Sierra turned to her. "What do you think? I'd like to. I mean, I'm only supposed to be staying until the whole Jared thing is dealt with, but I love it here. I think the children can have a wonderful life here – they've already settled at the ranch. The brothers all love them. I think this could be a better life for them than San Francisco."

Amelia nodded. "I have to say that I think you're right. And that's without even mentioning the fact that it looks like you and Wade have a future together and I don't see him leaving here."

"I know. Do you think that's bad, though? I don't. It's just who he is. I feel like I should be worried because if I want to be with him then it'll have to be on his terms, kind of. But it's not like that. It's just how it is. He is who he is, and this place is his life. His family's here. He built the lodge and the guest ranch from nothing. I couldn't and wouldn't expect him to give it up."

Amelia reached over and patted her hand. "It's okay. I get it. I don't know if you're trying to justify it to yourself or to me. But it's okay. I think it's right and normal. Now, if he were trying to *make* you give up your life to be with him that'd be a whole different matter, but he's not – is he?"

"No! He wouldn't."

"I didn't think so. And honestly, Sierra. I think you'd be better off here."

"You do?"

"Yes. You never made much of a life for yourself at home, did you? I mean of course, you have me." Amelia flashed her a grin. "But other than that, your life revolved around the business, because you were part of the family, and the gallery because they made you. You were much happier by yourself painting most of the time. And we won't even mention that the last year Jared took over your life."

Sierra stared out the window, thinking about that. "You're right. And if I want to paint, even if I want shows, Cassidy's here. It's not as though there's no art scene at all and I don't know anyone."

"Exactly."

"What about you, though?"

"What about me?"

"I can't imagine moving away from you."

"Who says you'd have to?"

"You'd move here, too?"

Amelia shrugged. "Yeah. If you wouldn't mind. I can work from anywhere. I spend most of my time alone anyway. I can go back to San Francisco whenever I want." She waggled her eyebrows. "And I love the scenery out here."

Sierra laughed with her. "You mean the mountains and the big sky or the Wranglers and cowboy hats?"

"Both."

"Wow. Does this mean that you're on the lookout?"

"Maybe."

"Oh, my gosh! Has anyone caught your interest?"

"Maybe."

"Tell me! Who?"

"Nope. I want to see if the interest is mutual first. You know me. I like to take my time and weigh my options."

"Until you decide. And then you're all systems go until you get what you want – whether that's with guys or in business or anything."

Amelia laughed. "Yep. And I want to be sure about this little infatuation of mine before I make any moves."

"Ugh. I may die of curiosity if you don't tell me."

"You won't die. I promise you. Not today anyway."

Sierra chuckled. "Well, Wade said I have to make sure that I bring you back with me tonight. He's grilling burgers for his brothers, and he said that you have to come."

"Really, did he say why?"

"Just that he feels kind of guilty that you're here, but I haven't seen you much because of him, and that it'll be fun to have you over as well, not just the brothers."

"Okay."

Sierra gave her a puzzled look. "Why do you look disappointed?"

"I don't! I'm not."

"Oh, my gosh! Is it one of the brothers?"

Amelia didn't answer.

"It is, isn't it?"

"I'm not saying a word."

Sierra scowled at her. "That's not fair! You're far too good at keeping secrets. If I guess right, will you tell me?"

Amelia laughed. "Nope. I'm not telling you anything until I know if there's any point in me being interested. And as far as keeping secrets goes, you know it's what I do. I have to."

Sierra blew out a sigh. It was true. Even after all the years that they'd been friends, she wasn't exactly sure what Amelia did for a living. She worked alone on her computer, and she was acutely aware of everything to do with computer security. Computers and phones. She said that she helped out big companies, and sometimes law enforcement, but other than that it was difficult to get her to talk about her work. Over the years, Sierra had learned not to ask.

That thought made her wonder for the first time, whether she might be able to track people – people like Jared and Lori. She turned to look at her friend as they sped along the highway between mountains that towered on either side and loomed closer together as they approached the pass.

"Have you tried looking into Jared's secrets?"

Amelia glanced at her before turning her focus back to the road. "I have."

"Did you find anything?"

She blew out a sigh. "I wasn't hiding things from you, Sierra. I was hoping that I might be able to track him down. I wanted to have something concrete before I brought it up."

"What have you found?"

"Are you sure you want to know?"

"Absolutely."

"Okay. Well, not everything I did is legal. So …"

"That's okay."

"It seems that he and Lori were in on it together from the beginning. They were talking before you ever got together with him."

"Wow!"

"Yeah. I can't believe that she fooled us both so completely. And I figured out how he was syphoning money out of the company."

"You did? Have you told Barney?"

"Like I said, Sierra, not all my methods are exactly legal. But I did manage to get my findings into the hands of the investigators Barney hired. You should be hearing from him soon about that."

"Okay." Sierra's heart was pounding. "That's good. Thank you." But she had to ask the most important question. "Do you know where he is?"

"No. But I think I'm close to finding out. He's smart. He's using burner phones and staying off the grid." Amelia chuckled. "I'm glad you know what I'm up to now. I can tell you, and I'm sure you'll be pleased to hear, that he popped up in Minnesota a couple of days after the wedding. I couldn't figure that out for the life of me – why he'd go there. I got a kick when you told me what Tyler had done with your cellphone."

Sierra had to smile. "Do you think I can tell Tyler about that – if I don't tell him how I know, of course."

"Sure."

Sierra blew out a sigh. "But you don't know where he is now?"

"Unfortunately, no. I know in the movies they make it look easy to track a person's every move. But it's not that simple, and especially not when you're working alone. After Minnesota he popped up in North Dakota."

Sierra frowned. "That's coming back this way."

"I know but it's not exactly around the corner. I would have told you if he was anywhere close. And to be honest, that's part of the reason I came up here. I don't think he'd be stupid enough to come after you, but I want to be close by."

"Well, I appreciate it. Thank you."

"You can thank me if I manage to help bring him in."

Sierra nodded She could only hope. Dax's concern that Jared might try to take the children niggled at her constantly. She'd never forgive herself if something happened to them, if Jared even scared them; they'd been through enough already.

Chapter Twenty-Four

Wade checked his watch. It was twenty-past four. He'd expected Sierra back a while ago. She'd called earlier to tell him that she and Amelia had gone over to Bozeman, and he was glad that she was getting out and about – especially when she'd said that she was going to an art supply store. But he'd thought that she'd be in a hurry to get back to the kids.

He went out to the back deck to check on the grill. He needed to relax. She was no doubt enjoying herself and there was no rush. He smiled at the thought that he was getting clucky like he'd told her he might when she came up with her mama duck theory.

Still, he checked his phone again to see if he'd missed a text from her. Nothing. He turned when Tanner appeared in the doorway that led out from the kitchen.

"You want a cold one?"

"Sure."

Tanner came out and handed him a beer with a smile. "Have you seen Ford in there with them?"

Wade had to laugh. "Yup. Ain't he cute?"

Tanner laughed with him. "I wouldn't have believed it if I hadn't seen it for myself. Uncle Ford! Who'd have thought it?"

Wade chuckled. "Don't give him too much of a hard time. He loves it, and so do the kids. Every time they see him now, they grab a book and drag him toward the nearest armchair. When Maya learns to read, I'm going to give Ford most of the credit."

Tanner grinned. "I love it. You know what I love the most, though?"

"What?"

"I love that we were all wrong about you and kids. You're amazing with them. We all love getting in on the act with our special thing: Ford with the reading, and me with the ponies, and Ty in the kitchen. But you? You're a natural. It's like you're the dad we all wished we had."

Wade's smile faded. "Yeah. That's about the only thing I have to go on."

"What do you mean?"

"That I have no clue what being a good father looks like – because we never had one. All I know is to do the opposite of what he would."

"Nah. Don't give the old bastard that much credit. You're not doing the opposite of him. He hasn't contributed a damned thing – not even by default. You're awesome at being a dad because of who you are. And who you are – the man you've become – is in spite of him, not because of him."

Wade held his gaze for a long moment before turning away. They rarely talked about their dad. He didn't want to dwell on the subject. "Are you sticking around for a while or are you working behind the bar at Chico tonight?"

"I'm working but I'm not on till nine. I figured you'd have the kiddos to bed and want to be rid of us all before then anyway."

"I wasn't going to give you a hard time. I get it. I don't imagine you had much time for the ladies while you were deployed. You're making up for it now."

Tanner grinned. "Yeah. It's just fun."

"I know. What do you think of Amelia?"

Tanner held his hands up. "Oh, no. Just because you're ready to settle down and become a husband and a father and all that good shit, don't go looking at me."

Wade laughed out loud. "Whoa! Calm down. That's not what I was asking. I just ... I don't know. She's been a good friend to Sierra. I just wondered what you make of her. I can't figure her out. I keep thinking that she should be mad at me for hogging Sierra's time, but she's ...cool. She gets it. She doesn't mind. She's okay off doing her own thing."

"I wouldn't worry about it. Not all chicks are demanding or clingy, you know."

Wade made a face at him. "I guess not."

Tanner laughed. "Yeah. From the couple times I've talked to her she strikes me as smart, independent and I don't know just ... like you say, content doing her own thing. I think she's here for Sierra if she needs her, but happy to entertain herself if she doesn't."

"Yeah. I invited her to come tonight." He checked his watch again. "Whenever they get back."

"Quit worrying, would you?"

"What's he worrying about?" Ford asked as he stuck his head out the kitchen door.

Wade scowled. "Right now, I'm worrying what the kids are up to. You were …"

Ford laughed. "Jesus! Calm down, would you? They're fine. Ty's with them."

Wade gave him rueful smile. "Sorry."

"It's all good. In fact, it's awesome – the way you are with them. They were asking what time Sierra's going to be back."

"I'm hoping she won't be too long now."

Tanner gave Ford a look that Wade didn't understand. "They went to Bozeman and Amelia's coming back here with her."

Ford nodded but didn't say anything.

"That's not a problem, is it?"

Ford shrugged, and Tanner laughed.

"What's going on?" Wade asked.

Tanner pointed his bottle at Ford. "I think that our big brother is the one who has the hots for the lovely Amelia."

Wade's eyebrows shot up. "You do?"

Ford shrugged. "I wouldn't exactly put it that way. I happened to comment that she's cool, and since Tanner only sees women as a way to spend the night, he assumed that's what I meant."

Tanner just laughed. "Don't try and talk your way out of it. Tell me you wouldn't go there if you got the chance."

Ford rolled his eyes and turned to go back inside. "I'm going to hang with the kids. I know I'll get a more intelligent conversation out of them."

"Wait!" Wade called after him. "Ignore Tan. Is he right?"

Ford turned back around and shrugged. "Sure. I find her attractive. But that doesn't mean that he's right. I don't see what the big deal is."

Wade startled when his phone rang, and he pulled it out of his back pocket, expecting it to be Sierra. It wasn't. He didn't recognize the number.

"Wade MacFarland."

"Wade, it's Luke. Luke Wallis."

"Oh, hey Luke. What's up, bud?"

"I'm not calling for a chat. I'm at work. Do you know Amelia Danforth?"

Wade's heart started to pound. Luke calling about work couldn't be good – he was a deputy with the sheriff's office. "Yes. She's Sierra's friend. Why?"

"Is Sierra with you?"

"No. She's out with Amelia. What's going on, Luke?"

His brothers were staring at him now. He could feel the blood drain from his face as he gripped his phone to his ear.

"We don't know yet, Wade. They might be fine."

"For fuck's sake, Luke! Tell me."

"Okay. There was a report of a vehicle turned over just this side of the pass heading eastbound. A gray Tahoe."

"Shit. That's what Amelia's driving."

"Yeah."

"Are they hurt? Where are they?" Wade was striding into the house; he needed his keys. He needed to go to her. He could only hope that she wasn't badly hurt, that Amelia wasn't.

Luke's next words stopped him dead. "We don't know."

"What do you mean you don't know?"

"The vehicle was empty, Wade. No, driver, no passengers."

"What the fuck?"

"Put it on speaker." Ford spoke calmly but forcefully beside him.

Wade did as he asked. "You're on speaker with me, Ford, and Tan."

"Okay," Luke said. "I've just come on shift. It was only when I heard the name Amelia in the handover that it clicked that it might be Sierra's friend. The vehicle was overturned. When units arrived on scene, there were no occupants."

Ford frowned. "And that's all you've got?"

"All that I know so far. Listen, I'll call you back when I can. Deacon's calling us all in for a briefing."

"Thanks, Luke."

Wade shook his head in an attempt to clear it. Ford was rubbing his fingertips to his temples.

Tanner was frowning. "What the hell?"

Ford met Wade's gaze. "Do you think it's Jared?"

"What else could it be?"

Wade's heart was still pounding. It was a rapid, steady beat. The immediate panic had subsided. What he felt now was determination. No way had he found Sierra just for something to happen to her now. He needed her; their kids needed her. And he was going to do whatever it took to find her and bring her home.

~ ~ ~

Sierra opened her eyes, but everything was fuzzy, so she closed them again. She could maybe snooze for another few minutes. She turned onto her side and that brought her mind into focus. She wasn't in bed. She was lying on a hard floor. She opened her eyes again. The room slowly came into focus. She was in some kind of cabin, but not the kind she was used to. This was much more rustic. It smelled musty and the light was dim. There was only one window, but it seemed to be boarded up from the outside. The floor was cold and dirty. It *was* dirt. She sat up then had to close her eyes again until the dizziness passed.

"Sierra?" Amelia's voice was quiet off to her left.

"Amelia! What's –?"

"Shh!"

Sierra covered her mouth with her hand. It all started to come back to her. They'd been on their way back from Bozeman. They'd had a lovely day. As they drove back over the pass, Amelia had kept checking the rearview mirror so often that it made Sierra wonder what was wrong. When she'd turned to look back, Amelia had grabbed her arm and told her not to.

She'd said that she thought Jared was following them. Sierra had to close her eyes again as it all came back in flashes. Amelia hitting the gas and tearing down the Interstate way too fast. The big black SUV that had been even faster and pulled alongside them. Seeing a man's face leering at them – it wasn't Jared. The momentary relief she'd felt before he swerved in front of them, running them off the road.

She touched her head gingerly; there was a gash, and her fingers came away tacky with blood. She felt queasy as she remembered the way the world had turned upside down when Amelia's Tahoe had hit the guardrail and flipped over.

"Are you okay?" She had to know that Amelia wasn't injured.

"I'm fine," Amelia whispered. "You took the worst of it. Are you okay?"

"I think so. I cut my head. Where are we?"

"You don't remember anything?"

"Not after we went off the road." She tried to push to her feet, but Amelia grabbed her arm.

"We need to stay as still and as quiet as possible. If he hears us, he'll know we're awake."

"He? Jared?"

"Yeah."

"What? How?"

"He arrived less than a minute after we crashed. You were unconscious. Is your head okay? It looked bad."

"I think it is. I'm dizzy and I have a headache but I'm okay."

"Good. Jared pulled you out of there and put you in his van. I thought he was going to take you and leave me. But he came back and got me too."

That surprised Sierra; she would have expected Amelia to fight him. She was tough like that.

She heard her friend sigh. "I couldn't do a damned thing. I was trapped in my seatbelt and the bastard punched me in the face and knocked me out. I think he broke my nose."

"Amelia!"

"Shh! And don't get too upset about it. I have a feeling that a broken nose is going to be the least of my worries when he comes back."

"What do you think he wants?"

"All he's ever wanted. Your money."

Sierra closed her eyes. "He can't get it if he kills me."

"No."

The way Amelia whispered that one word filled Sierra with dread. "What are you thinking?"

"That you're right. He can't get your money if he kills you. So, he'll threaten to kill me unless you give it to him."

"Oh my gosh, Amelia! No! I'll give it to him."

"Sierra. I love you, but you're not that stupid."

Sierra felt panic claw at her throat. "No. I'm not. As soon as I gave him what he wanted, he'd kill us both."

"Yeah. But I don't see any way out. He's going to come back soon. He's not going to want to waste any time. I'd guess that he dumped us here until we come around, but he'll be back to check. We should see if there's any way out of here, but even if there is, we don't know where we are."

Sierra took a deep breath. "There has to be a way out. If there's not a way out of this cabin, then there's a way out of this situation. No fucking way am I going to let that bastard kill us. I won't let him kill you because of me. And I just got the life I always wanted but never dreamed I'd have. No way is he going to take it away from me."

Amelia chuckled quietly. "Well, damn! Finally! Listen to you curse, girl! I always figured that you'd come out fighting if you had to. I'm glad I wasn't wrong."

"You weren't wrong. I mean it, Amelia. I never needed to fight for anything before. But I do now. And I don't intend to lose." Her heart was pounding, her head felt as though someone was sticking knives in it. But Sierra felt a strength coursing through her veins that she hadn't known before. "I have everything to fight for now, Lia. We're getting out of this. I promise you."

"Awesome. Any ideas how?"

She looked up at the window and over to the door. She wanted to check them both out. But Jared might be on the other side of that door and as soon as he heard them moving around, he'd come in ready to do whatever he planned. She shuddered. She needed time to think before she had to face him. What could she do?

She had no idea. But she had to think of something. She couldn't die here. The thought of leaving Mateo and Maya now that they were finally safe, the thought of never seeing Wade again. How sad he'd be. He would have done anything he could to save her life.

Wait! He had done something that might just save her life – hers and Amelia's. She lifted her arm and looked at the fuchsia-pink plastic watch. It might be a bit garish, but she'd grown to love it because Wade had given it to her. She loved it and him even more as she pressed the button on the side three times and held her breath as she waited. She didn't totally understand how it worked. Wade had told her that it didn't need to connect to her phone – which was a good thing because she had no idea where that was – it should be able to find a signal by itself and send the SOS message – to the email contacts she'd entered, and to the emergency services. A wave of relief mixed with hope washed over her when she felt the vibration that indicated the message had been sent successfully. Now all she could do was hope that it would get through to Wade and the police, and that they'd be able to get here – wherever here was – before it was too late.

Chapter Twenty-Five

Wade gripped his hat between his hands and stared at the highway ahead as Ford drove them up to town. They'd left Tyler with the kids – they were baking cookies. The plan had been to surprise Sierra with them when she came home. Now … no, he refused to believe that she wouldn't be coming home.

She had to be okay. He closed his eyes at the thought of her in Amelia's Tahoe as it flipped and rolled off the road. He could only cling to the fact that if she'd been killed in the accident, if either of them had, the police would have found them still inside the vehicle. If this was somehow Jared's doing, and he had to believe that it was, he must have taken them. But where – and how the hell were they going to find them?

His heart thudded to a stop, and he pulled his phone out of his back pocket. He opened his email with shaking fingers, but there was nothing from Sierra. Nothing from the security company where he'd bought the tracker watches.

"What've you got, bro?" Tanner asked from the backseat.

"Nothing. I'm just hoping that she's going to manage to get a message out."

Ford glanced over at him. "Shit. You're right. I forgot about that stupid-looking watch you gave her."

Tanner took his own phone out. "I've got nothing either."

"Who did you add as her contacts?" Ford asked. "Did you say it was five people? Damn, Wade. I know I wasn't exactly enthusiastic when you showed me that watch, but God I hope I was wrong."

"So do I."

"How does it work again?" asked Tanner.

"All she needs to do is press the button on the side three times and it should send out an email notification to all five of her contacts. That's the three of us, Barney, and Dax. It also notifies emergency services. All the alerts will give her location."

"That's awesome!" said Tanner.

"It will be," Wade hated what he heard in Ford's voice even before he said the words, "if she can use it."

Wade closed his eyes. She wouldn't be able to push the button if she was unconscious. It'd do her no good, then.

Ford glanced over at him. "Sorry, bro. We have to hope for the best. Even if she was knocked out in the crash, if Jared took her, it has to be because he wants something from her. He won't get anything while she's out cold. When she wakes up, she'll send the signal. She'll do it."

"Yeah." Wade gripped his hat tighter. He had to hold on and believe that she would.

When they got to town, Ford parked in the lot behind the sheriff's office. Luke greeted them as soon as they walked through the door.

"What have you got?" asked Wade.

"Not much to go on yet," Luke said grimly. "Like I told you, the vehicle was empty. It's a rental under the name Amelia Danforth." He met Wade's gaze. "The officers on scene retrieved Amelia's purse – and Sierra's. There was a set of tire tracks in the dirt leading up to Amelia's vehicle and away again. Someone took them."

"Yeah, and we know who."

Luke held his gaze. "You think it's the guy Sierra was supposed to marry?"

Wade was glad that he didn't need to explain the situation. Luke had been a friend since kindergarten. He was bound to have heard all about Sierra and why she was here. "Yeah."

"Come on through. All I know about Sierra is what I've heard through the grapevine. It's probably all I need, but I want you to tell me everything you know – about her and about, what's his name?"

"Jared. Jared Hanson."

Wade and his brothers started to follow Luke into an interview room, but they all stopped and reached for their phones at the same time. Wade held his breath until he saw the email alert he'd been hoping for.

"We've got her!" said Ford.

"Thank fuck!" said Tanner.

Luke turned back and looked at them. "What's going on, guys?"

Wade held his phone up. "She has a tracker with an SOS alert. We just got her location."

"Where is she?"

Ford was tapping at his phone. "In the foothills of the Crazies."

The three of them turned and ran back for Ford's truck.

"I'm right behind you," Luke called.

Just as they reached the front door of the building, the sheriff, Deacon, stepped out in front of them. "What's going on?"

Wade dodged around him. "We found her." He wasn't going to stick around to talk about it. "There should be an alert coming in from Silverstone Security Services."

To his relief, Deacon didn't try to hold them up. But he did call a warning after them. "The deputies will be right behind you. You know the score, guys — you have to stay out of the way and let them do their job when you get there."

Wade didn't even dignify that with a reply. As far as he was concerned, it was *his* job to get Sierra out safely. A quick look at his brothers told him that they felt the same way.

Then he heard Deacon bark, "Luke! I'm riding with you."

They all piled into Ford's truck, and the tires squealed as he pulled out of the parking lot.

Tanner looked out through the back window. "Do you think Deacon's going to try and keep us away?"

Ford checked the rearview mirror and shook his head. The next moment, sirens blared, and Luke's cruiser pulled past them. Ford let out a short laugh. "Nope. Looks like they got the location. My guess is that Deacon came himself because he knows the score. No one's going to be able to keep us away, so he's not going to let his deputies take the blame for whatever goes down. He'd rather be there himself."

Wade could barely focus on the conversation. He just needed to get to Sierra.

~ ~ ~

Sierra huddled closer to Amelia. It must have gone dark outside now; there was even less light in the room than there had been earlier. She checked her watch again. It had only been half an hour since she sent out the SOS message, but she didn't know where they were or how long it would take Wade or the police to come.

"How's your head?" asked Amelia.

"Throbbing." Sierra gingerly touched the big lump that had formed around what had to be quite a gash, considering how much blood there was in her hair. "How about you? Do you really think that he broke your nose?"

"I do."

It wasn't light enough to see properly anymore, but Sierra felt Amelia reach up to touch her face.

Then she heard her draw in a big breath. "If we get out of this, I'm going to have it fixed. I've toyed with the idea of getting a nose job for years."

"We're getting out of this, Lia. I refuse to let that man kill us."

Amelia chuckled quietly. "I'd never in a million years have wished for either of us to be in a situation like this, but I love seeing what it's brought out in you. Right up until the day of your wedding, you were letting Jared run your life. In a way, he was killing the Sierra I knew."

"I know. But everything's different now. And I don't just mean that our lives are literally on the line. I mean that the stakes are so much higher. I've just found the life I always wanted and I'm not going to let him take it away. I want to live – here, in Montana, with Wade and Mateo and Maya, and you – when we get out of this, you have to stay, Lia. Promise me?"

"I promise you that if we get out of this, I'll move up here."

"When not if."

"Okay, when. But if we're going to get out, we need to have some kind of plan. He's going to come back and he's going to want something. Maybe all he wants is to kill us – to get revenge for you screwing up his plans."

"No." Sierra's heart felt as though it might beat out of her chest. She was terrified, but she knew Jared. "He doesn't just want to kill us. I mean, I'm not stupid, I'm sure he plans to. But he'll want more than that. He wants money, as much of it as he can get. He'll want me to transfer it over to him or something."

"I agree that he wants your money; it seems that's all he ever wanted. But if you transfer it to him and then they find your dead body, it'd be obvious what had happened – that he was the one who killed you."

Sierra closed her eyes. "Nobody's going to find my body –"

"Yeah. He'll probably get rid of us where we'll never be found. Bury us out in the wilderness or –"

"Stop!" Sierra realized too late that shouldn't have said it so loudly. She continued in a fierce whisper, "I mean our bodies aren't going to be found because we're still going to be walking around in them – alive!" She started to shake when she heard a rattling at the door. It sounded like a chain was being removed.

She could make out the whites of Amelia's eyes as she turned to her. "If he hurts me to make you do what he wants, let him, okay? Drag it out as long as possible. Wade will get here before it's too late. I know he will."

Sierra grabbed her friend and hugged her tight. She couldn't speak through the tears and fear that choked her throat.

The door swung open, and Jared stood silhouetted against the light from the next room. "Sierra. Amelia. I hope you enjoyed your nap. I'm glad to hear you're both awake. We have some business to take care of."

Sierra could only stare at him. Her ability to speak, even to think rationally, fled when she saw that he was holding a belt – did he plan to beat them with it? She had no idea, but she knew she was about to find out when he grabbed her by her hair and dragged her to her feet.

"You owe me, bitch, and you're about to pay up." He dragged her out into the larger room, where he shoved her down onto a dirty sofa.

Sierra knew she should be trying to think about what she could do, but for some reason her mind chose to focus on the room. The floor in here was dirt, too. It was a log cabin, with one window and one door. The door looked as though it led outside – to freedom.

She screamed and tried to fight Jared off when he grabbed her again, this time by the throat. His eyes looked crazed as they met hers. "You're going to die today, Sierra. But first you're going to make me a happy man."

She gasped in shock, and his hand tightened around her throat as he laughed. "You think I'm going to fuck you? That's one thing you don't need to worry about. You see, Sierra, you're too frigid for my taste. You could have learned a thing or two from your friend, Lori – she knew how to please a man. She took it any way I wanted to give it to her."

Sierra could only stare at him. She was on the verge of passing out; she wasn't getting enough air, and his fingers were only tightening around her throat as he spoke. When he stopped, he released his grip, and she gulped in big breaths. Her brain finally processed what he was saying. He was talking about Lori in the past tense. She wanted to hope that he only meant he wasn't with her anymore.

His hand closed around her throat again and she grabbed it with both of hers, trying to get him off. She had to fight. Her head jerked to the side when he struck her, but he didn't let go of her neck. It took her a few moments to focus again. "Aren't you going ask about your friend? Don't you care what happened to her? I'm surprised at you, Sierra."

When she dared to look at his face, what she saw made her blood run cold. He was smiling the cruelest smile she'd ever seen. "Lori outlived her usefulness, but only by a few days."

Sierra gasped and started to struggle again. This time, Jared let go of her. "You should thank me, you know. She sold you out. She did everything I wanted her to." His smile faded. "It's your fault she's dead. If you'd gone along with the plan, I would have left her safe and well when I left."

"I thought … I thought that you and she were going to … that once you had the money, you'd be together."

He laughed. "That's what she thought, too. Tell me, Sierra. Why are women so stupid?"

She wouldn't have been able to answer even if she'd wanted to. His hand closed around her throat again. This time he looked into her eyes as he brought his other hand up and used both of them to encircle her throat. Darkness started to creep in around the edges of her consciousness. Perhaps he'd changed his mind. Perhaps she was going to die right now. An image of Wade and the children filled her mind. No. She couldn't leave them. She tried to struggle, and to her amazement, Jared let go.

"You surprise me. I didn't expect you to fight." His smile almost looked genuine before it turned cold again. "You might even make this fun." He picked the belt up and then set it down again. I was going to use this around your neck, but I like it this way better, it feels more … intimate. Here's what's going to happen. We're going to get on my laptop and you're going to log in to your accounts and give me access."

She shook her head, but he just laughed. "Oh, you are, Sierra. That's why Amelia's here. I'll bring her out in a minute. Don't worry, she won't miss out on the fun. I just wanted to give you a taste of what she's going to go through if you don't do as you're told."

Sierra searched his face, not understanding. He closed his hands around her throat again, and she tried to fight him off again, but it was no use. He squeezed tighter and tighter until her lungs and her head felt as though they were about to explode, and the darkness started to take over.

He seemed to know just the moment to release the pressure, leaving her lying on the dirty sofa, gasping for air. "Demonstration over." He glanced through the doorway to where Amelia was still sitting. "Now, it's her turn. I wanted you to know what you'll be doing to her if you don't do exactly as I say."

Sierra's mind was racing. She didn't want Amelia to be strangled to death, but he couldn't take it too far. He had to know that if he killed Amelia, she'd never do what he wanted.

He raised his eyebrows. "You have more backbone than I gave you credit for. I can see that you're weighing up whether I'll actually kill her. And you're right, it'd be stupid of me to do that; she's my bargaining chip, if you like." He laughed as if he'd said something hilarious. "In case you doubt me …" He stood and went to a canvas duffle bag that sat on the floor near the door. He came back with his hands behind his back and when he brought them around in front of him, Sierra cowered back at the sight of the big, jagged-looking knife. "I had thought to keep things civilized. But if you need blood and gore to convince you, this should help."

"No!" She finally found her voice.

"Good girl. Now, wait here while I bring her."

Sierra glanced back at the room Amelia was in. It dawned on her for the first time that neither of them was tied up. She was free to move, and Amelia had been ever since Jared had brought her out here. This was probably going to be the only chance she got. She ran for the duffle bag, hoping against hope that Jared had something else in there that she could use as a weapon.

She'd reached the bag and was rifling through clothes when she heard Amelia scream, and Jared shout, "Bitch!" Then there was a thud that sounded like someone had hit the floor. Sierra's trembling fingers closed around cold, hard metal that could only be one thing. She managed to pull back the slide to check it was ready. Relief washed over her as she pulled the pistol out and stood.

"Put it down, Sierra, or I'll kill her."

She spun around and aimed at Jared. He pulled Amelia in front of him and held the knife up to her throat.

"Drop the gun or I'll kill her."

"No. You won't. If you kill her, I'll shoot you."

"Drop it, Sierra. You don't even know how to use it. For all you know, the safety's still on."

A sense of calm came over her, and her confidence came through in her voice. "My brother was a Navy SEAL. He wanted me to know what to do if some asshole ever tried to hurt me. Safety's off and there's one in the chamber." She couldn't help a small smile when she saw the fear on his face.

"Shoot him, Sierra!" Amelia tried to duck to give her a clear shot, but Jared kept hold of her, and Sierra saw a red line appear on her neck.

She raised the gun. He was taller than Amelia; she had to trust her aim and … She froze at the sight of movement behind Jared. It was Wade!

The next moment, everything seemed to happen at once. Wade grabbed Jared's arm and dislodged the knife from his hand. Amelia fell to her knees. Tanner came out from the other room to help Wade, and Ford burst in through the front door.

Jared somehow wrestled himself away from Wade, and Sierra screamed. But she needn't have worried. Wade's fist landed in Jared's face, and he went down, out cold.

Then there were policemen in the room, and Ford was on the floor with Amelia, holding her and gently examining her neck and her face. Sierra rushed forward.

"The knife … Did he … Are you?"

Amelia looked pale and she was shaking visibly, but she smiled. "I'm fine. Or I will be after I get a nose job."

Sierra couldn't help it, she started to laugh. It took her a moment to realize that she sounded hysterical. By the time she did, Wade was there, closing his arms around her, holding her to him, pressing his lips into her hair, telling her that she was okay, that everything was going to be okay. And this time, she knew that he was right.

Chapter Twenty-Six

When Sierra stirred beside him, Wade tightened his arms around her and drew her closer, needing to feel her safe and warm, not only in his arms and in his bed, but in his life. He'd known that he loved her even while he thought he was only going to be her rebound guy. Now, he knew that he'd do whatever it took to be with her for the rest of his life. To take care of her and Mateo and Maya. To become a family. They had their kids already – and there was no question that they were *their* kids. But he wanted them to be a real family. He wanted to make it official. He wanted to marry Sierra and for them both to adopt Mateo and Maya.

Sierra looked up at him over her shoulder. "Good morning."

He dropped a kiss on her lips. "Good morning, darlin'. How are you feeling? The bruises on her neck were fading but they were still very visible. They made him wish that he'd taken the gun from Sierra and shot the bastard himself.

She turned over and touched his cheek. "Better than you are, if the look on your face is anything to go by."

He made himself smile – it was no great hardship when he was looking at her. "Sorry. I was just thinking about what he did to you." He gently traced his finger over her neck. "It makes me want to break into prison and kill him."

She sighed. "A part of me wishes that I'd pulled the trigger."

"No. I'm glad you didn't. Don't get me wrong; I wish he was dead. But I'm glad that you don't have to live with having killed him."

He felt her shudder. "You're right. That would be hard. I just feel like I should have finished the job."

He dropped another kiss on her lips. "You did a great job! You're a little badass!"

She chuckled, and the sound of it tugged at his insides.

"I'm serious, Sierra. When we were waiting outside trying to figure the best way to get in without making the situation worse, I had visions of him holding the two of you at gunpoint, not the other way around. Deacon's still pissed that we didn't wait for his go ahead, but the second I heard Jared tell you to drop the gun I knew you had the upper hand, and we could help."

"I don't know about the upper hand. I was scared to shoot him for fear that I'd hit Amelia, and scared not to for fear that he'd cut her throat." She shuddered again. "She's going to have a nasty scar."

Wade tipped her chin and smiled at her. "Apparently, she's going to ask if the surgeon can do anything about it when she gets her nose fixed."

"Really? When did she say that?"

Wade waggled his eyebrows. "It's what she told Ford."

"Oh! Do you think …?"

Her question was cut off by a tap on the door. They smiled at each other, and Wade called, "Come on in."

The door swung open, and Maya peeked her head around it.

"Do you want morning snuggles?" The first morning after what had happened with Jared, Wade had tried to get Sierra to sleep in. He'd at least wanted her to stay in bed while he got her coffee. When he'd come back, he found both kids sitting on the bed with her. They'd been scared when they saw the bruises on her neck and her other injuries. Wade had joined them and the four of them had snuggled together, reassuring each other that they were all okay.

Maya grinned and nodded rapidly.

"Come on then." As soon as he said the words, she was scampering across the bedroom and climbing up onto the bed, and Mateo appeared in the doorway. Wade nodded at him, too. He came more slowly than his sister but climbed up on the bed just as eagerly.

Once they were all sat up, leaning against the headboard, Wade smiled at Sierra over the kids' heads. The way she smiled back made him want to ask her here and now. It was the perfect moment. But he still hadn't figured out if it was too soon. How could it be fair to ask her to marry him when she'd been through so much in such a short time? She needed to find her way again – to figure out if what she felt for him was real. To know if she wanted him forever, or if he really was just her rebound guy, albeit one who'd played more of a role than either of them had expected.

Mateo leaned against his side and looked up at him. He looked so serious that Wade frowned. "What's up, little man?"

Mateo shook his head and looked away.

Sierra shot Wade a worried look. "I hope you know that if there's something bothering you, you can always talk to us, Mateo."

He looked at her and then back at Wade, then he wrapped his arm around his sister's shoulders and nodded.

Wade waited, hoping that he'd tell them what was wrong. But the silence lengthened, and he still didn't speak.

Wade knew better than to push the kid. He'd tell them whatever it was when he was ready.

He watched as Maya snuggled closer to her brother. His heart raced when she put her lips to Mateo's ear and covered her mouth with her hand. She was talking?

Wade looked at Sierra in wonder. Her hand was over her heart as she watched Maya whisper to her brother. When she looked up at Wade, her eyes were filled with tears.

When Maya finished whatever she was saying, Mateo nodded. Then he reached for Sierra's hand and Wade's. Wade watched as he brought their hands together, and then he and Maya placed theirs on top.

Maya was smiling and nodding eagerly. Mateo took a deep breath and then looked up at them again. "Maya wants me to tell you, and I want to tell you also. That … we want … if you want …"

Wade held his breath. He didn't know what was coming, but he knew it was something big.

Maya nodded at Mateo, urging him on, but he looked worried now.

"What's wrong, little man? Whatever it is you can say it, and whatever you need, we'll try to help."

Mateo frowned. "Maya wants us to be a family now. She doesn't remember our mom, and our dad was … not good." The kid visibly swallowed. "We love you."

Wade's heart melted in his chest, and he heard Sierra let out a little sob and breathe, "We love you, too."

Wade nodded, "We do."

Mateo relaxed a little, but something was still bothering him.

"What is it?" Wade asked. "What else?"

Mateo hung his head and spoke into his chest. "Maya wants me to ask if you will be our mom and dad. But you're not married. And I don't know …" He let the words trail off and the silence they left behind echoed all around them.

Shit. He'd just told them that whatever they needed, he'd try to help. But he couldn't help them with this one – not without putting Sierra in a position that he didn't want to force on her – not yet.

He slowly raised his gaze to meet hers. She looked … scared. But what was she scared of? That he'd want to get married, and she didn't? That she'd be letting the kids down? As he looked into her eyes, he thought he knew the answer – she was scared that he didn't want to marry her. It looked as though there was a storm raging in the gray depths; flickers of emotion shone like lightning. He didn't want to ask her for more than she wanted to give, but that would be better than leaving her hanging, than not making it clear once and for all that he loved her with all his heart and wanted to marry her and be with her forever. He opened his mouth to say it all, but she held up her finger, and he stopped.

"We would love to be your parents." She smiled down at the kids. "That's what I've hoped for from the day I heard about you. I wanted to bring you home with me and be … your mom."

Maya flung her arms around Sierra's neck and said very quietly, "Mom."

Wade squeezed his eyes shut to keep the tears in. He felt Sierra's fingers tighten around his. "I know that Wade loves you, too. And he's already told me that he wants to be there for you." She squeezed tighter as she continued, "We're not married, but that doesn't mean he can't be your dad. But if the day ever comes when he wants to marry me, I'll say yes in a heartbeat." She looked back down at the kids, as if she were telling them, but he knew her words were meant for him. "He thinks that it's too soon to ask me. Because – as you know – I was supposed to marry another man not so very long ago."

Maya touched the bruises on her neck, and Mateo said, "The one who did that to you."

"That's right. The one who did that." She met Wade's gaze before she spoke again. "I think that Wade believes that he's doing the right thing by giving me time. He's such a good man, he never wants to rush me or put pressure on me. He's taught me to be sure that I make my own decisions and that I only base them on what I want." She smiled and a tear rolled down her face. "He needs to know that he taught me well, and that I've decided that I want to marry him just as soon as he wants to ask me. I don't want to wait. I could have died last week, and I don't want to waste a single day. I know the life I want. I want to be his wife and I want to be your mom and for him to be your dad and for us all to be a family just as soon as we can."

Wade couldn't keep a tear from spilling over and rolling down his cheek. He leaned over the kids and kissed Sierra. "I love you."

She smiled through tears of her own. "I love you, too."

He didn't know if she looked expectant or if he was just imagining it. This was the perfect moment, except for one thing. He didn't have a ring! His mind raced. What could he use? He didn't want to let the moment pass by, but he didn't want to ask her without putting a ring on her finger. It wouldn't feel real.

She brought her hand up to brush her hair out of her eyes. Her smile was fading fast, and her cheeks were tinged with pink. Shit. She'd gone out on a limb for him, and he was leaving her hanging. His eyes landed on her watch. It might look tacky, but it had saved her life, and it was about to save his.

"Can I see your watch for a second?"

She gave him a puzzled look but took it off and handed it over. He worked off the loop that held the end of the strap in place and gave the watch back. She still looked puzzled as she put it back on, and both kids were watching him curiously. He slipped the loop over the tip of his finger. It should work. It might be too big, but it would go on.

This was it, then. He grinned at the three of them and then got out of bed. He held up his hand to stop Mateo when he got up to follow him.

He walked around to Sierra's side and got down on one knee on the floor. The kids crowded against her as all three of them looked down at him with wide eyes.

"Sierra." His voice sounded rough and gravelly, but he pushed on. "Sierra, darlin'. I think I've loved you since the minute I laid eyes on you. I didn't think someone like you would give someone like me a second glance." He reached for her hand, and she gripped his fingers tight. "When I first met you, I thought you were someone who needed my help; I thought I could help you out by showing you how you deserve to be treated and by making you see just how special you are. It's only been a short time, but you've stolen my heart and I don't ever want you to give it back. I'm going to love you until the day I die." He looked at the kids. "I'm going to love you guys till the day I die, too. I promise that I'll always be there for you." He looked back at Sierra. "I didn't want to push you for this. I didn't want to ask you too soon. But I trust you to know what you want. So, I'm asking you, will you marry me? Say you'll be my wife?"

Tears were streaming down her face as she nodded. "Yes! I'll marry you."

He slid the pink piece of plastic onto her finger, and she laughed. "It fits! That has to be a sign."

He laughed with her. "Yeah, it's a sign that I'm the luckiest guy on Earth. I have to be, to get you as my wife, and you two as my kids."

He climbed back onto the bed and wrapped his arms around Sierra. Maya wriggled her way in between them and Mateo kneeled up and put his arms around their shoulders.

Wade swallowed back more tears when Maya looked up at him and nodded, and the first words she ever spoke to him were, "I love you."

"I love you, too, baby girl." He smiled at Sierra. "And I love you, darlin'." He put his hand on Mateo's shoulder. "And I love you, little man."

Sierra laughed. "I love you all!" She held up her hand with the piece of pink plastic wrapped around her finger. "When I woke up this morning, I didn't expect that I'd be getting engaged today."

Mateo leaned back and spoke solemnly. "Unexpected love is the best kind of love." He met Wade's gaze. "My new dad said so."

Wade wrapped his arms tighter around all three of them. He might have told Ford that if the right woman came along, he'd want to marry her. But he hadn't been looking for a wife and certainly not for kids. And yet here he was – happier than he would have believed possible with his unexpected love;

;

A Note from SJ

I hope you enjoyed Wade and Sierra's story and getting to know the MacFarlands. As you probably noticed, the siblings are all angling for books of their own – and they'll each get one. But they'll have to wait their turn. Next up will be Janey and Rocket – I can't wait to share their story with you.

With Summer Lake, I gave the older characters their own series in Summer Lake Silver. I'm not going create that separation with the MacFarland Ranch series. There is a whole bunch of older characters who will get their own books. We met Ace, and Frankie's brother, Maverick, in Spider. You've seen glimpses of Deacon and Emmett in Wade and Sierra's story. And there are a couple of other guys whom you haven't even met yet. So many books; so little time!

And if you're one of the many people who notices the details I miss, you might be wondering about the eldest MacFarland brother, Cash. (Ohh … Cash!). You've heard several mentions of him, and yes, he will be getting his own books. Yes, bookS – plural. According to him there will be three, but we're still in negotiations about that. I may talk that number down – he may talk it up – who are you betting on?!?

The man has taken up residence in my head, you have him to thank for the whole series. He's masterminding everything, I'm just – mostly – doing as I'm told.

Please let your friends know about the books if you feel they would enjoy them as well. It would be wonderful if you would leave me a review, I'd very much appreciate it.

Check out the "Also By" page to see if any of my other series appeal to you – I have the occasional ebook freebie series starters, too, so you can take them for a test drive.

There are a few options to keep up with me and my imaginary friends:

The best way is to Sign up for my Newsletter at my website www.SJMcCoy.com. Don't worry I won't bombard you! I'll let you know about upcoming releases, share a sneak peek or two and keep you in the loop for a couple of fun giveaways I have coming up :0)

You can join my readers group to chat about the books or like my Facebook Page www.facebook.com/authorsjmccoy

I occasionally attempt to say something in 140 characters or less(!) on Twitter

And I'm in the process of building a shiny new website at www.SJMcCoy.com

I love to hear from readers, so feel free to email me at SJ@SJMcCoy.com if you'd like. I'm better at that! :0)

I hope our paths will cross again soon. Until then, take care, and thanks for your support—you are the reason I write!

Love

SJ

PS Project Semicolon

You may have noticed that the final sentence of the story closed with a semi-colon. It isn't a typo. <u>Project Semi Colon</u> is a non-profit movement dedicated to presenting hope and love to those who are struggling with depression, suicide, addiction and self-injury. Project Semicolon exists to encourage, love and inspire. It's a movement I support with all my heart.

"A semicolon represents a sentence the author could have ended, but chose not to. The sentence is your life and the author is you." - Project Semicolon

This author started writing after her son was killed in a car crash. At the time I wanted my own story to be over, instead I chose to honour a promise to my son to write my 'silly stories' someday. I chose to escape into my fictional world. I know for many who struggle with depression, suicide can appear to be the only escape. The semicolon has become a symbol of support, and hopefully a reminder – Your story isn't over yet

Also by SJ McCoy

The Davenports
Oscar
TJ
Reid
Spider

Remington Ranch Series
Mason
Shane
Carter
Beau
Four Weddings and a Vendetta

A Chance and a Hope
Chance is a guy with a whole lot of story to tell. He's part of
the fabric of both Summer Lake and Remington Ranch. He
needed three whole books to tell his own story.
Chance Encounter
Finding Hope
Give Hope a Chance

Love in Nashville
Autumn and Matt in Bring on the Night

The Hamiltons
Cameron and Piper in Red wine and Roses
Chelsea and Grant in Champagne and Daisies
Mary Ellen and Antonio in Marsala and Magnolias
Marcos and Molly in Prosecco and Peonies

Summer Lake Series

Love Like You've Never Been Hurt
Work Like You Don't Need the Money
Dance Like Nobody's Watching
Fly Like You've Never Been Grounded
Laugh Like You've Never Cried
Sing Like Nobody's Listening
Smile Like You Mean It
The Wedding Dance
Chasing Tomorrow
Dream Like Nothing's Impossible
Ride Like You've Never Fallen
Live Like There's No Tomorrow
The Wedding Flight

Summer Lake Seasons

Angel and Luke in Take These Broken Wings
Zack and Maria in Too Much Love to Hide
Logan and Roxy in Sunshine Over Snow
Ivan and Abbie in Chase the Blues Away
Colt and Cassie in Forever Takes a While
Austin and Amber in Tell the Stars to Shine

Summer Lake Silver

Clay and Marianne in Like Some Old Country Song
Seymour and Chris in A Dream Too Far
Ted and Audrey in A Little Rain Must Fall
Izzy and Diego in Where the Rainbow Ends
Manny and Nina in Silhouettes Shadows and Sunsets
Teresa and Cal in More than Sometimes

About the Author

I'm SJ, a coffee addict, lover of chocolate and drinker of good red wines. I'm a lost soul and a hopeless romantic. Reading and writing are necessary parts of who I am. Though perhaps not as necessary as coffee! I can drink coffee without writing, but I can't write without coffee.

I grew up loving romance novels, my first boyfriends were book boyfriends, but life intervened, as it tends to do, and I wandered down the paths of non-fiction for many years. My life changed completely a few years ago and I returned to Romance to find my escape.

I write 'Sweet n Steamy' stories because to me there is enough angst and darkness in real life. My favorite romances are happy escapes with a focus on fun, friendships and happily-ever-afters, just like the ones I write.

These days I live in beautiful Montana, the last best place. If I'm not reading or writing, you'll find me just down the road in the park - Yellowstone. I have deer, eagles and the occasional bear for company, and I like it that way :0)